# Alidor

Written by Matthew Hillsdon

Self Published

First Edition

First published in Great Britain in 2021

Copyright © Matthew Hillsdon 2021

ISBN:978-1-7398601-0-3

A record of this book is available from the British Library.

Cover illustration: Bobooks
Edited by: Emma Chiswell-Saunders

For my lady of light, whose beauty goes before her, fair face that makes eyes water. In a dream you found me, one that I wished never to wake, but I have woken now, and for years I did search for my lady of light. Found her I did, as lost as I, my hand in hers I was healed. Old wounds sealed and forgotten, lost to time, for the past is long dead, remembered by few, but here with you I feel new life bloom. Hand in hand we went on into our new land, to Alidor we come together hand in hand.

Prologue
A short history of Alidor, as told by the Seers.

The elves believe the most powerful beings in the universe are the eternal spirits, or gods as they call them. Most believe they formed the universe itself, and the one known as Norsea created a world she named Alidor, and gifted it to her chosen people, the high elves. They were the first beings to walk her new world. Created by Norcea using her own cosmic energy to manipulate the cells in stars to create life. When they were ready she cast them down to the planet below. The first of these high elves awoke to find nothing but a world covered in sand and dust, but with Norcea guiding them from the heavens they filled the dead world with life. Barren plains became forests and grassland. Where there were dry, dusty plains, rivers and streams ran. With them came more new life. The high elves influence over the land was much stronger then their god had created them to be, allowing other life forms to evolve at an incredible rate. This, however allowed her chosen to persuade others to take on the tasks they had been given. She watched as her high elves grew weary of caring for her world, but Norsea did not act. She just watched as another god's eyes turned to her world, seeing a world of light he could consume with darkness. He gave the secrets to creating intelligent life to an unknown high elf, who then hid himself under the earth, and twisted this gift to create the orcs. Made to be the high elves opposite, with a love for war and destruction. As tall as a high elf but far stronger, built solely for war. After a century of hiding the orcs came up from the caves of a place known as the Blood Works, ruled over and lead by the high elf who made them, who would become known as the Dark Seer. Under his rule, orcs swarmed elf lands, leading to the death of most of the high elf population, who after years of peace had no defence against orc rage.

Humans were created by the high elves to be slaves and soldiers. High elves being immortal had no desire for war, or battle. In the forth age of the elves, after thousands of lives had been lost to the orc invaders. The council of Seers, five high elves who are said to be the most powerful and wise of all, decreed they would create a mortal army to fight their wars and defend their lands. Declaring no elf would die in battle again. With the help of the wizard June, an odd dwarf mage, who studied the orcs, dissecting them and using all manner of torture and enchantments to learn how to make an army of his own. Using this magic, he created an army of ten thousand humans who were born in the underground caverns below the Crown city. With fair faces and slim builds like the elves, but fierce, war hungry and mortal like the orcs. The Crown city itself was barely that, it was built to be a dock city but when no lands were found in the southern seas it was forgotten. The buildings made of rotting wood and the only people living above ground were normally in hiding. The Seers used these criminals to test their new soldiers, when they were ready, they sent them above ground to retake the city. Their human army took over the city in a few hours, they killed mercilessly causing the Seers to see this as a great success. Using the new army they reclaimed most of the land lost to the orcs and for almost one hundred years the humans would be slaves to the elves, and die in their place.

The House of Hargo was chosen by Seer Elidom Godborn himself to lead the army of the Crown City. The head of their family, Galivn Hargo was given the title King, along with the Crown City to rule over. On the condition they would use it to improve their army, which he did. He hired the dwarves of the Iron Mines to create the finest weapons and armour for his troops. The Crown City soon became the largest fortress in Alidor, but when Galivn died, the title was passed to his only remaining son. Harold, who hated the elves and all magical life. He demanded the elves free all of the humans of Alidor, or he would turn their own army against them, knowing few would still fight for the elves without their King's blessing. The elves had little of their own army, after relying on the humans for so long. The council of Seers eventually gave in, and freed their human slaves, who quickly joined the ranks of Harold's army. Not satisfied with freeing his people, Harold soon broke his word. He wanted revenge on all elves, so Harold started a war against all magical creatures and sent his army to begin in his own words, *cleansing wherever can be found of magical life.* They weren't alone in this war, by their sides many of the soldiers had wolf companions. Huge beasts that unlike the humans were loyal to a fault. The humans were a great army alone but with the wolves at their side, they where almost unstoppable.

The elves knew something had to be done to stop the humans before they made it over the Lavender Lake. If they did defeat the garrison there, the elves would be lost. Seer Elidom Godborn the head of the council of Seers, traveled to every corner of his kingdom to find aid for the elves. He did better than he dared he would. King Harold's hatred had been inflicted on so many races that armies came from all over Alidor, the dwarves of the Iron Mines and the beasts of the Crimson Grove were the first to respond. Elidom knew they would come to their aid but hatred for the humans spread far, and many more joined his cause. The greatest of all were the dragons who had been enemies, but after losing so many to human hunters they were left with little choice but to fight alongside the elves.

Elidom lead his new army to the Crown City to lay siege, hoping to cut the head off the snake, but King Harold's army was waiting before the city on the plains of Nore. The over fifty thousand strong army stood confidently in formation when Elidom's army of mostly elves and dwarfs approached. As their smaller force of barely thirty thousand marched onto the dusty plains, unbeknownst to Elidom crows had sent word to the human King of what flies with them. For crows has always be rather loyal to the Humans following their armies and cleaning the fields as they went.

## The Unlikely Allies

Harold knew this army was on its way, and now knowing what flew with them, he sent his wolves away so as not to risk losing them to the dragons. For month's now his force had been beaten back by Elidom's new army leading to much of the human population to return to the city for safety. He was waiting on top of the battlements of the huge stone walls of the rebuilt city. Elidom moved to the front of his army with the Wizard June by his side. He raised his hand and with that, the dragons came down from the skies, raining fire on the men below. Harold stood on the walls of his city and could do nothing as dragon's fire ripped though his army. The elves then began to fire arrows into the burning army as the dwarves marched forward. The remaining men ran for the cover of the city, but fire blocked their way. All fifty thousand men outside would die trapped between fire and arrows. By the time the dwarves reached the human lines the battle was over, the ones that remained begged for mercy but were shown none by the elves. Rain began to fall as Elidom prepared to move into the city and rid the world of their accursed creation.

The Wizard June began walking toward the city gates which were now ablaze, but the rain and mist of the sea was helping to put out the fires in the city, June raised his staff. Elidom seeing this began to run to June, but before he could reach him June slammed his staff to the ground with a thunderous roar. The earth around the city walls began to shake splitting in two and the land divided. June pointed his hand towards the city now a small island, with a push of his hand it began to drift away from Alidor. Elidom reached June, fuming with anger wanting his revenge. He held his sword to June's neck and yelled, 'Why would you? Why would you save them? After all they have done?'

'We created them for war and that's what they did, now I want to know if they do something else,' and with that, he vanished leaving his staff behind. Elidom not happy with the idea of the humans ever be able to return instructed the mages of Accultian to create the King's wall, a huge magical barrier going to the bottom of the sea and high into the sky to keep the humans caged on their island, which had now drifted away out of the sight of even an elf.

Elidom took the title of King of elves, a new position. For the council of Seers would control the new elite elf army that was being made, from only the finest soldier's amongst the elves. Lead by Seer Marlos La Sore, who had rose to great fame for slaying the Dark Seer, but the King was now to see that they were never be used or needed. He endeavoured to bring all to peace so what is now called the human's war could never happen again.

June's wish that the humans would forget about war and live in harmony did not come to pass. After finding out there was no way off the island riots began. A group calling themselves the Redeemer's rose up and began to challenge the King's line. This lead to a civil war that after twenty three years the Redeemer's were on the verge of winning. They attempted to hunt down all members of the Hargo family, but a young girl was able to sneak out of the city and get to the edge of the ocean. She found a basket on the shore and took her bag from her back placing it in the basket. She opened it to reveal a newborn baby inside. The girl stroked the baby's face and then pushed him away into the ocean. In a vain effort to save the child perhaps, everyone that had tried to pass the King's wall had failed, but for some unknown reason this baby's basket just sailed through as if it was being guided.

# The Unlikely Allies

# The Unlikely Allies

## Chapter 1
## The Fang

The sun rose over the Fang, bringing the warm summer air with it. Flowing from the East Sea over the desolate, dead, grey ground of the Plains of Nore. It made its way through the lush, green grass surrounding the forest, rising to knock the old leaves from the ancient oak trees. Moving along the shoreline, where waves crashed onto the pebble beach before the Fang, as a pack of wolves stalked the shore in search of an easy meal. 'What's that thing?'One of the wolves mumbled to himself. He moved over to a bit of seaweed on a rock that appeared to be moving. He pulled the weed away to find it wasn't covering a rock, but a worn wicker basket with a malnourished baby inside. 'Hey! What you found?' Another wolf shouted as he ran over, followed by others. 'I don't know. It looks like an elf pup,' the first wolf replied. 'It looks like a nice snack to me, let's eat it, before the others get here!' The first wolf moved in to bite off the child's head, but before he was able to, the basket was swept out from under his jaws. Another wolf had pulled the child away and put the basket between her front paws. She had bright white fur with a black line over her left eye. She bared her sharp teeth at the wolves in front of her, staring them down with her deep brown eyes. 'You fool,' she snarled, 'This is no elf! This is a human pup.' The others moved in on her.

'That's not human. They're long gone. Now give me my kill, I found it,' The first wolf proclaimed with drool running down his jaws, hungry for his snack. 'This pup is not for eating!' She barked back holding her ground as they circled her.

Then an almighty howl came from the forest. The wolves turned to see a humongous jet black wolf walking out of the undergrowth. He howled down to the beach with such force it shook the leaves from the surrounding trees. He was Balvor Mammoth Slayer, Descendent of Barramore the Brutal, Lord of

12

the Fang. 'Salene What's going on?' He barked down at the female wolf on the shore. The other wolves backed off and went back to hunting, not wanting to deal with the wrath of their alpha. Salene picked the basket up in her jaws and ran to Balvor. 'Where did you find that?' he asked.

'It was on the shore, I got to him just in time, he's human right?' her angry tone had been replaced by one of sheer excitement. 'Yes it seems to be,' he replied, sniffing the child who lay there sleeping. 'You should put it back.' He turned to walk away, but Salene blocked his path. 'We can't just leave him my love,' Salene said, trying to pry on her mate's softer side. 'The humans would not show such favour to our deformed pup,' Balvor said sternly. 'Our pup is not deformed,' she snapped at him, 'humans and wolves were allies long ago, who's to say if they would, but if we leave him he will die out here, and I see no need for that,' Salene argued and with that took the basket back in her jaws and walked off into the forest. 'Fine, I want nothing to do with that thing,' Balvor grumbled under his breath as he followed his mate back into The Fang.

The pair made their way to the centre of the forest. Many wolves began poking their heads out of their dens to see what Salene was carrying. Wolf dens were terribly basic, nothing more than large holes in the ground filled with grass and leaves to make them more comfortable. Salene placed the basket in front of her den and took the child softy in her jaws, placing him in the grass bed next to her own tiny pup. He wasn't like the other wolf pups. He was tiny for his age and still had patches of skin showing where his light brown fur hadn't grown. 'What do you intend to do with it now? You know what the elves will do if they find out there's a human here,' Balvor said as he joined Salene outside the den. 'I intend to care for him my dear, the elves have no reason to come here. They'll never need know about him' Salene said turning to look into her den. Her own pup had woken, and the two were now playing. The puppy jumped around the child whilst he tried to catch the little wolf's tail unsuccessfully. 'See, and it will do Billy good to have a brother.' She was smiling from ear to ear, too happy to see her pup playing to care about the consequences. 'You should name it, the others will be less likely to eat it if it has a name,' Balvor groaned, realising he had no say in the matter. 'I'll call him Hilly. It will fit nicely with Billy,' she announced.

'Hilly and Billy?' Balvor replied, unimpressed.

'Yes, they're great names,' she said, smiling and feeling very proud of herself, 'and as for the elves, you shall have to speak to the ranger and come to an understanding.'

'The ranger's aid does not come for free. You know what he will ask,' Balvor grumbled.

'Yes I know, but you have put off the inevitable for years now, we have hidden in these woods for far too long.'

'Fine, I'll tell the others,' Balvor said, sitting up and walking off back down the path.

The Fang was the nine hundred acre forest the wolves lived in. Shortly after the human's war, many wolf packs feared the elves and other races would put them to death for fighting alongside the humans of the Crown City. For safety, they joined together under the rule of Barramore the Brutal. He had stood beside King Harold Emra at the head of the human's army. Barramore led them to live in the forest close to where the Crown City used to be, and after a few years of living there in peace Barramore was approached by a wood elf ranger who offered the wolves' ownership of the forest. In return, they would have to defend the nearby town of Noress should it ever be needed. Barramore agreed to his terms and renamed the forest The Fang. He was then seen as the saviour of the wolves and since then, a wolf of Barramore's blood has always led the pack, Balvor was a descendent of Barramore and a popular leader whose reign had until now been faultless. He hoped this was enough to convince the others to turn a blind eye to his mate's choice to raise the human pup. A decision he wasn't happy about himself and could not understand, however it was not Salene alone that bound him to care for the human. The wolves' own laws forbid any wolf to harm or enable a human to be harmed. Any human who may come to a wolf asking for aid could not look away. Likewise, in human law of the past, no matter how much hatred and cruelty King Harold's army inflicted on other races of Alidor, wolves were always treated as equals. The last thing Balvor wanted was the blood of a human on his paws.

Balvor continued walking down the path until he came to a small pond surrounded by mossy boulders. Most of which had a tired wolf sleeping on top. Balvor walked through the pond and leapt up onto the biggest boulder. He laid down with a groan. A smaller dark brown wolf called Jerrest hopped up onto the boulder beside him. He only had one ear, losing his left years ago when he and Balvor were only pups. 'What's the matter boss?' Jerrest asked. 'It's Salene,' Balvor replied with a sigh.

'What she do now?' Jerrest wondered. Before Balvor could tell him about the baby, he caught sight of the hunters that had Salene cornered on the beach. They were making their way to the pond, led by a rather unpleasant wolf called Fengal. He had a black greying coat and his face was covered in scars. 'Well, have you told them yet?' Fengal shouted to Balvor.

'I was just about to,' Balvor said, sitting up on his Boulder. 'Salene found a human pup on the beach and intends to raise it as her own,' Balvor announced, raising his voice to be certain they all heard, the ears of the wolves raised, never expecting to hear such a thing. 'She didn't find anything! My hunters found it, the pup belongs to me,' Fengal barked as his hunters began to circle the other wolves at the pond. 'Salene has done you a favour Fengal, you know the rules about eating humans. If she hadn't taken it, and your hunters had killed it then we would be here discussing your punishment,' Balvor said calmly. 'We don't have to eat it, but it has to die if the elves found out they'd kill us all, you're endangering the whole pack,' Fengal barked as he made his way into the pond. 'The decision has been made Fengal there's nothing more to talk about,' Balvor said. 'That child will bring doom upon us and when it does, I shall have your head for it Balvor,' Fengal barked. Hearing this, Jerrest leapt into the pond in front of Fengal. 'Well, we better kill you now then, can't have the boss watching his back all them years,' Jerrest growled at his new enemy.

'Enough, this discussion is over! Salene will raise the boy. We will hide him from the world, none will know of him but members of our pack,' Balvor said. With that, he leapt off his boulder and began walking back towards the path. But Fengal wasn't done. 'Will we really be led by a wolf who can't even control his own mate? The only reason that bitch wants it is because she can only have deformed disgu...' suddenly, before Fengal could finish Balvor grabbed him by the back of the neck and forced his head under the water. Before Fengal's hunters could help, they were blocked by Jerrest and the rest of Balvor's hunters. Fengal was frantically struggling for air, making him swallow more of the dirty pond water. He felt his lungs begin to fill just as Balvor pulled him out and threw him to the ground beside the pond. Balvor walked over to Fengal and asked, 'Do we have anything else to discuss?'

'No boss,' Fengal said, coughing up the water as he did.

After his altercation with Fengal, Balvor made his way to the outskirts of The Fang and sat beneath a tree to overlook the Plain's of Nore. He looked up into the trees above him and saw a crow sat there staring back. 'I need you to find the ranger for me, tell him we must speak,' Balvor said.

'CAW foolish wolf, he cannot just be summoned especially by you CAW,' the crow squawked.

'Get him, and tell him the pact will be broken if he does not come,' Balvor ordered.

'CAW fine, but he will not be happy. I have warned you wolf CAW,' the crow said, flapping his wings and taking off. With that, Balvor returned to the dens and waited.

Three months passed with none but the wolves knowing of the human until the ranger finally arrived at The Fang. When he did, Balvor was already waiting, he had caught the ranger's scent long before he had reached the forest. 'Why have you summoned me? The crow didn't say much, just that you wish to break our pact,' the ranger asked as he got down from the white horse he rode. 'We must change the pact you and my ancestor made, I do not wish to break it,' Balvor said.

'For what purpose?' the ranger asked. Balvor stared at the wood elf before him and prepared himself. 'Three moons ago in the month of the steed, my mate found a child, a human child' Balvor announced. The ranger put his hand to the sword on his belt. 'Hand him over' the ranger demanded as anger swelled in him. 'No. You know our laws tell us we cannot let the boy be harmed,' Balvor replied.

'Your laws are not mine. Hand over this child Lord of the Fang, or I shall return with my rangers, and we will take him,' the Ranger said. 'I will not hand him over, and you will have to burn down every tree in The Fang to find him,' Balvor roared. The ranger drew his sword. 'I am not playing dog. Hand him over, if you don't and the Seers find out they will burn your forest with your wolves in it,' the ranger argued, as he held the long sword with its silver blade shining in the darkness. 'Enough of this,' a voice said out of the shadows of the Fang. They both turned to see another figure covered in smoke with his face and body hidden under his old brown cloak, the stink of pipe weed coming from the pipe hanging from his mouth. The smoke concealed him and had dulled Balvor's senses letting him sneak up on the pair. 'What are you doing here?' The ranger said, rage fuming from him. 'I heard you were travelling here and wondered what it was about. Seems I got here just in time,' the smoke covered figure said. 'This is not your concern, get out of here!' The ranger shouted to him.

'Oh I don't know about that, sounds to me there is an agreement we can all come to here,' the smokey figure said.

'I agree last time we spoke ranger you asked me to join your group. Well I will, if you can promise me the boy will be left with us, we will keep him in the Fang, none but us will ever know of him,' Balvor said.

'True, your skill would come in use, but if the Seers find out they would slaughter you wolves. They hear nothing from your people these days, they have forgotten about you and that is

# The Unlikely Allies

for the best. If they ever hear of this human their eyes will turn back to the Fang and nothing I can do will help. The elites will wipe you out,' the ranger warned, lowering his sword to his side. 'I am sorry, but this is how it must be.'

'Maybe…maybe not. What if I stay and watch over the wolves?' the figure queried.

'How could I trust you to watch them?' the ranger asked. 'I am not immortal like you woody, I am getting old. There are ruins of a farm to the southwest of here. I think it will make a nice place to grow even older. I shall buy it and watch over the wolves and human from there. Our group will only know the truth of the human. We already have so many secrets, one more will not hurt. In return, Balvor will join us and shall answer the ranger's call whenever it comes, but you should know our work takes us far from our homes and into the darkest places this world has. You must ask yourself Fang Lord, is protecting this child worth this? You have a charmed life now. All you have to do is cast the child aside, and it will be that again' the figure stated. 'If you will watch over them and if you Balvor, agree to join, I will agree to this also, but it is as this old fool has said, this will change your life. Eyes will turn to the Fang someday with the human here,' the ranger said.

'In truth, if you had come the same day we found him, I may have handed him to you. Now I would never give him over, he is one of my pack now, my son. I will join you and I will be there when you call, and I will keep the boy here, he will never leave The Fang,' Balvor said. The ranger turned and pulled himself back onto his steed. 'Then we are agreed. I shall send the crow when I have need of you, until then I hope to hear nothing of this place,' the ranger said and with a glare to the figure he sped away. Balvor turned to address the smokey figure, but he had already vanished.

## Chapter 2
## The Hunt

Fifteen years went by and Salene stuck to her word, raising the human boy as her own. She'd watched her son's growing into young adults, never once regretting her decision. Billy's fur had grown out, he now had a thick light brown coat and a white fluffy belly, sharing the deep brown eyes of his mother. He was still a lot smaller than the other wolves that after fifteen years stood almost as tall as a horse. Billy, however, was still just the size of a domesticated dog. The small wolf had one thing going for him though, his speed. He could already outrun the fully grown wolves of the pack, and was a lot smarter than many gave him credit for. Taking on every challenge that came his way without complaint. Hilly had grown into a young man with scruffy black hair and a slim athletic build. He wasn't nearly as fast or as energetic as his brother. He'd commonly be found passed out in a tree from smoking too much pipe weed or doing anything possible to avoid work. The only thing he put effort into was stealing, it being the only way he could get normal everyday goods like clothes. He'd become an expert at sneaking into the merchant coaches that used the road through The Fang heading to the pub at Noress. The landlord of the pub was, as the wolves would say, so crooked he'd sell his fur, which meant a vast variety of goods were moved through The Fang allowing Hilly to procure everything he would need. He was the complete opposite of his brother in almost every way, but the pair were absolutely inseparable.

'Our first hunt.' Billy bounded around, unable to contain his excitement. 'I know! Calm down you grasshopper, you'll make me drop my sword,' Hilly said. Clinging to his leather scabbard, which held an old Elven short sword. He also had a dagger with a curved blade and a black handle tied to the back of his belt in another scabbard. Just a couple of the treasures he procured

19

along with his black long-sleeved tunic and trousers he wore, that were covered in the dirt of The Fang. 'Do you remember what we planned?' Hilly said.

'Don't worry, I can easily out run the others. I'm worried about you keeping up on two legs,' Billy joked.

'Well, if this goes to plan I won't have to do any running,' Hilly smiled. The wolves their age weren't exactly nice to the pair. Billy was constantly teased about his size, and Hilly was quick to anger. When the fighting started Balvor's howl was all that would stop them, but they would show them all today, the first day of Summer. The young wolves who wanted to join the hunters of the pack, race to see who can bring in the biggest game in the quickest time. Balvor would constantly tell the boys the tale of when he won the hunt by duelling a mammoth alone. The boys rushed to meet the others to the east of the nest of dens, four other wolves were already sat in front of Balvor, surrounded by the rest of the pack. Balvor saw his sons at the back of the crowd. 'Get over here you fools you're late,' he barked at the boys. They pushed their way past the rest of the wolves and ran to stand in front of their father with the others who was still giving them a disapproving glare. Then he turned to the crowd and spoke. 'You have all come here because you want to join my hunters and provide for our pack, before you can do this you must first prove you're worthy, show us you can track and hunt your pray alone. Whoever returns with the best prey in the quickest time will be the one joining my hunters,' Balvor announced to the hunter hopefuls. 'On my howl the race will begin.' Hilly turned to Billy,

'Are you ready? You remember what to listen for?'

'Yes I know just don't fall,' Billy smirked. With that Balvor's howl rang out the other wolves and Billy shot off into the darkness of the woods. 'What are you doing boy? Go!' Balvor shouted at Hilly who was just casually walking along. 'Alright I'm going,' Hilly said as he began jogging off after the others, but only until he was out of sight of the wolves back at the dens, then he went back to strolling through the forest. After a few minutes he came across a large old oak tree. 'This one should do,' he said aloud to himself. Standing next to the huge tree, he pulled the dagger from its scabbard and dug it into the bark. He hauled himself up using the dagger as a foothold and began climbing. It was an easy climb as there were a lot of branches and indents in the bark, so he was quick reaching the top. Once there he could see to the east where beyond the waves the Crown City had been banished and encaged. West was Noress a small farming town surrounded by wheat fields, whose inhabitants had become fond of the wolves they lived beside. North and West were the elf lands of King Elidom Godborn and the Seers. All the brothers knew of these lands were through tales. Hilly balanced himself on a branch where he could see the tops of the trees. He couldn't see much below, the leaves were too thick but he didn't need to look down at the forest floor. He looked around watching the treetops, until he saw one waving about like something was shaking it. 'There you are,' Hilly said. He pouted his lips and made a call of a Skag owl.

Billy had gotten ahead of the rest of the pack, who seemed to be putting more effort into keeping up with him than hunting. Then he heard Hilly's owl call. 'Finally,' he mumbled, picking up his speed and darting to the left. He was soon out of sight of the pack behind him. 'Alright, where is it then?' Billy slowed down as he heard a grumpy groan coming from behind the bushes in front of him. 'Okay Hilly, if you let this thing eat me, I'll kill you,' Billy said, preparing himself as much as he could before leaping through the bush. On the other side was a Wood troll scratching his back on a tree. Wood trolls are massive, over thirty feet tall monsters, with moss and weeds growing on their dirt like skin. They kill whatever crosses their path, but stayed away from the dens because they knew a group of wolves could easily bring them down, but one little wolf away from the dens was an easy kill. He lunged towards Billy with a roar, his huge green moss covered hand stretching out to grab him, he quickly jumped out of its way. As the beast stumbled and fell, Billy howled as loud as he could before turning to run. The troll was soon on his feet roaring in anger as it ran after Billy, who was having to keep slow, so the troll didn't lose sight of him. Another owl call came from the left. Billy turned to go to where the sound was coming from as the troll grew even more frustrated. He was pushing over trees and smashing through rocks in a vain attempt to catch the little wolf. Then Billy heard a monstrous roar and looked back to see a log flying through the air. The troll had uprooted a tree and tossed it at Billy. He jumped, dodging it with seconds to spare as another log landed to the ground, right in front of his paws, blocking his path. The troll was right behind him. Billy looked up to see the troll's face looking down at him, his yellow rotting teeth ready to crush down on the wolf's little bones, but then Billy saw Hilly's dagger in the side of the tree next to him. *Ha, that's lucky*, the little wolf thought. Hilly drew his short sword and jumped from the tree landing on the troll's head, he positioned his sword and drove it through the beast's soft skin and into its skull. It stumbled for a second, then fell back and smashed to the ground dead, throwing Hilly onto the floor next to Billy with his now broken short sword. The blade had snapped off and embedded itself into the troll's head, leaving Hilly with just the handle in his hand. 'Well, that worked.' Hilly smiled, tossing the handle away. 'Why did you wait so long? It could have eaten me,' Billy shouted.

'I was just waiting for an opening, you're fine, don't whine, and we're definitely going to win the hunt now,' Hilly said. 'So how do we get it back?' Billy asked as he realised the true size of the beast. Hilly burst out laughing and said, 'I honestly didn't think of that'.

The boys were the second hunters to get back to the dens. Morla, an older wolf with dark brown fur and teeth too large for his jaws was the first. He was not a friend of the boys who had elected to hack the leg of the troll off and cut it in two. Billy was dragging the foot along the ground whilst Hilly was struggling to carry the beast's thigh on his shoulder. It would still be bigger than anything the others could have caught. 'What is that?' Morla said as they dropped the body parts down in front of their father. 'That is the leg of a wood troll,' Billy announced proudly.

'And you expect the pack to eat that muck,' Morla said, growling under his breath. He had just brought back a small deer, not enough to beat their troll, and wood troll meat was hardly muck, once the dirt like skin is removed the meat beneath is the sweetest the Fang has to offer. 'You can't use that,' Morla barked.

'What's the problem Morla? Is it 'coz we didn't bring the beast's knob back for you?' Hilly joked.

'Enough,' Balvor said, 'he's right, you can't use this. You two broke the rules you must hunt alone, not in a pair as you did,' Balvor barked displeased with his sons. 'Father, we didn't break the rules. They say we can't be together on the hunt, at no point whilst the troll was living were me and Billy together. He just happened to run across my path whilst the monster chased him down,' Hilly said, trying his best to save their victory.

'Don't try to worm your way out of it Hilly, I heard you making your damn bird calls. You may think my ears are old, but I hear all that happens in the Fang. One day you will find yourself without the other, having to rely on your skills, which is what this race was about.' With that, Balvor turned to greet the other competitors. Hilly stormed off, furious with his father's decision. Billy followed him as Morla grinned to himself.

'We did kill a wood troll, that's still something we can boast about at least,' Billy said after they were far enough away from the others. 'I'm sorry I should have just let you do it by yourself, you could have still shown up Morla easily,' Hilly sighed.

'It's alright. I only wanted to do it with you anyway, and you'd never pass without me,' Billy laughed.

'Who was it that killed that troll?' Hilly said, smiling back at his brother. 'Since we're in trouble already, we could go sneak into the village,' he said wanting to show his brother there were no hard feelings. 'Yes, Wasiz's new stuff should have dried out by now,' Hilly said running into their den. It was extremely comfortable compared to the rest. Dug into a large mound big enough for them to dig out a window as well as a door, tall enough for Hilly to walk through without having to stoop. It was a good distance away from the others so as not to be disturbed.

## The Unlikely Allies

They had placed animal furs over it, covering the floor and walls. A silver candelabra holding three burning down white candles illuminated it, giving their den a warm glow. After running in, Hilly reappeared with a filthy hooded black cape which he threw on over his shoulders and put the hood up, so it covered his human ears. With that, the boys headed off through the forest towards Noress.

Chapter 3
The Drunken Goblin


The boys got to the edge of the forest just as the sun was setting.
'Come on, we're almost there,' Billy said, as he ran ahead of
Hilly. He could see the village, Noress was a mile or so walk
through the wheat fields from the outskirts of The Fang. It only
had a few wooden buildings. It was more of a large farm than a
village. The largest building was the tavern, or pub, as the locals
called it, The Drunken Goblin. The only stone structure in
Noress, from the outside it looked like an old elven temple with
huge metal doors and colourful stain glass windows of the God
Norcea's earth spirits. The inside, however, was very different. It
was normally full of centaurs and elves, most of them were
farmers apart from the few dwarven traders passing through on
their way to Orashson. The boys made their way to the Drunken
Goblin, but didn't go to the front door. Instead they went to head
around the back, but before they could, a young wood elf jumped
out as if from nowhere. Clad in green silk that seemed to dance
as she moved with a worn brown coat thrown over her shoulders
for warmth. 'Does your mother know you two are out?' she
spoke with a smile. 'Mary!' Billy barked, and jumped up at her.
'Where have you been? You've been gone so long. I really
missed you. Did you bring me something back with you?' Billy
asked, too excited to see her to think of just one question to ask.
'Calm down puppy,' Mary said while scratching his chin. 'I've
been in Meceller looking after my mother, it took her longer to
get better than I had hoped,' she replied.
    'You should have found yourself some honest work
instead of coming back here,' Hilly remarked as he made his way
to the cellar door. 'Oh, I found plenty of work, but it wasn't very
honest, and you know that old fools lost without me,' Mary
laughed. 'You can't be a whore forever,' Hilly said as he bent
down to lift open the metal door to the cellar. 'I'm not a whore,'
Mary snapped at Hilly. 'I'm a lady of leisure,' she added proudly.

# The Unlikely Allies

She then waved goodbye and began skipping to the main door of the Drunken Goblin. Hilly pulled open one of the cellar doors and the two walked downstairs into a dimly lit, smoke filled cellar. There were a few candles, a dresser, and a couple of stools inside. The smoke was coming from an old Goblin who was sat in a rocking chair with a long crooked wooden pipe hanging out of his mouth. His dark green skin was covered in boils and scars from where he'd scratched the boils. Goblins normally have two large teeth protruding from their bottom jaw, this goblin, however only had one, the other had been broken off. He wore a brown filthy top and tattered trousers. To unknowing eyes he had the appearance of a tramp. 'Is that a dirty little wolf I smell?' The old goblin groaned as the boys walked in. 'Ha be nice Wasiz, he can't help it,' Hilly said, laughing with him. Billy shrugged off his comment and asked, 'What's that you're smoking? Smells good!'

'It is, it's a new strain of my pipe weed', Wasiz said, coughing on the smoke as he did. 'My farmers just finished drying it out. I had a couple of Pixie friends of mine lend me some of their fancy dust and I mixed it with the soil,' Wasiz said, taking another huge pull of his pipe. 'I must say, it's quite a success,' the stoned goblin continued. Hilly walked over to a drawer in the dresser, opened it, and took out another pipe. 'Fill it up then' Hilly said, pointing the end at Wasiz.

'You boys got the money for the last one yet?' Wasiz asked. 'We paid that off! We spent two nights keeping imps off your fields, you still owe us.' Hilly said pointing the pipe at the old goblin again. 'Well, I guess you did do a good job, but don't tell anyone I'm giving you handout's though,' Wasiz said, filling Hilly's pipe from a bag full of pipe weed beside him. 'Who could I tell anyway? You won't even let us in the pub,' Hilly said, lighting his pipe using the candle and taking a puff. He took it from his lips and coughed on the smoke. 'Blimey! That's strong!' he said, holding the pipe down, so Billy could try some. 'You know why human. If the rangers found you here, they'd have all our heads and that's nothing compared to what your mother would do to me,' Wasiz said.

'They're already mad at us anyway. We failed the hunt,'
Billy slurred his little head was already spinning from the pipe
weed. 'Don't worry about that now,' Hilly said while trying and
failing to blow smoke rings. 'Tell us a story Wasiz,' Billy begged.
Wasiz took a big puff on his wooden pipe and blew out a perfect
ring of smoke. 'What tale would you like to hear?' The old
goblin had two great loves in his life, one was The Drunken
Goblin and the other was telling stories and over his long life
he'd amassed hundreds. 'Something with romance,' Billy replied.

'What! No something with action and loads of fighting,'
Hilly said. 'Well, I think I have a good one you'll both like, it's
called Madness of the Iron King,' Wasiz said.

'Oh, sounds good, is there a lot of battles?' Hilly asked.

'Don't interrupt boy, just listen.' Wasiz snapped.

'The madness of the Iron King. It was the year six hundred and
sixteen and the now King of the Elves Elidom Godborn, then a
seer, was seeking aid to build an army. An army needed to defeat
King Harold and your ancestors. His first stop on this quest was
to the Iron hills, where the dwarves live, ruled over by King Lex
Darum. Elidom knew that the dwarves magical siege engines
would help turn the war in his favour. But King Darum refused
Elidom not wanting to drag his people into a war he believed the
elves had brought upon themselves. This led Elidom to play upon
the love dwarves have for gold, a love many races share. The
Iron hills are filled with just that, iron. No gold has ever been
found there, however Elidom had control of a fairly large gold
mine on the outskirts of the weeping woods. Elidom offered this
mine to the dwarves in return for their aid. Once the war was
won, Elidom would hand control of it over to the dwarves. King
Darum jumped at this offer, his love for gold was far greater than
the love he had for his people. After ten years of fighting
alongside the elves, the war was finally won. King Lex Darum
returned home with his army and waited for Elidom to return to
hand the mine over to him. Months and then years went by, Lex
growing ever more frustrated. Every message he sent to the elves
never returned. Lex soon came to realise the high elf was not

going to keep his word, but he feared going against Elidom. He had fought alongside him, he knew his power. He could turn the King of the Iron Hill's to dust with a click of his fingers, so Lex locked himself away and began work on a weapon that would make him more powerful than Elidom could imagine. He spent seven years locked in his forge until finally he emerged holding a sword in the human's katana style. To insult the elves even more, he named his sword the Kalarumba a dwarven word, that in our tongue means God Slayer. Without a second thought, he assembled his army, left his loving wife and six young sons and prepared to march, through the Weeping Woods. As they made their way through the bamboo woods, Lex thought he saw something moving above them. Then arrows started flying down from the tree tops in all directions. Lex looked around to see his thirty thousand strong army being cut down. They weren't ready for an attack so close to home, many didn't even have their armour on. To make things worse Lex could not see who or what was firing the arrows, his only hope was to use his new sword. He grabbed it and tried to pull it from the scabbard, but it was stuck. Lex pulled with all his might but the sword wouldn't budge, it remained locked in its scabbard, he then felt a sharp pain in his back. He was hit. An arrow had gone straight through his iron armour and embedded itself in his left lung. He knew this was his end. As his lung filled with blood and the light faded from his eyes. That was when the sword removed itself from the scabbard and began to glow blood red. The last thing the King of the Iron Hill's saw was this red glow, which soon spread covering the whole of the weeping woods. When the light finally faded, there was nothing left; no bodies, no attackers, no king, it was as if they were never there and the great weapon he had created was never seen again.'

'That was a great story Wasiz,' Billy said, now laying on his back on the floor. His little head was still spinning from the pipe weed. Hilly was lent up against the wall, almost asleep still with the pipe hanging from his mouth. 'Well, I hope you learnt the lesson of the story young wolf,' Wasiz said.

'Yer of course I did, but just in case I need to explain to Hilly later.'

'You boys must learn to pay attention, the lesson is look at what you have before you go chasing a dream, a warm bed in a safe house is worth more than any gold mine,' Wasiz said, with that, there was a large bang above Wasiz's head and a trapdoor above him was flung open and Mary's head appeared through it. 'There's a ranger here!' She announced.

'What?' Wasiz said, leaping out of his seat. 'Why are they here?' He pushed his rocking chair back and pulled the rug up to show another trapdoor in the floor. He opened it and the boys could see it was just a crawl space, nearly full of pipe weed. 'Get in quickly before they come down!' Wasiz ordered.

'They never come here, whatcha do?' Hilly said, rubbing his now red eyes. 'Well, them pixies may not have been friends of mine,' Wasiz answered with a smirk. 'You idiot, the rangers must have seen one of your thugs. You should have asked us to get it,' Hilly grunted. The boys squeezed into the crawl space. 'You'd have cost too much,' Wasiz replied as he slammed the door down, pulling the rug and chair back over, just as the cellar doors were swung open with a loud bang as the heavy doors hit the ground. Wasiz sat back in his chair as a wood elf walked down the stairs into the smokey room. The goblin looked up at the wood elf and smiled when he realised who it was. 'Lord Balmoth what brings you to my humble home old friend?' Wasiz said, standing to meet the wood elf. Lord Balmoth wore a dark green cloak over his lighter green ranger uniform, with the ranger's emblem of a leaf on the breast pocket and a two handed sword hanging from his black belt with a red jewel in the hilt. Hilly, and Billy could only see the outline of the wood elf through the slits in the floorboards. 'Don't worry Wasiz I'm not here to put you in the stocks, I'm here on more serious matters,' Lord Balmoth said. Pulling back his hood to reveal his pointy wood elf ears and his short brown hair. 'There's smoke coming from the Blood Works. I believe the orcs have left and are massing for something. I was hoping you might know what.' Balmoth was being blunt with Wasiz, but he was clearly too preoccupied to worry about pipe weed. 'I don't, I've had no word from the South,' Wasiz said, relighting his pipe.

'I may be wrong, but you should be safe, take your girls and go to Meceller for a while, my family will keep you safe.' Billy was listening intently to their conversation until he heard a rustling next to him. He turned to see Hilly filling his pockets with pipe weed, 'What are you doing?' Billy whispered.

'You'd be doing it too if you had pockets,' Hilly whispered back, smirking. Billy looked back through the crack to see Lord Balmoth staring right back at him. 'Wasiz you better tell whoever's down there to come out, or else I'll have to poke my sword into the floor 'till I find them,' Balmoth said menacingly tapping the top of his sword. A worried look shot over Wasiz's face as he got up and pushed his chair back. 'Wasiz I've never seen you so pale, who is under there?' Balmoth said now quite interested in what his old friend was up to. Wasiz removed the rug and Hilly forced open the trapdoor. 'Well, the last thing I expected to find here was you,' Balmoth said, quickly catching sight of Hilly's human ears as he pulled himself out of the crawl space followed by Billy 'or a wolf at that.'

'Are we in trouble?' Billy asked.

'No, you're lucky today, you're the sons of Balvor are you not?' Balmoth said.

'We are. How do you know our father?' Hilly asked.

'We have a deal where you're concerned Hilly. Your father was meant to keep you in the Fang, and you were only meant to watch' Balmoth said glaring to Wasiz.

'I can explain Balmoth,' Wasiz said.

'Later you old fool, we have more to discuss. You two, my son James is outside wait with him and once I'm done I'll escort you back to your father,' Balmoth said waving his hand to jester to them to leave. Hilly grabbed his cloak, and the pair made their way to the stairs. 'Be safe, Wasiz,' Billy said like he always did.

They walked back up the stairs out into the chilly night air. As they did, Hilly saw a couple of bright white horses tied to tie rings attached to the Drunken Goblin. Then, in the darkness, he noticed a young wood elf lent up against the wall, 'Who's there?' The wood elf said, as he heard them coming, moving from the wall into the light shining through the stained glass windows. The pair could now see his green ranger uniform, short messy light brown hair and, more importantly the bow he held in his right hand with an arrow pulled back by the other. Seeing this, Hilly instantly put his hand to the back of his belt to find his dagger, but before he could remove it Billy spoke up. 'That ranger told us to wait for him out here,' the little wolf spoke quickly before either of them did anything foolish. 'That's Lord Balmoth to you dog,' James said, but stopped when he saw Hilly's ears. He had forgotten to put his hood back up. 'Wait, you're not an elf, what are you?' James asked, still staring at Hilly's ears. 'Right, I'm not an elf, and he's not a dog,' Hilly said, hand still on the handle of his dagger. 'What are you then?' James asked, pulling his arrow tighter in his bow. 'Put your bow down boy!' Lord Balmoth's voice bellowed out as he emerged through the cellar door. 'Who are they father?' James inquired as he lowered his bow, clearly getting frustrated that no one was answering his questions. 'This is Hilly and Billy, they're sons of the Lord of the Fang. I have to escort them home, you're to head to the Cove without me, tell them I'll be there by dawn,' Balmoth replied as he untied his horse. He pulled himself on top and then held his hand out to Hilly and Billy to help them on. 'I'm alright, I'll run faster than any horse,' Billy said.

'Ha! These are Meceller horses dog. They're the fastest land creatures in Alidor they could even outrun a dragon,' James said as he mounted his horse. 'My brother's the fastest creature in Alidor and he's a wolf you woody.' Hilly was interrupted by Balmoth's hand grabbing his shoulder and pulling him onto the back of his horse. 'That's enough. We don't have time for you to squabble,' Balmoth said as Hilly's arms instantly locked around his waist terrified he was going to fall off. He'd never been on a horse before, living in the Fang there was never a need. 'We should stay together father, I'll come with you to The Fang,'

James suggested. 'No, head for the Cove. You'll be more use there,' Balmoth ordered.

'Fine, but I think this is a bad idea,' James said then he whipped his reins and began riding southeast for the Cove. Balmoth did the same, but toward The Fang.

'So, what do you want to talk to my father about?' Billy asked as he ran alongside Balmoth's horse. 'That is for your father and I to discuss. Are your dens still near the centre of the forest?' Balmoth inquired. 'Yes, but they'll smell you before you get that close,' Billy said.

'Good, that should save some time, is your brother alright?' Balmoth asked, Hilly still had one hand firmly gripping Balmoth's waist, but his other was covering his mouth, desperately trying not to vomit. 'He's fine, what's the Cove?' Billy asked, not too worried about his brother. 'So many questions for a little wolf, it's a fort we use for scouting, nothing special,' Balmoth replied, as they reached the edge of the forest. 'I can't take it, let me off I'll walk,' Hilly said, coughing through his hand. Balmoth tugged on his reins and the horse stopped. Hilly pulled his leg over to get off, but as he did the horse moved again, and he slipped off and fell hard onto the ground, landing on his back. Billy wandered over to him. 'You okay?' he asked.

'I'm never riding a horse again,' Hilly said, sitting up and rubbing his back. 'How far is it now?' Balmoth asked.

'Not far they probably know you're here by now,' Billy said. 'I certainly do.' Balvor's voice came bellowing out of the dark forest, he emerged from the undergrowth with a furious face. 'Where have you two been? Your mother's worried sick. She even sent Jerrest out to look for you,' Balvor barked before turning to Lord Balmoth, 'It's good to see you old friend, thank you for bringing these two home'.

'It was no trouble, I was on my way to speak to you anyway,' Lord Balmoth replied. Balvor then turned his attention back to his son's, 'You two get back to your mother now. I'll decide what to do with you later.' Hilly pulled himself to his feet, and the pair started making their way back to the dens, but only until Hilly was sure he was out of sight of the pair, then he pulled his dagger from his belt and embedded into a tree. 'What are you doing? We're already in too much trouble,' Billy said, but it was too late. Hilly was already on his way up the tree. 'I just want to find out what they're talking about. It might be about me,' Hilly said, proving he was more vain than anything. Once he was high enough, he began making his way along the branches until he was back in earshot of his father and Lord Balmoth. 'Did he tell you they took down a wood troll today?' He could hear his father saying, 'If they'd have only followed the rules,' Balvor continued. 'They're boys, you give them rules they go out of their way to break them. I have the same problems with my son,' Balmoth said they both laughed and joked for a while before Balmoth's voice changed to a more serious tone, the same he had used with Wasiz. 'I worry the orcs may be on the march soon. If Noress is attacked, your hunters will be called on to fight,' Balmoth said. 'We will defend the town if the need arises but why wou…' Balvor stopped mid sentence and began sniffing the air. 'There's another wood elf in the Fang, and he's bleeding.' With that, the two of them shot off through the forest. Hilly got up and quickly made his way back to Billy. 'What happened? What they say?' Billy asked as Hilly leapt from the tree and pulled his dagger from it. 'There's another wood elf bleeding somewhere they ran off to find him, can you smell anything?' Hilly asked. 'No, my nose isn't as good as dads do you think it's that James?' Billy replied.

'I don't know, we need to get back to mum come on!' Hilly said.

The boys rushed back to find Salene sat in front of their den. 'Where have you been? I've been waiting for you two to come home for ages,' Salene said as they ran up to her.

'Mother, something's wrong. There's this wood elf who knows dad and this other wood elf who's bleeding,' Billy said getting far too frantic. 'Calm down, where's your father now?' Salene asked, but before they could tell her Balvor came charging through the dens with James on his back. 'Salene quickly take the boy,' he said as Salene and the boys ran over to him. 'What happened who's this?' She asked as Hilly pulled James off his father's back and lay him on the floor. He had a wound on his stomach that looked like an arrow had hit him. 'What happened ranger?' Hilly asked.

'Cove gone,' James answered as he fell unconscious. Hilly took his cape off and ripped it to make a bandage, wrapping it around James covering his wound. 'Salene take everyone who can't fight and go to Meceller now,' Balvor said.

'Wait, tell me what's going on? What happened to the ranger?' Salene barked.

'It's the orcs Salene, the orcs are here now get the pups and go!' Balvor said turning to the rest of the pack that had now gathered around them. Before he could say anything, they heard the drums. So loud, they sounded like the footsteps of giants. 'Hunters to me,' Balvor roared. Hilly picked James up putting him on his mother's back. 'What's going on?' Hilly asked.

'It's Okay we just have to get to Meceller,' Salene said, then she looked to the rest of her pack, 'Anyone who isn't a hunter follow me,' Salene barked. Balvor had now formed a line with his hunters, and the drums were getting louder as Fengal took his place beside him. 'Never been up against orcs before boss,' Fengal said, clearly scared. Balvor looked to his family. Salene was leading the others away, hopefully to safety. He worried he'd never see his foolish pups again, glancing back to his hunters he spoke. 'We must fight this day to save the pack we must fight, if the pack lives on we live on,' Balvor roared followed by the rest of his hunters. Their howls drowning out the Orc's war drums, then they charged.

Salene and the others had gotten out of sight of the hunters. Hilly ran over to James, who was still passed out on Salene's back. 'Why have orcs come here ranger? Wake up and tell me what's going on?' Hilly shouted.

'Stop it Hilly, he's passed out you can shout all you want when we're safe,' Salene said.

'Orcs! there are orcs ahead of us,' a voice screamed, then Billy saw them. They had dark green skin with red markings all over their bodies. They wore little clothes, some had armour others just rags, but they were all huge and terrifying. 'Hilly, take the ranger quickly,' Salene said. Hilly pulled James off her back and put one of his arms around his shoulder to hold him up. 'Get to Noress and hide there. I'll come and find you, go!' Salene barked as she charged at a group of four oncoming orcs. Hilly saw her rip the head clean off one sending the others flying before turning to his brother, 'Come on, we hav...' Hilly said as something hit him from behind and sent him crashing to the floor along with James. An orc had knocked him down with his fist. Billy looked up at the orc now towering over him, he tried to run, but his legs were frozen from fear. The orc raised his axe to decapitate Billy, but before he could, Hilly leapt onto the orc's back and dug his dagger deep into the orc's neck, its green blood gushed out covering Hilly's face as he pushed the orc to the ground. He grabbed his brother by the scuff of his neck. *These gits are everywhere we can't run* he thought to himself, then a hollowed out tree caught his eye, 'but we can hide, Billy get the woody in that tree,' Hilly said tugging on his brother's scruff to get him moving. Billy quickly grabbed James shoulder with his teeth and dragged him to the tree. Hilly followed, dragging the corpse of the orc he just killed. Once inside, Hilly used the orc's large body to block the gap and hide them away.

The Unlikely Allies

## Chapter 4
## Old Enemies & New Allies

The boys sat inside the tree for what felt like hours. They couldn't see passed the corpse of the orc to look at what was happening outside, but they could still hear the orc's war drums. The howls of the wolves had stopped soon after they hid themselves away. They remained there in silence until the sun finally began to rise. 'Where am I?' James said, finally waking back up. 'Hiding in a tree,' Billy whispered.

'Why what happened?' James asked, clutching his stomach to find the bandage Hilly had made that was now soaked with his blood. 'You tell us ranger everything was fine 'till you showed up,' Hilly said.

'The Cove, it was burning when I got there. They ambushed me and got me with a crossbow bolt as I ran,' James said, pointing at his wound, 'I'd never have got away if it wasn't for Jenna.'

'Who's that?' Billy asked.

'My horse, soon as I got hit she started charging back to father dodging every bolt that followed. Where are they? Last thing I remember is him putting me on a wolf,' James replied.

'Don't know what happened to him, or our parents, or our whole pack,' Hilly said, trying to keep his voice down encase any orcs were still outside. 'Did you see where mother went?' Billy asked. 'No, I lost sight of her when this git hit me,' Hilly said punching the back of the dead orc. 'I hope they're okay,' Billy said, not being able to take his mind off his parents and the rest of his pack. 'They'll be fine, you saw mum charge the orcs. She ripped them apart. They must have made it out, she only left us because she knew we'd be okay. We can look after ourselves, others in the pack can't,' Hilly said hoping to keep his brother calm. He didn't know how much of what he was saying was true, but he hoped it was. 'We need to get out of here,' James said, moving forward to push the body out the way. 'Quiet, someone will hear,' Hilly said, grabbing James by the shoulder, then Billy started sniffing the air. 'What is it?' Hilly asked.

'I think I smell orcs. I don't know they're not like elves, orcs seem to all smell different,' Billy said, worry creeping into his voice. Hilly pushed the orc's head aside a bit, just enough to see. He could see more corpses scattered around, orcs and wolves. Then a group of five orcs came into view, 'I can see them, stay quiet!' Hilly said.

'What are they doing?' James asked.

'I don't know, shush…' Hilly said, putting his finger to his lips. The orcs walked closer, and Hilly could see them clearer. There were four walking around a fifth who had his hands bound behind his back and a noose tied around his neck, wearing nothing but a loin cloth to cover his waist. The group walked over to the tree opposite the one the boys were hiding in. 'This one will do for the scum,' one orc spat and the one holding the end of the rope tossed it over a branch of the tree. 'They're going to hang that orc!' Hilly said, quickly turning back to the others. 'Good, one less for us to worry about,' James scoffed.

'We need to save him. Can you use your bow?' Hilly said quietly, pulling his dagger from his belt. 'What? Why do you want to save it?' James wondered, trying hard to keep his voice down. 'If we save him, we can get him to tell us what's going on, he might know a way to get to Noress without running into any more of them,' Hilly explained, 'Billy you get the one on the right I'll go left.'

'Fine, but I do this under protest,' James said. Hilly looked back at the orc he was now hanging in the air gasping for breath. 'We have to go now, ready?' Hilly said, turning to Billy.

'Yer I'm ready. I want to get back to the others,' Billy said. 'Okay this is mad but let's do it,' Hilly ordered, pushing the dead orc out of the way. He shot out to the left and ran at the orc in front of him. Billy darted to the right and quickly got to his target. He jumped up at the orc, before he knew what was happening the little wolf had ripped out the orc's throat. James had pulled himself up and lent on the tree by the time Hilly made it to his target. The orcs were still stunned, but this one still had time to swing his mace, luckily Hilly was quicker. He ducked under the mace, sliding across the ground and using his dagger to cut the tendon at the back of the orc's leg, making him fall to his knees. Hilly swiftly stood up behind the orc and rammed his dagger into his neck. James drew an arrow back in his bow and shot at the orc holding the noose tight. The arrow hit him right in the eye, and he fell to the floor dead, dropping the rope sending the orc they were hanging falling to the ground. James quickly let off another arrow, dispatching the final orc who had turned to run away. Hilly pulled his dagger from the neck of the orc he had killed and looked at his brother, whose jaws were dripping with green orc blood. 'Well, I'm amazed that worked,' Hilly laughed.

The orc they had saved pulled himself up, and walked towards the orc that had been holding the rope tight around his neck. When he reached his body the orc raised his bare foot and began slamming it down on the orc's head, turning his skull and brains into a pile of mush. The orc they had saved had dark green skin that showed the many battles he had fought in by the scars over his body, with long black greasy hair, and bright blue eyes that all his people shared. 'That's enough scum,' James said, pulling another arrow back in his bow. The orc stopped and turned, looking at the boys, still not saying a word. He just looked each of them up and down. They all remained still for a minute until the orc finally spoke, 'Why did you save me?'

'We need to make it to Noress, can you get us there without running into any more of your lot?' Hilly asked.

'And if I say no?' the orc said.

'Then I'll just put you down here,' James threatened, pulling the arrow tighter in his bow. The orc stepped forward towards Hilly and turned for him to cut the rope binding his hands. 'I will get you there. I, unlike the others, still believe in the honour of a life debt, but it would be futile,' the orc said.

'Why's that?' Hilly questioned, cutting the rope. Once the rope was removed, the orc strode over to the body of the orc Hilly had killed. He was the closest to his size. He removed the grey trousers and leather sleeveless jacket it had on and began to put them on, along with the dead orc's boots, belt and mace. 'They would have raided it by now and be on their way to Meceller,' the orc said.

'What? They can't be going to Meceller you orcs would never stand against the rangers there,' James replied.

'That's what the dwarves at Orashson hoped too, but we took that city and sixty thousand orcs remain. You woody's in your wooden forts have no hope to hold back the horde,' the orc replied taking a sword off the floor and attaching it to his belt.

'Who are you to know so much? Your leaders don't tell grunts things like this,' James protested.

'I am Mor Ash,' the orc said proudly pounding a fist to his chest, he looked at the boys expecting them to have heard of him. Hilly and Billy hadn't, but when they saw how pale James had gone, he clearly had. 'You're the brother of Ore Ash the War chief, right?' James said.

'I am,' Mor answered.

'Then why were they hanging you?' Billy asked.

'I refused to fight at that Woody fort, so my brother ordered I be imprisoned, but once he left the others took it upon themselves to try to hang me,' Mor said.

'If what the orc's saying is true, it will be a slaughter. My entire families there, we need to warn…' before James could finish talking, his head spun, and he couldn't hold himself up any longer. He slipped off the tree and fell to the floor as the boys ran over to him. Hilly rolled James onto his back and pulled up his shirt, seeing the bandage he had made that was now drenched in blood. The skin around the wound had turned a sickly green, which seemed to be spreading over him. 'Please leave me, get to Meceller warn them,' James spoke in a whisper, drifting in and out of consciousness. Mor walked over and looked down at James, 'How was he hurt?' Mor enquired.

'I think he said it was a crossbow bolt,' Billy barked.

'If it was one of ours, it will have been poisoned, he'll need Mangas root to cure it,' Mor said.

'How long does he have?' Hilly wondered.

'A day maybe, if he's strong,' Mor replied. Suddenly, James' hand grabbed the scuff on Billy's neck. 'Stop, just get to Maggie, my sister please.' With that, James' grip loosened, and he passed out again. 'How long will it take them to reach Meceller?' Billy asked.

'Three days if they run,' Mor answered.

'Don't even think about it,' Hilly warned, trying his best to rebandage James' wound. 'I can get there in a day. He's right we have to warn them,' Billy barked.

'The rangers did nothing to help our pack Billy. We need to stay together,' Hilly argued, desperate to convince his brother not to go. 'His father tried without him we'd still have been sitting with Wasiz getting high, don't worry I can easily make it there before the orcs,' Billy said.

'Mum would be mad if we did nothing, just don't get yourself killed for a load of rangers,' Hilly said, forcing a smile. 'I won't, I'll be back in a couple days, long as I can find my way. Where will you be? I won't be able to sniff you out unless you're with these two,' Billy asked. Hilly sat back and thought for a second. 'We'll go to Noress,' Hilly said.

'I told you they will have sacked it,' Mor grunted.

'So they should have moved on by now. Wasiz has hiding spots all over that town. He has to be alive, and he has every herb you can think of, he will have what James needs,' Hilly said. 'This is foolish,' Mor said with a grunt.

'Are you helping or not?' Hilly snapped. Mor didn't say anything, he just lent down and lifted James over his shoulder with one hand like the young wood elf weighed as much as a leaf. 'Okay, so we've got a plan, just don't stop running, not 'till you're safe.' Hilly said, wishing there was another way.

'It will be fine, just watch yourself with the orc,' Billy said. Then Hilly threw his arms around his brother. He let go, and with a nod to Hilly, Billy turned and shot off through the forest before his mind could be changed.

Hilly waited there until Billy went out of sight before turning to catch up with Mor. 'Why did you have to come here, what did wolves ever do to you?' Hilly asked as they made their way through the forest back to Noress. 'The wolves have done plenty to us orcs, them and the demons nearly drove us to extinction, but it surprised me when Ore ordered the horde here after that Woody fort,' Mor said.

'Why didn't you fight?' Hilly asked.

'There was barely a warrior there, mostly women and children. There's no honour in killing them, it would have sullied my glory,' Mor said.

'Then why go there? Why leave your home in the first place?' Hilly said.

'Truthfully, I do not know. This man, I think he was an elf. He showed up, called himself the Dark Seer or something like that. I don't know what he spoke to my brother about, but soon after he assembled the horde and ordered us to take Orashson. The blood works were emptied, and the horde marched as they did in days of old,' Mor said.

'So you fought against the dwarves,' Hilly asked, amazed. 'I did, they were mighty warriors. The battle lasted three days we had the greater numbers, but the dwarves had turned that city into a fortress, their siege engines are like huge metal beasts that spit fire,' Mor said as he made his way over a ridge. He stopped and turned to Hilly, 'We need to go around here,' Mor said gesturing to Hilly to walk the other way. 'Why are there orcs over there?' Hilly asked.

'No but...' Before Mor could finish, Hilly shot passed him and over the ridge. On the other side was a mass grave. The orcs had thrown all the wolves into a pile in a ditch, leaving the bodies of the hunters of the Fang piled up on top of one another. 'I'm sorry,' Mor said as Hilly ran down into the grave and started trying to move the heavy wolf corpses, desperate to find out if his parents were in this pile. Mor placed James on the floor and walked into the grave to help the struggling boy, who now had tears streaming down his face. Mor moved a few bodies aside to reveal the rest underneath. 'They're not here,' Hilly said still crying but hopeful his parents were still alive. Then he saw Morla dead at the side of the grave. If Balvor had made him and

Billy hunters, that would be him laying there now. 'He was only a hunter for a day,' Hilly said.

'Come on, we should keep moving, the woody won't last much longer,' Mor said heading back to pick up James.

'Hold on,' Hilly said, reaching into the mouth of one of the dead wolves and coating his hand in what little saliva was left. He climbed out of the grave and went over to James. He lifted his bandage and rubbed the saliva over his wound. 'What are you doing?' Mor asked.

'Wolf spit has healing qualities, it might help buy him some time,' Hilly said as he put the bandage back down. Mor lifted James back up and over his shoulder, and they continued on to Noress.

'So who's the Dark Seer?' Hilly asked, trying to take his mind off the grave full of his pack. 'Not a clue, didn't even see his face, he had black bandages covering his whole body. I thought he was blind,' Mor said, happy to try to take the boy's mind off the horrors of war. 'How did you know he was an elf?' Hilly asked.

'His frame, he was slim like an elf, well an elf or one of you I guess,' Mor said.

'What do you mean one of me?' Hilly said.

'Don't act as if I'm a fool demon,' Mor spat.

'I assumed you thought I was an elf, you didn't say anything?' Hilly said.

'Well, if I'm honest, I didn't want to say, I was worried you'd burst into flames and eat me,' Mor said.

'What? Why would you think that?' Hilly said with a giggle. 'That's what happened in the stories my mother told me when I was young, but seeing you back there it's clear you're no demon, just flesh and bone like all others,' Mor said. They both laughed a little, then Hilly smelt smoke in the air. Before Mor could say anything, Hilly ran off for the outskirts of the Fang. As he came charging out of the forest into the wet field, he could see Noress, it was burning. The flames had engulfed the wooden buildings, sending ash and smoke bellowing into the air. Hilly rushed further into the field until he could see the Drunken

Goblin. It was still standing, the stone building had withstood the fires. 'It's okay come on!' Hilly shouted, turning back to Mor who had just caught up with him. 'Wait, we have to move slow,' Mor said as they made their way closer to the town. Suddenly, Mor grabbed Hilly by the shoulder and pushed him onto the ground. 'Quiet, they're still here,' Mor whispered as he lay James beside him. Hilly picked his face out of the dirt and moved the wheat aside. He was just able to see the main door to the Drunken Goblin. A group of twenty or so orcs were standing around like they were waiting for something. Then the large metal doors of the Goblin flew open and an orc wearing a full set of iron armour and an iron helm in the shape of a wolf walked out of the doorway. With a battle-axe in one hand and a chain wrapped around the other, he gave a hard tug on the chain and pulled Wasiz from his home. The chain was wrapped around the goblin's hands. The orc kept pulling on it, dragging Wasiz across the floor, until he was at his feet. When Hilly saw Wasiz he instantly went to run to his friend, but Mor still had a hand on his shoulder holding him down.'I'm going to shove that helm right up his ass,' Hilly said through gritted teeth.

'Stay down, we can't fight them all,' Mor said.

'I'm not just going to watch him die!' Hilly protested, picking up a handful of dirt and tossing it in Mor's eyes. Mor let go of his shoulder just long enough for Hilly to slip away. He stayed low, hoping the wheat would keep him hidden. He stopped when he heard the voice of the orc. 'Tell me goblin what's there to watch here?' The orc said in a calmer tone than Hilly had expected. 'You may as well talk goblin, you and your friends will soon be dead, and your secrets will be meaningless,' the orc continued. 'Then why are you asking?' Wasiz replied as blood dripped from his mouth. The orc kicked Wasiz onto his back. 'Die then watcher filth,' the orc said, raising his battle-axe and slamming it down into Wasiz's chest. Before Hilly knew what he was doing, he had pulled his dagger and was charging towards the orc. 'Bastards!' Hilly screamed as he threw his dagger at the orc, but he raised his arm and Hilly's dagger ricocheted off his armour and landed on the floor. The other orcs had begun charging at Hilly who was now weaponless. He was done for, until Mor came running from the field into the oncoming orcs. 'Fight me you whelks!' Mor screamed, as he grabbed an orc by the neck throwing him at the others, he quickly pulled his short sword from his belt and plunged it into the closest orc smashing his mace around the head of the next. Hilly kept running past the others, his only target was the orc with the wolf helm. The orc raised his battle-axe as Hilly got closer. Once he was in range, he swung his axe, but Hilly ducked down and rolled past the orc, grabbing his dagger as he did. He immediately got back up and went to slash the leg of the orc to bring him down as he had done previously. Before he could the orc turned and kicked Hilly in the chest, throwing him across the ground leaving him in excruciating pain. That kick must have broken my ribs he thought. He tried to get back up, dagger still in his hand, but he was in too much pain to stand, so he started dragging himself along the ground. The orc, with the wolf helm was making his way towards Hilly as Mor continued fighting the others, suddenly a bolt of lightening shot down from the sky, hitting the ground outside the Drunken Goblin. As the light subsided Hilly could see Lord Balmoth standing in front of the metal doors, his silver long sword in hand. Some orcs fighting Mor broke off and ran to Balmoth. He lifted his sword and with a blink of an eye the orcs were dead, their heads flew into the air like balls. The orc that was going for Hilly saw this too and instead of staying to fight, quickly began running from the village. Hilly kept crawling along the floor until he made it to Wasiz. 'Hey you old fool,' Hilly said, lifting himself up to look down on his friend. 'Stupid human,' Wasiz choked coughing on his green blood. 'Inside a box under the bar. It's for you and your brother, get it,' Wasiz continued still struggling to talk. 'You can give it to me yourself,' Hilly said as he tried to stop the bleeding. 'Boy, I'll always be watching,' Wasiz said, then with a sigh he was gone. Hilly couldn't help but breakdown in tears again. Everyone he knew was dying. Before he could wallow longer, Balmoth ran over to him whilst Mor slew the last of the orcs. 'Where's James? Is he alive?' Balmoth shouted as he ran over.

Hilly was too distressed to reply. 'He's in the field, I'll take you to him,' Mor said. Balmoth glared at the orc and wondered why he was helping the boys, but was too concerned for his son to find out now. 'Show me where orc. Hilly take one of these for the pain,' Balmoth said throwing a small purse to Hilly. He opened it and it had yellow beans inside. He ate one and instantly the pain in his chest faded. Then he remembered what Wasiz had said. With the pain gone, he easily stood back up and made his way into the Drunken Goblin to look for the box.

Once inside, Hilly made his way behind the bar and began searching. Then he heard a noise from under the trapdoor behind the bar. He pulled his dagger back out, ready for whatever was inside, he flung the door back. 'Mary,' Hilly shouted.

'What's going on?' she said through tears, Hilly put his hand out and helped her up, throwing his arms around her once he was able. 'You're okay,' Hilly said.

'Wasiz sent me down there and said not to come out, what happened?' Mary inquired.

'The orcs killed him,' Hilly said.

'But your wolves, you're meant to stop this?' Mary cried.

'They attacked the Fang too, everything's gone,' Hilly said. 'Wait, where's Billy?' Mary asked, worried.

'He's fine, he went to get help. Don't worry he can look after himself better than I can,' Hilly said rubbing his chest, 'Wasiz said before he died there's a box here for me do you know what he meant?' Mary moved to the end of the bar, and popped out a panel to reveal a hidden drawer. She reached in and took out a small red box. 'I think he means this,' Mary said, handing it to Hilly. He opened it to reveal a small hourglass. 'Why did he leave me this?' Hilly said. Before they could talk more, Lord Balmoth burst through the doorway with James in his arms. He lay him on a table and pulled his bandage off. He took a herb from his pocket and rubbed it into James' wound, the green over his stomach started to revert to its normal colour. 'Is that Mangas root?' Hilly asked as Mor joined them in the bar.

'Yes, ran into an old friend on the way here. He claimed I'd need it,' Balmoth said. Hilly quickly put the hourglass in his pocket before Balmoth saw it. He didn't know what it was, but he knew he didn't want the rangers to know about it. 'Now, why do you have an orc following you around?' Balmoth asked when he was happy James was getting better. 'We saved him from a hanging, so he helped us get here. He also told us about their next target,' Hilly told him.

'Which is?' Balmoth asked, looking to Mor.

'Meceller,' Mor grunted.

'James sent Billy to warn them,' Hilly said.

'That's impossible, I saw your horde myself on the way here. They were heading back to Orashson,' Lord Balmoth announced. 'That's not what we were told, the orders were to take the Fang and head to Meceller,' Mor said.

'So the orcs a liar what a surprise,' Balmoth laughed, sarcastically clapping before drawing his sword. 'Best I end you here. Your lies may already have got that poor wolf lost to who knows what fate.'

'Stop it!' Hilly shouted, as he felt the pain come back into chest he got out the purse and ate another bean. Mary took the purse from him and looked inside. 'You can't keep eating these. They're Elin beans you'll get addicted,' Mary said.

'I saved his life, which means I own him,' Hilly declared.

'Fine, keep him as your pet for now.' Balmoth laughed, putting away his sword. 'D…dad,' James stuttered as he finally woke back up. 'Mary, get some water,' Hilly said as he went over to James, 'how you feeling ranger?'

'I didn't expect to wake, I thought you'd leave me,' James replied. 'Well guess your lucky wolves are so kind, humans however need paying,' Hilly said as the pair laughed a little. Then James remembered about the army heading to Meceller. 'Father, the orc said there's an army,' James said, but stopped when his father raised his hand to his shoulder. 'It's alright I know about that, but it was bad information. I saw them heading back to Orashson,' Lord Balmoth said. Then they all could hear a rumbling sound coming from the outside. 'That's horses I believe,' Lord Balmoth muttered, walking back outside followed by Hilly and Mary. The sun was now high in the sky, letting them look at the full extent of the damage. The village was devastated. The Drunken Goblin was the only building left standing, but the fires were going out because of the wet wheat fields surrounding the town. Lord Balmoth looked up the west road, where he could see three carriages surrounded by guards on horseback charging towards them. 'Oh no,' Balmoth said as the carriages pulled up, and the guards formed a circle around them. Then, to the surprise of all there, Billy jumped from the window of the middle carriage and bolted towards them.

## Chapter 5
### Hunter's Quest

Billy ran as fast as his paws could across the Plains of Nore trying desperately not to look back, but he couldn't help himself any longer. He stopped and peered back over his shoulder. The Fang looked so small before the vast grey ground of the Plains. He could also see smoke coming from where he thought Noress was and hoped everyone was alright. He thought for a second about running back, but he knew he had to keep moving to warn the rangers of Meceller. Just then, as he was about to speed off, he heard a strange rumbling noise coming from the dry, broken ground of the Plains. Billy stood back as the sound continued until the earth fell away, creating a small round hole in the ground. Before Billy could look in, a small hairless pink creature crawled out of the hole. He wore a small, well made, black vest covered in a grey trim, and a bowler hat, that was balanced between his long pink ears. 'Holt stranger! Who dare impede the journey of Bumbe?' the small creature said.

'Excuse me, but are you speaking to me?' Billy asked, since Bumbe stood with his back to him. He turned around and Billy saw his eyes were shut. 'Ah, there you are, name yourself stranger. For I am on a very important quest, and the noise your feet make have thrown me off and gotten me lost,' Bumbe said.

'My name is Billy, son of Balvor Mammoth Slayer I didn't think my paws made that much noise,' Billy said.

'Balvor you say, so you're a wolf of the Fang aye, well before you get any ideas us mole rats are extremely foul tasting,' Bumbe said as he tapped the ground with his feet, searching for his hole to make a quick escape from the wolf's jaws. 'Don't worry yourself, I haven't eaten for a while, but I'm not so hungry that I'd eat whatever you are,' Billy said.

'Whatever I am? What I am is a blind mole rat, Sir Bumbe the Third is my name, and it is one you should remember.

For once my quest is complete, the whole of Alidor will know that name,' Bumbe said proudly.

'What's your quest?' Billy asked, he was eager to get going but Sir Bumbe had pecked his interest. 'There are strange things happening in the underworld. Beneath your paws is a whole other world living in the earth, and we see and hear things you do not. To you, your paws move silently, but to my ears they are like boulders slamming the ground and I have heard footsteps like many, as if an army walks this way, but that is not all. Wherever these footsteps go the land dies, the soil becomes impossible to dig through, the roots of trees bleed and rot away leaking poisonous black sap into the soil. My people suffer, and I must find out why,' Bumbe said.

'I know nothing about bleeding trees, but I'm fairly sure I know what the footsteps you speak of are. They belong to orcs. They attacked the Fang from what me and my brother found out, they're going to Meceller now. I'm hoping to make it there before they do to warn them,' Billy said.

'Orc's you say, well yes that would explain the footsteps, but I have lived many years, thirty-six in all, and I have never heard of orc's being capable of such things. I am sure whatever infects the soil is not their doing, magic is the only thing that could infect the ground to this extent… wait, Meceller is where you head you say?' Bumbe asked.

'Yes and I cannot waste any more time,' Billy said.

'Wait lad! Wait, you have aided me by telling me of the wolves and orcs, so I shall aid you and tell you to carry on north as you do, and you will come to the Lavender Lake not the Meceller you seek,' Bumbe said.

'What? So, I've been running the wrong way?' Billy sighed.

'Not quite head northwest for a few miles, and you will find a track that will lead you the rest of the way, just be sure to go west. I have travelled to Meceller many times, and it is the course I take,' Bumbe said.

'Thank you, I hope I can still make it in time,' Billy said.

## The Unlikely Allies

'No thanks needed, good luck to you wolf. I have got my bearing now and shall be off. Also, happy I am to have made a new friend of the Fang in days as dark as these,' Bumbe said, hopping back into his hole and with a tip of his hat he vanished underground. Billy looked back to the Fang once more and then sped off, following the directions Sir Bumbe had given him.

He went on for more than twenty miles, not slowing for a second, until he finally came upon a dirt road. To the side of the road was a wooden post that a large black crow had perched on top of. As Billy walked onto the road, the bird squawked. 'CAW! What's this here? CAW!' Billy looked up at it, shocked.

'I didn't know crows could speak,' he replied.

'CAW! And I have never seen a dog as small as you speak. CAW!' the crow answered.

'Fair enough, but must you squawk every time you speak,' Billy asked.

'CAW! Yes I must, I cannot help it. Rude dog very rude dog! CAW!' the crow cawed.

'I don't have time for this, just tell me Meceller is west along this road right?' Billy demanded.

'CAW! I won't say, get lost for all I care, rude dog CAW,' the crow squawked. Then, further ahead on the road, the pair saw three carriages and a large group of cavalry riding with them. 'CAW! Elfie's CAW!' the crow said, flapping his wings. At first, he thought they might be rangers, but then he saw their bright gold armour. 'Who are they?' Billy shouted up to the bird.

'CAW! Better run dog, the Seer's guard come. CAW!' the crow squawked as he flew away, leaving the little wolf to deal with the elves charging towards him. They must have seen him because a group of six riders rode ahead, galloping towards Billy. One carrying a white banner with an emblem of a golden griffin on it. He thought about running, but these may be just the people he was looking for. If he'd already found someone to tell about the orcs, he could get back to his brother a lot quicker, and hopefully, they wouldn't be as odd as the others he had met today. Before he knew it, the group of riders had reached him and circled him, 'Do you speak dog?' One of them asked from behind the slits on his golden helm. 'I do, and I'm a wolf of the Fang, not a dog,' Billy snapped back, fed up with being called a dog. 'No way, Fang wolves are huge, he's lying,' another rider said.

'I'm not. The Fang's been attacked by orcs, a ranger sent me to warn Meceller they're on their way there next,' Billy barked. 'What orcs? No one's buying this story dog. Hey can I skin him, he'd make a nice coat for the wife?' the riders joked and teased the little wolf whilst the three carriages continued to approach. The ones at the front and back were plain white coaches with drawn white curtains hiding whoever was inside. The one in the centre was painted gold with golden carvings running around the top and the sides, like golden roots wrapped around the carriage holding it together, framing the door and four windows. Unlike the others, it was completely spotless, dirt seemingly just bouncing from the bodywork. All were being pulled by grey Meceller shire horses, four to each. As they approached, a young girl's head popped out of the window of the middle carriage. 'What are you doing to that dog?' the girl shouted. 'It's nothing your Highness. he's just telling stories,' a rider said as the girl gestured to her driver to stop and all the carriages came to a holt. She opened the door and stepped out. She looked a bit younger than Billy, with long light brown hair tied in a plated tail and bright red rosey cheeks, she was a wood elf but looked different to the others he had seen, wearing a long blue gown that trailed behind her as she walked. She rushed over to Billy. 'He's so adorable,' she said, stroking Billy's head. Billy was taken aback for a second by how nice the girl smelled, but he soon remembered why he was there. 'Please I'm not lying, orcs are heading to Meceller, a ranger called James Balmoth sent me,' Billy replied. 'Wait, James sent you? Maggie!' the girl said, turning to her carriage where another older girl had come out. She had shoulder length brown hair and a long green dress that matched the colour of James' uniform and was nowhere near as fancy as the other girls. 'Do you know this wolf? He said your brother sent him,' she continued.

# The Unlikely Allies

'Wait. You're Maggie?' Billy said, jumping passed the girl to Maggie. 'James told me to find you,' he ran to the girl, not believing his luck. 'James should be with my father,' Maggie said. 'He was, but the orcs attacked, and he got hurt,' Billy barked as the other girl walked up behind him. 'What? he's injured, where is he?' She panicked.

'He's with my brother, they were heading to Noress to find him help,' Billy answered.

'Princess, please let me take a horse and find out if what the wolf's saying is true,' Maggie asked. Billy looked at the girl and finally realised that she was royalty. The Princess turned to her riders. 'We need to go to Noress,' the Princess ordered.

'But my lady, it would add a day or two to our journey and if what he speaks is correct we may run into this orc army,' a rider said. 'Well, you can return to the academy without me then and see what my father says then,' the Princess said sternly to the rider. 'As you wish my lady, turn the carriage around,' the rider shouted. 'Come on, get in,' Maggie said to Billy, and he jumped up into the carriage. It was just as lavish on the inside as it was on the out. The walls were painted with a warming violet, along with the roof that had two bronze lanterns hanging from it. Billy jumped up onto the cushioned red seat next to Maggie, and the Princess sat opposite. The carriage turned and Billy heard the whip of the reins and the rider shouting orders. 'I'm sorry I forgot to introduce myself, I was just so excited to see an actual wolf, although I heard you were bigger,' the Princess said. 'That's okay, I've never met a princess before, and we are bigger, well the others are. My father would tower over your riders,' Billy replied. 'My name's Emma, well Princess Emmalin Godborn of the Elfin people and the city of Duniesa,' she said sarcastically. 'Well I'm just Billy. Saying that if my parents are gone, guess I'm the Lord of the Fang,' Billy said, realising this was too much for the little wolf. He cried trying hard not let the girls see, but they did. Maggie put her arm round Billy and started rubbing his chest. 'It's alright, we just have to get back to our brothers, and it will all be okay,' Maggie said trying to comfort the little wolf.

## Chapter 6
## The Golden King

Hilly ran down to Billy as fast as he could with broken ribs. Once Billy was close enough, he leapt up into Hilly's arms. 'You're still alive!' Hilly said, putting his brother down. Lord Balmoth and the others followed Hilly out of the Drunken Goblin. Maggie flung the door of the carriage open and quickly made her way to James, who was now standing but was using his bow to keep himself balanced. 'What have you done to yourself? You look half dead, you had me worried you were dead, you stupid boy!' Maggie said, scolding her younger brother before turning to her father. 'And you, why is he even out here? He should have been with us getting ready for the academy, mother's going to be furious,' but Lord Balmoth wasn't paying attention to his daughter, he was watching the Princess who was walking towards Hilly and Billy. 'Well, is this your brother then?' Emma asked as her cheeks became even redder, barely able to make eye contact with the young boy before her. 'He is Princess,' Billy replied. 'But he's not a wolf?' Emma shyly asked.

'No, I'm a human. Thank you for bringing my brother back,' Hilly said, holding his hand out to the girl. When he did, the riders moved in closer to him. 'Did he say human, your highness?' the lead rider asked. The Princess ignored her guard and put her hand out for Hilly to take. He took her soft hand with his own and Hilly pulled her in tight to him. The riders drew their swords as he did and pointed them at Hilly. 'Release the Princess human or lose your head!' the lead rider shouted.

'That's not needed,' a light voice said coming from the last carriage in the row. The curtains had been pulled back, and a pale face peered out of the window, then the door opened and a high elf man stepped out. He was wearing a clean white gown with hair so long and blonde it looked like it was glowing, and ontop of his head he wore a crown of white gold. 'Put your swords away,' the man said, and the riders did as he ordered.

## The Unlikely Allies

'My King, I had no idea you were travelling with us,' the lead rider spoke with a tremble. 'I know I wanted to surprise my daughter on her arrival at the academy. It seems this side track of hers has flushed out the only human left in these lands,' the King said walking towards his daughter who was still standing so close to Hilly she could feel his breath on the top of her head. Hilly let go of her hand and stepped back from her as Lord Balmoth quickly moved to stand behind Hilly and Billy, whilst King Elidom moved to the side of his daughter. The boys noticed how much longer his ears were compared to a wood elf. He was much taller too, standing at least a foot taller than Lord Balmoth. 'What is this Balmoth?' Elidom snapped.

'I can explain my King,' Balmoth replied.

'Can you? Can you tell me why a human child stands here before me. Can you tell me why this settlement is burning? Why there are orcs on my lands? Can you tell me all this Balmoth?' Elidom exclaimed his anger was increasing by the second, he then turned and lead Emma back to his carriage. He waved his hand for Balmoth to follow. Once they were away, the riders showed little interest in Hilly and Billy, all apart from the lead rider. Then Billy saw Wasiz on the floor. 'What happened?' He asked. 'An orc had him in chains when I got here, I tried to save him,' Hilly said as he fell down to his knees clutching his chest.

'Well Balmoth explain!' Elidom said once he was sure only the three of them could hear. 'You explain!' Emma said, interrupting him, 'why are you even here?'

'It's like I said. I just wanted to surprise you,' the King replied. 'Nonsense! You were against me even going to the academy, you're just here to find a reason to drag me back to the Seer's tower,' Emma said. Her trip to Meceller was her first trip without her father in tow, that was at least what she had believed. 'That's enough. We will talk about this later. Wait in your carriage,' the King ordered as he turned back to Lord Balmoth, but she just stood there with her arms crossed glaring at him. 'Well, explain!' Elidom said, snapping at Lord Balmoth once again. 'You asked me to make a lasting peace with the wolves. I did. Barramore and I made a pact that lasted until his descendent Balvor summoned me and sought to change the agreement.' Balmoth said he'd always feared the day he'd have to explain his actions. 'I guess that's when this boy showed up, was it?' Elidom asked. 'It was. He said he'd break the pact unless I could ensure the safety of the boy, the laws of the wolves bound them to protect the child. I didn't think one human could make any difference, so I allowed it,' Balmoth said. Then, out of the corner of Elidom's eye he saw Mor, standing in the doorway of the Drunken Goblin. 'What of the orc? Why does he still live?' Elidom asked, intrigued. 'The boy's managed to get him to help them, not to sure how myself yet, but he got them here. Hilly said they saved his life, but if that's the true reason the orc aids them, I am not certain. Adding to that, I also believe he's the brother of Ore Ash the war chief of the Blood Works,' Balmoth said. Then Emma saw Hilly hunched over the ground, clearly in pain, she quickly left her father's side and went back to the boy. Elidom turned to call his daughter back, but before he could, Balmoth put his hand on the King's shoulder to stop him. He turned back to the ranger. 'We could send them to her?' Balmoth said.

'What's wrong with him?' Emma asked.

'It's nothing, Mary give me a bean,' Hilly said.

'You can't have any more they'll make you ill,' Mary replied, walking over. The Princess was taken aback by the way she was dressed, but she quickly pushed this thought from her mind and looked back at Hilly. 'Tell me what happened, I might be able to help,' Emma said.

'Think I broke my ribs when that orc kicked me,' Hilly winced as the pain grew worse. The Princess rubbed her palms together then pressed them to Hilly's chest but nothing happened. 'That's strange,' Emma said looking down at her hands. Then Mary saw a glow coming from Hilly's pocket. She slipped her hand in without the Princess seeing and pulled out the hourglass, quickly slipping it under her silk shirt. As soon as it was

removed, the Princess's hands became covered in a blue glow.
'Well that was unusual,' she said.

'What are you doing?' Hilly asked as she moved her
palms over his chest. 'I'm finding what ribs you have broken,
and I'm going to try to fix them,' Emma replied.

'You can do that?' Billy asked.

'Yes, but I'm not great at it, so it might hurt a bit,' Emma
said as the glow from her hands grew brighter. Then Hilly began
to feel the pain subside. 'They're good as new. You had two
broken ribs. You're lucky to be alive, they could have splintered
and pierced your lungs,' the Princess added.

'That's amazing,' Hilly began to thank the Princess, but
before he could, Billy interrupted them. 'I can hear them talking
about the pub, sounds like the King wants to tear it down,' Billy
said. 'What? They can't do that!' Hilly exclaimed.

'If the owner died and didn't leave it to anyone, it falls to
the King and I can't imagine my father wishes to own a brothel,'
Emma said.'This place is not a brothel,' Mary snapped.

'Not now Mary,' Hilly muttered, standing up and running
over to James like his ribs were never broken. He grabbed him
by the shoulder. 'Come on ranger, time to pay up,' he said as the
two of them went back into the Drunken Goblin.

Elidom and Balmoth made their way back over to the girls and
Billy. 'The King has come to a decision regarding you and your
brother Billy,' Balmoth announced.

'Which is?' Billy asked, worrying what Balmoth would
say. 'You are both to attend the Ranger's Academy. I'm close
friends with the Headmistress there. I'm sure she will find some
use for you two,' Balmoth said.

'Really? That's great. You'll love the academy Billy,
you'll learn so much,' Emma said.

'So I could be a ranger?' Billy asked.

'Maybe if you pass the tests, and she allows you to train
there,' Balmoth said. Then Hilly came storming out of the pub.
'Balmoth read this,' Hilly ordered, shoving a crumbled piece of
paper into his hand. Balmoth looked at it and instantly

recognised James's handwriting. 'I Wasiz owner of the Drunken Goblin and all the surrounding farms hereby leave my entire estate to Mary Kalon,' Balmoth read the note aloud. Mary looked shocked and was sure the King wouldn't be fooled by this crude attempt at a bequest. 'Well, you knew the goblin Balmoth is it in his hand?' Elidom asked. Balmoth looked at Hilly then back at his King.'It is my King,' Balmoth said.

'Good, well that settles that then. Now we have spent too much time here we should be off. These lands don't feel the same as they used to,' Elidom said, looking around at the corpses scattering the town. He and Balmoth boarded his carriage. 'Come on! You can ride with me,' Emma said. Her, Maggie and James went to get back on. Before Hilly could go, Mary threw her arms around him. 'It was the hourglass that stopped her magic,' Mary whispered. 'What hourglass?' Billy asked. Mary took it from her silk shirt and gave it back to Hilly. 'Wasiz left it to us,' Hilly said, 'Are you sure?'

'Yes it was glowing. Oh, and that Princess likes you too,' Mary said, giggling to herself. 'What? No, she doesn't?' Hilly mumbled going bright red. 'Hilly, Billy, come on, get in,' the Princess shouted. 'You go on, I'm going to get a ride with one of these handsome boys in gold,' Mary said, walking over to one of the riders. 'Well, make sure it's the horse you're riding then,' Hilly shouted to her as he climbed in the carriage and sat down next to James. Billy jumped up to sit between Maggie and Emma, then Hilly saw Mor still standing before The Drunken Goblin. Had the King forgotten about him, or was he just not bothered with him? Then he heard Balmoth call Mor over to the King's carriage. Mor walked over and Balmoth put out a hand to help him in, his colossal frame could barely fit through the door. He sat down beside Balmoth wondering his fate as the drivers whipped the reins.

'My son told me what you did for them, I wanted to thank you,' Balmoth said. 'It's not needed. They saved me, I owe them a life debt' Mor replied.

'What do you think will happen to you now? Mor was it?' the King asked.

'I expect you to torture and kill me,' Mor said bluntly. 'Well, that's just ghastly. Others may go that way, but Balmoth thinks you can be a lot more useful to us than that,' Elidom said. Mor turned to Balmoth. 'I don't know what help I could be. All I know of my brother's plans I have told, you may not believe me, but it is the truth.'

'That is fair. I was short with you back at the Drunken Goblin. I do not believe you led the boys here under a falsehood. You have shown me something I have never seen from one of your people. So, we will talk as friends and I shall not ask questions of your kind but this one. I need to know why you left the Blood Works?' Balmoth said.

'That I can at least say. He called himself the Dark Seer. Many of mine had never heard the name, and when the boy asked me the same question, I said the same. But my brother and I are entitled and elders have told us tales of old, that others cannot hear, to ready us for his return. So when he came orc's would not bow, but fight for their glory, but my brother did not stand instead bowing to him, and now the dark lord has returned the orcs he created are now his once again,' Mor said.

'I knew it, he's back! Elidom he was never killed,' Balmoth exclaimed. 'We don't know that yet, this person could just be using the name,' Elidom said.

'How do you know of him?' Mor asked, shocked that they seemed to know this Dark Seer. Elidom waved his hand as if to say this is Balmoth's problem. 'That's not your concern at the moment. What should be is those boys, I have worries about their safety. Even at the academy they require a guardian to help keep them safe,' Balmoth said.

'You want me to watch over them?' Mor queried.

'It's that or a dark damp cell in the tormented cliff. Do you accept?' Balmoth asked.

'Yes, it would be better than being in chains, but you should know these boys, your son included, will need more than a mighty orc to protect them. The orc who ran from the battle, he is known as Oshan the executioner. He was the reason I was hung from a tree, and he was also the one who brought the Dark Seer to the Blood Works. The Dark Lord will now know of the human and those who aid him,' Mor said. Then they heard laughing and shouting coming from the Princess's carriage. James came alongside the King's carriage, riding his horse. 'Dad, Jenna found us,' James shouted, smiling ear to ear. Then Billy shot passed, 'Keep up ranger,' Billy yelled.

　　　'That's cheating,' James said, rushing to catch back up to Billy. 'Told you he was faster,' Mor heard Hilly shout. The King leaned out of the window to see Hilly hanging out of the open door of the Princess's carriage cheering on Billy, joined by Maggie and Emma leaning out the windows. Elidom saw his daughter smiling like he never had before and could only worry.

Chapter 7
Tailor's Hope

The carriages carried on charging down the road, Billy and James had finally stopped racing each other. James was now sat beside the driver on the Princess's carriage whilst Billy was lent up against Hilly fast asleep like the girls. Hilly, however, was just staring out of the window. He couldn't stop thinking about how everything had changed. A few nights ago he barely had a worry in the world, now he was in a carriage with a Princess, had no idea where his parents were and was going to some academy. *What even was an academy?* He thought to himself as the carriage went over a bump shaking the Princess awake. She rubbed her eyes and saw Hilly staring out of the window. 'Are you okay?' she asked sheepishly.

'Not really,' Hilly said trying to force a smile on his face. 'Are you scared? I would be,' Emma asked.

'No it's not that I've just.. I've lived in The Fang my whole life. I always wondered what else was out there, but now I'm here I just want to go home,' Hilly said.

'I'm sorry,' Emma said putting her hand on Hilly's knee.

'Why? It's not your fault and if it wasn't for you who knows where Billy would have ended up,' Hilly said.

'Guess Norcea was smiling on us,' Emma smiled.

'I don't think your god keeps an eye on wolves,' Hilly joked. 'Don't worry my father will find out what happened and Balmoth's the best ranger there is, I'll make sure they do all they can to find the rest of your pack,' the Princess said sternly.

'Do you really believe they're gonna help us?' Hilly replied placing his hand on top of Emma's. 'Of course they will they must want to stop the orcs as much as you,' Emma said.

'I don't need their help, me and Billy will find who did this.' Hilly said letting go of Emma's hand.

'Wake up,' James shouted from the driver's seat and banged on the roof. 'What is it?' Billy asked waking from his sleep.

'It's the East gate over the Lavender Lake. We're stopping here to rest the horses and will head for the academy in the morning,' James said jumping down from the carriage as it came to a halt. The boys got out and they were instantly amazed by what they saw. They had stopped at the entrance to the stables in a small village known as Lonas. A handful of homes were scattered about before the great gate. At least sixty stories, with two huge towers on either side covered in stone Gargoyles and Golems, which incased the eighty foot iron Portcullis and drawbridge, that spanned the whole of the gorge over the Lavender Lake. 'It's incredible,' Hilly said staring up at it.

'Is everything this big outside The Fang?' Billy asked looking at Maggie. 'No this was built during the human's war,' Maggie said quickly stopping when she saw Hilly was listening, not wanting to create tensions in the group. 'It's okay Wasiz told us a lot about the war. I just didn't believe half of it,' Hilly said as Balmoth and Mor appeared ahead of them. 'Inside, get to bed girls,' Balmoth ordered as the King made his way into the tower followed by his guards. 'Wait what about them?' Emma asked pointing at the boys. 'The King said they are to go in the barn,' Balmoth ordered. 'Have fun with the horses guys,' James said laughing as he led Jenna over to a trough. 'He's also ordered you to stay with them James to make sure they don't disappear into the night,' Balmoth said with a smile.

'Thats so unfair,' James uttered under his breath.

'I'll see you in the morning try to sleep,' Emma said patting Hilly's arm. Then her and Maggie made their way to the tower door. Balmoth simply nodded at the boys then followed the girls. 'Hilly,' Mary said appearing behind him from nowhere. 'Here, one of the riders gave me this,' she said handing a worn wooden pipe to Hilly. 'Thanks may as well get wobbly if we're sleeping in a barn,' Hilly joked.

'I just wanted to cheer you guys up,' she said pulling Hilly to his knees so she could hug the both of them. After a few seconds she let go and stood back up. 'Here, I found you a chain for the hourglass too,' Mary said handing the silver chain to Hilly. She turned and began walking to the tower. 'See you in the morning,' she said waving her hand.

'Wait why don't you have to go in the barn?' Hilly said.

''Ladies' of leisure don't sleep in barns,' she giggled skipping towards the door. 'Come on,' Mor said leading the boys into the barn.

It was large and run down. It didn't even have doors, but was at least full of hay so they'd have something soft to sleep on. Mor walked in and sat down on a hay bale. Hilly sat down on the straw covered floor leaning up against the wall and started filling his pipe with what was left of the pipe weed in his pocket, most of which had fallen out. 'What did they want to talk to you about?' Billy asked Mor.

'About you two and the Dark Seer,' Mor replied.

'What did they want to know about us?' Hilly asked.

'They asked me to be your garden while you're at the academy,' Mor said, laying back on the hay bale.

'You mean guardian,' Billy suggested.

'Yer, that was it,' Mor grunted.

'You don't have to. I was just trying to stop them killing you when I said you were my slave,' Hilly said, Billy was rummaging through the hay and soon reappeared with a lantern in his mouth. 'I knew I could smell wax,' he said, placing it next to Hilly. 'You could really smell that?' James said in disbelief as he walked Jenna into the barn. 'You're not bringing that thing in here,' Hilly shouted to him.

'The main stables are full of the elite guard's horses,' James said. 'Then put it outside,' Hilly ordered.

'Leave her alone, she's had a hard day. Here,' James said, reaching into his pocket and throwing an arrow head to Hilly. 'Fine, just keep her away from me,' Hilly struck the arrowhead on the side of the lantern to create a spark that lit the wick of the candle inside. 'So, did you agree to be our guardian?' Billy asked Mor. 'I did. To be honest, I didn't think I had much choice, you're not the only ones who can't go home,' Mor said, closing his eyes. 'What did you tell them about the Dark Seer?' Hilly asked. 'Who's that?' James wondered.

'Ask your father, I'm going to sleep,' Mor said.

'What you mean, like the Seers?' Billy questioned, 'Mor Mor,' Billy continued putting his front paws up on the hay bale, but Mor was already asleep. 'How can anyone fall asleep that fast?' Billy said, amazed. Hilly lit a piece of hay on the candle, using it to light his pipe and taking a puff. 'Oh great here comes Makron,' James said. Billy looked, and he could see the lead rider walking towards the barn, still wearing his golden armour and helm, with a backpack flung over his shoulder. 'What is it?' James shouted to him. 'You twat's that's what, the King's ordered me to stay out here and watch the Princess's new pets,' Makron said, stepping into the barn throwing his backpack to the floor. 'That's why I'm here'.

'The King's worried you might let them go.'

'Yeh right, he's just punishing you for getting your dad to get you this assignment. Take your armour off too or are you too scared of the human?' James said, poking and teasing Makron. He removed his helm to reveal his short, light blonde hair and bright blue eyes. 'What about you? Not like I'm the only second year getting a job off my father, the last thing I heard the head had suspended you,' Makron said, pushing James back. 'Calm down, we're done fighting for the day,' Hilly slurred, looking up at Makron. Then he noticed how much taller he was than James and his ears were much bigger, more pointy, like the King's. 'What's that smell?' Makron asked.

'The best pipe weed in Alidor, want some?' Hilly bragged, holding the pipe out to Makron. 'That's illegal,' Makron scoffed. 'It's only illegal because the goblins are the only ones who can grow it and elves don't like goblins, that's what Wasiz would say anyway,' Hilly said.

'That's not true,' Makron said, sitting down. James sat down too, and the four made a circle around the lantern. 'Let me try,' James asked, holding his hand out for the pipe.

'You should be arresting them, not smoking with them woody,' Makron snapped.

'There's more important things going on than pipe weed Makron,' James stated as he took a puff and coughed, quickly passing it back to Hilly. 'That's what your dad said to Wasiz,' Billy added. 'Yer he's been saying that a lot lately, not just about pipe weed of course. How did you know the goblin anyway?' James asked, rubbing his eyes. 'He was friends with our father and once we were old enough, he started giving us jobs on his farm,' Billy replied.

'What did you mean by second year?' Hilly asked Makron. 'You really are stupid human,' Makron laughed.

'Don't be like that, we're both starting our second year at the academy when we get there,' James answered.

'Well I am. He still has to beg to get back in,' Makron said to James. 'So we'll be first years?' Billy pondered.

'You should be. I'm not sure what class they're going to put you in though,' James replied.

'What are the classes?' Hilly asked.

'Well, there is the rangers which is what I'm in, Makron's in the elite guards class and the girls are in the home economics class,' James said.

'How do they choose what class to put you in?'

'It's simple wood elves become rangers, elves, and high elves like me become elites and the elf girls go to Home Economics,' Makron said.

'So you don't get to pick, that seems unfair,' Hilly said.

'You sound like the girls,' Makron laughed.

'So where do wood elf girls go?' Billy asked.

'They don't get to go. Maggie's only here because she's Emma's handmaid,' James said.

'A job she shouldn't have, it should be an elf, but the princess kicked up such a fuss when Maggie was not allowed to go with her,' Makron said.

'That really set your father off didn't it?' James joked. 'He's probably still complaining now,' Makron said as he reached into his backpack pulling out a loaf of bread. He ripped a chunk off and went to eat it. As he did, he saw Hilly and Billy staring at the bread they hadn't eaten since before the hunt and the pipe weed was making them even hungrier. Makron tossed the bread over, 'Pass it 'round,' he said.

'Thanks,' Hilly said quickly, taking a bite out of the loaf then ripping a piece off and passing it to Billy and throwing the rest over to James. The boys enjoyed their meagre meal, laughing and joking with each over until they finally fell asleep.

'Wake up,' James said, shaking Hilly awake.

'What's wrong?' Hilly asked, worrying the Orcs had caught up with them. 'We're leaving ahead of the others. Come on, get up,' James said, throwing Hilly a ranger's green hooded cape. 'Where's Billy?' Hilly asked, reluctantly pulling himself up and throwing the cape over his shoulders. 'He's playing with the Princess,' James responded as the pair walked out of the barn to see Billy on his back with the Princess scratching his belly. When the Princess saw Hilly, she quickly stood up and brushed the dust from her long red silk dress. 'Good morning,' she shouted over to Hilly and James. 'Morning Princess, new dress?' James teased. 'Did you sleep ok? It wasn't too cold out here, was it?' Emma asked Hilly, ignoring James completely. 'It was fine. I'm used to sleeping outside,' Hilly said.

'Well, father told me you were being sent off early with Lord Balmoth and well, I just wanted to make sure the elites gave you a good horse,' Emma said, pointing to a huge grey stallion tied to a post. 'That's a big horse,' Hilly said, shocked.

'Yeah, I helped her pick one,' Billy grinned.

'Thanks for that,' Hilly grumbled through gritted teeth. Then the door to the left tower flung open and Lord Balmoth came strolling out with Mor. The pair were talking and laughing like they were old friends, Balmoth turned his attention to the Princess. 'My lady, your father says you should be upstairs preparing,' Balmoth shouted down to her as he waved his horse over. 'I hope I see you both soon,' Emma said before walking back to the tower, giving Balmoth a grumpy glare as she did. Balmoth pulled himself onto his horse and shouted, 'Rangers line up.' James and two other rangers made a line in front of him standing to attention. 'That means you two as well,' Mor said to Hilly and Billy. They both moved over and Billy sat next to Hilly in the line, 'What do you mean rangers?' Hilly asked.

'You and your brother will be in the ranger class. You'll be given the rest of the uniform when we get to the academy. The cloak will have to do for now,' Balmoth said.

'What if we don't want to be rangers?' Hilly said, then Mor quickly slapped him on the back of the head. 'It's being a ranger or have their Seer's pick your fate, and they're not known for being as kind as this King seems to be,' Mor grunted.

'So the King wants us to be rangers?' Billy asked.

'Not exactly. He unlike me was more willing to have you sent before the Seer's, but the young princess got quite the strop on when she found out you may not be going to the academy,' Balmoth said. 'Anyway, this is a briefing, not a social call. We are to head to the academy, but first we need to go to Tailor's Hope. A professor Leonardo Wileby is there. We need to escort him to the academy. Now mount up,' Balmoth ordered with that the other rangers rushed to get on their horses, but Hilly had more questions. Before he could ask them, Mor grabbed him by his shoulder and pushed him in the direction of the horse Emma had left for him. 'Just mount up, we can talk on the way,' Mor said. 'Fine,' Hilly whined. He put his hands on the horse's saddle and tried to pull himself up, after a couple of failed attempts Mor grabbed him by the waist and threw him ontop of the horse. 'I hate these things,' Hilly said, taking the reins in his hands and shaking them, trying to make it move. James trotted up beside him on Jenna. 'It's easy just tap his side with your foot to make him walk, whip the reins to make him move faster and pull them in the direction you want to go,' James directed, doing his best to try to help Hilly. 'Yer easy, just throwing up I'm worried about,' Hilly said. 'Open these gates!' They heard Balmoth shout, then the huge iron gates began to slowly open. The drawbridge lowered to meet with the one on the other side. 'Come on, we'll get left behind,' Mor said mounting a horse of his own and whipping the reins to catch up to Balmoth. James did the same, but before Hilly went to follow he looked down to Billy. 'We could run you know, we could just go looking for our pack?' Hilly said. 'I think we should stay with them the rangers are our best hope of finding the others,' Billy said.

'I don't want to become a ranger Billy, and I don't want to ride a bloody horse,' Hilly said fed up with not getting his own way. 'And I don't want to be Lord of the Fang, but we don't have a choice now,' Billy said sternly, staring into his brother's hazel eyes. 'Fine, we go along with them for now until we think of a proper plan, okay,' Hilly said, Billy agreed.

'Wait, where's Mary gone?' Hilly asked, looking around for her. 'She left with some traders that were heading to Meceller, she said Lord Balmoth tried to get her to cross the river with us, but she wouldn't go without her mother,' Billy said.

'Do you think we'll see her again?' Hilly worriedly asked. 'Don't worry, she's smarter than the both of us and Wasiz put together, and she promised she would find us once her mother was safe,' Billy replied. Hilly then lifted his leg and tapped the side of the horse and he began moving forward. He trotted slowly onto the old iron bridge with Billy beside him, 'What's taking so long?' Mor shouted from up ahead.

'This is as fast as I need to go on this thing, thank you,' Hilly remarked. James rode up beside Hilly's horse and slapped it on the rear. With that, the horse shot off. Hilly held the reins tight and did his best to steer it toward Lord Balmoth's group. His horse darted past them, with James and Billy close behind. James caught up with Hilly and grabbed his reins, pulling them back to slow his horse. 'What you do that for?' Hilly shouted.

'I'm sorry, I didn't think you'd be that bad at riding,' James said, tying Hilly's reins to the back of his saddle. 'Just hold on, I'll do the rest,' James said.

'You will have to learn to ride soon to be a ranger,' Lord Balmoth shouted from behind. 'I don't think I'll make a very good ranger,' Hilly mumbled.

The group made their way over the bridge and onto a paved stone road which went in two directions. One west following the

# The Unlikely Allies

Lavender lake, the other to the north. 'Which way are we going?' Hilly asked. 'West, it won't take long to get there on horse back,' James said. 'What's north?' Hilly asked.

'The high elve's golden city,' Mor said in jest.

'And the academy and a lot more,' James added.
'Golden city?' Hilly said, full of interest, causing Billy to look up at him with a disapproving stare. 'It's not a golden city, just one gold tower,' James replied. Lord Balmoth lead the group onto the west road, and they galloped alongside the gorge that divided Alidor. At the bottom of the ten mile drop the Lavender Lake ran. The water was so clear the boys could see the fish swimming below as they looked down into the gorge. Unable to be fished the fish had grown to incredible sizes, so that even from so high they could be seen clearly. 'Hilly, you better keep your hood up when we get to Tailor's Hope. We don't want to attract unwanted attention. You better keep your face covered too, Mor,' Lord Balmoth said, handing a black cloth to Mor to cover his face with.

For sixty miles they rode, until the group approached Tailor's Hope. The town was bustling with people. Hilly noticed the townsfolk looking over at them as they came into town. He quickly pulled his hood tighter over his ears, hoping no one would notice him. He had never been anywhere that was this crowded before. Lord Balmoth leapt down from his horse and was surrounded by a group of admirer's. 'Excuse me sir, but are you Lord Balmoth Commander of the rangers?' one girl shyly asked. 'So much for not wanting to draw attention,' James muttered. 'I am my lady,' Balmoth said, smiling to the girls.

'Do you think you could help us? I'm searching for a man called Leonardo Wileby do you know where I might find him?' Balmoth asked.

'I know of him, although he is a rather peculiar person and I don't know what you'd need of him. He lives in the centre of town. We can take you there,' another girl said taking hold of Lord Balmoth's arm. 'Excellent, you two come with me, James you and the others stay with the horses,' Balmoth ordered, and the other two rangers followed him whilst James tied up the horses. Hilly gingerly slid off his horse doing his best to keep his hood up. 'Getting used to it yet?' Billy asked as Hilly put his feet back on the floor. 'I'll never get used to riding these things,' Hilly said, looking passed his brother to Mor who also had his hood up and the cloth covering most of his face. 'Hey Mor you and the Lord seem to be getting close,' Hilly said as Mor walked closer to the pair. 'I'm doing same as you boy, trying to keep the woody's nice, so they don't behead me,' Mor said, checking James didn't hear. 'You still haven't told us what you said to him about the Dark Seer,' Billy asked.

'I told him all I could about that Dark Seer but other than that we...' Mor was cut off by a huge explosion.

'What was that?' James shouted, running over with his bow ready. They could see thick black smoke bellowing out into the sky, coming from what looked like the centre of town. 'I smell blood,' Billy said.

'Lead us there,' Hilly ordered and Billy shot off, leading the group into a maze of stone buildings until they made it to the centre of the town where the market was. 'It's him,' Mor said as he glanced around the side of a building, pulling the sword and mace from his belt. Hilly looked and in the centre of the burning market stalls stood a man all in black with black bandages covering his face. Suddenly, Lord Balmoth appeared behind the man and swung his sword down, hoping to catch him off guard, but the man quickly turned and grabbed the blade of Balmoth's sword in his left hand. 'Tut tut Richard sneaking up on people how rude,' the man said. Then a purple glow appeared on his right hand, and he slammed it into Balmoth's chest, throwing him into the burning market stalls. James ran out firing arrow after arrow at the man, but he simply put up his hand deflecting them all. Then with a wave James's bow was pulled from his hand, shattering into pieces. 'Enough of this, come out I know you're hiding out there human. I hope that traitorous Orc is still with you too,' the masked man said.

'Billy stay hidden and wait for your chance,' Hilly ordered as he walked out to join James with Mor. 'Why do you want me?' Hilly said, pulling his hood down and removing the rangers cape. Mor did the same, not wanting to die with his face covered. 'So it's true there really is a human, do you realise how many orcs I killed because I thought them to be lying?' The man said like it was a joke. 'And you Mor Ash your brother will be the one to pay for your betrayal,' he continued.

'Your fights with me, not my kin,' Mor said.

'And you human, I don't know where you came from, but because of a couple of orcs seeing you they took it as a bad omen and rushed back to Orashon like a bunch of deranged cowards.' The man said in such a way that if his mouth was uncovered, he would be spitting in anger. 'Well, that explains some things, but it don't tell me why you had Wasiz killed?' Hilly asked. 'Oh, I killed a friend of yours. I'm sorry but lets be honest boy, I've taken more from you than one feeble old goblin,' the man said raising his glowing purple hand. Two black shadows appeared in front of him, one shadow then took on the appearance of Balvor lying on the ground wounded. The other took the form of the orc wearing the wolf helm. Balvor's shadow lay there, barely able to move, but Hilly could just about make out his jaws moving like he was saying something, but the shadows were silent. The orc's shadow began to move over to Balvor battle axe in hand. 'Stop this now,' Hilly shouted to the Dark Seer. 'There's nothing to stop, this is the past, nothing but a memory. There's no changing this, no saving your pack nor your father.' As the Dark Seer said this, the orc's battle axe slammed down onto Balvor. 'I will gut you,' Hilly screamed, pulling his dagger from its sheath. 'No you won't human you will die here,' the man said, creating a fist with his glowing hand. The purple light over it darkened and sparks shot from it. 'First you die, then I kill the orc and lastly the son of the great Richard Balmoth,' the man said raising his hand. 'Stay behind me,' Hilly exclaimed.

'Why?' James asked.

'Just do it,' Hilly barked as the man shot a purple beam of shadows at the group, but as it got close, Hilly's hourglass glowed. Then the beam was stopped by an invisible shield created by the hourglass, protecting the three of them from the

Dark Seer's attack. 'How did you do that?' James asked Hilly, looking at him shocked. 'I'll tell you later,' Hilly said.

'How did you do that?' the Dark Seer shouted, clearly frustrated, or even worried Hilly had some mysterious ability. This caused him to lose focus, and he didn't notice the little wolf making his way around the side of him. This was his chance. Before the Dark Seer could react, Billy leapt up and drove his fangs into the masked man's throat, but to his surprise there was no flesh beneath the cloth. Billy landed on the ground on top of the pile of black clothes and cloth the man had been wearing. 'Where is he?' Hilly said, running up to Billy.

'I don't know, he disappeared,' Billy said.

'It's shadow magic. He was never here in truth, just in spirit,' Lord Balmoth said as a man helped him to his feet and walked him over to the boys. He was badly hurt, his leg was clearly broken, and he was bleeding all over. 'This is Leonardo Wileby by the way,' Balmoth said gesturing to the man beside him. The man wore a white long jacket with a smart grey tunic and trousers which suited his short blonde hair. His nice attire, however, was now stained by Balmoth's blood dripping on him. Before they could say another word, the towns folk came out of hiding. One instantly screamed seeing Mor standing in the centre of town. 'An orc!' one man called out as a group of soldiers ran in, making a line in front of the group. 'Well, you guys showed up late,' Hilly said, turning to the soldier's with a cheeky grin.

'A human too,' another man cried in shock.

'Who are you to have such interesting friends, my Lord?' Leonardo said to Balmoth. 'Don't wind them up Hilly' Balmoth demanded. 'You're in no condition to deal with this Richard, don't worry I'll take care of this,' Hilly said, smiling to him.

'So much for keeping him a secret,' Balmoth said.

'My good people don't fear me and my companions,' Hilly said to the crowd forming in front of him, raising his arms in the air. 'My name's Hilly, son of Balvor the Mammoth slayer, and yes, I am the only human in Alidor,' Hilly declared.

'What's he doing?' James said, leaning down to Billy.

'I'm not too sure,' Billy said.

'Me and my brother Billy lived happily in the Fang, with our pack but a couple of days ago our home was invaded. Our family killed by the same man who attacked your charming town, because of him me, and brother may be all that's left of our pack. Now because of him, many of your people now lie on the ground before us,' Hilly said gesturing to bodies scattered around the market, then he saw the bodies of the rangers he'd been riding with. 'Now you may not trust humans, you may not trust wolves or that ugly orc standing there before you, but you can trust we will save our fangs for the real enemy, I hope you will too,' Hilly said. The elves of the town calmed, and the guards gingerly lowered their weapons. One removed his iron helm and walked towards Hilly, whilst James bandaged Balmoth's leg. 'I believe I should thank you, I suppose,' the elf soldier said, holding out his hand to Hilly. He shook the man's hand and said 'No thanks needed, it's just a shame we didn't get the man responsible for all this.' Looking up to the elf, he only seemed a handful of years older than Hilly. 'Me and my men aren't exactly used to seeing orcs and wolves in our town,' the man said.

'And where were you and your men Landon, when this fiend attacked my shop?' Leonardo said, pointing to his destroyed workshop. 'I thought the explosion was in the market,' Billy said. 'No, Lord Balmoth had just been in my shop a second then that masked man showed up, all I remember after that was waking up in the street,' Leonardo replied.

'So he wasn't after me? It was you!' Hilly said looking up at Balmoth. 'We can talk about this later, we must hurry to the academy' Balmoth said.

'No,' Hilly said, blocking his way. 'This guy attacked the Fang to kill our father, then he attacked Noress to kill Wasiz, now he attacked this town knowing you'd be here picking up the professor. The only reason you're still alive is us. We don't leave this town 'till you tell us why he's hunting you all down,' Hilly insisted. Balmoth looked at the boy standing in front of him, he was right he had a right to know but how much to tell him. 'Come on, there's a tavern over there, I need a drink' Balmoth said. Mor came over and helped him into the tavern beside Wileby's workshop.

The group went in and sat at a round table, Captain Landon continued to the bar and got a large bottle of Dwarves' whiskey along with several glasses and brought them over to the table. 'Here, on the house, least I can do,' Landon said.

'You own the pub?' Billy asked.

'No but being Captain of the Guard gives you some perks,' Landon said.

'We can't stay here long, you need your wounds looked at,' James said to his father.

'I think I have something in my bag for pain,' Leonardo announced, reaching into his large carpet bag he had brought with him. He pulled out a bronze injector with a huge needle on the end. 'No, thank you,' Balmoth quickly said.

'Why don't you get the wolf to lick you,' Mor said as he threw back shots. 'What?' James wondered.

'Wolf spit has healing qualities, Hilly covered you in it when you were poisoned.' Mor laughed.

'You did what?' James said shocked.

'Can you please all shut up!' Hilly said sternly, his eyes were still locked on Lord Balmoth. 'He's right, we should all discuss what we now know,' Balmoth said.

'Right, you start,' Hilly demanded, he would not let Balmoth talk his way out of this. 'Where to start, as you know I was the one who made the pact with your ancestor to defend Noress, then later when your father came to me to discuss you, but when he did, I sought for something in return from him,' Balmoth said. 'What was it?' Billy asked.

'That he'd join the watchers,' Balmoth announced.

'That's just a story you told me and Maggie when we were kids,' James added.

'No boy, they were true. We are a group of people from a wide range of races created by myself and King Elidom after the first orc invasion,' Balmoth said.

'What did you do?' Mor asked.

'We were spies, I ran the group with the Headmistress of the academy,' Balmoth said.

'She's in on this too,' James said, shocked.

'Yes quiet boy, we started just the two of us then the dwarf Banburry Bale joined us, then the goblin Wasiz. After the human's war we were ordered to disband by the King and go our separate ways. Instead, we decided on watching over our races, but we'd only act if their actions would cause the world to go to war again. You see, we'd all seen and done horrible things in the human's war, things we can never atone for, but we never wished to go back, never wanted our children to fight like we did. We wanted to stop the world turning into a bloodbath once again. Then a while later your father joined the group' Balmoth said.

'So he's dead now because he was in your group,' Hilly asked.

'Only us watchers and the King know who the others are. Not even the King knew of your father at least that's what I thought, but now the head and I are the only watchers left, and I know it can't have been one of us that sold out the others,' Balmoth said.

'What about the dwarf?' Hilly wondered.

'I assume he died in the attack on Orashson,' Balmoth said. 'Did he have grey hair and talk with a stutter,' Mor asked. 'Yes,' Balmoth replied.

'He is dead then. He's the only one of the dwarves the Dark Seer made a show of killing, had the whole horde watch as Oshan beheaded him,' Mor said still throwing back shots.

'Did he say anything before he died?' Balmoth wondered. 'He may have, I was too far back in the crowd to hear,' Mor said. 'Is Oshan the one with the wolf helm?' Hilly asked 'He is, he's my brother's head executioner, or I should say the Dark Seer's now,' Mor said.

'How do you know it's not this Headmistress then?' Billy asked. 'I know it couldn't have been her. If she wanted to kill them and me she'd have done it with a click of her fingers and a smile. That's why I know it's not her, that's why I set a trap this morning when I announced our plans to come here, I did that so the elites would hear,' Balmoth said.

'This was all a trap, that's why you accepted my application all of a sudden, to use me as bait,' Leonardo said in shock. 'We will pay for the damage to your workshop,' Balmoth said. 'My workshop. People are dead Balmoth!' Leonardo exclaimed. 'I didn't expect an explosion,' Balmoth replied.

'No, but you knew this man has an army of orcs. You were expecting this town to be wiped out,' James shouted, clearly angry at his father. 'Who do you think it is?' Hilly said, ignoring the others. 'I can't be sure yet but at least it shows the elite's may have someone feeding information to the Dark Seer,' Balmoth said. 'The elites, you mean that Makron from last night?' Billy said. 'When did you meet him?' Balmoth wondered.

'In the barn the King sent him to keep an eye on them,' James replied. 'Really well that's interesting,' Balmoth said.

'Why?' Hilly asked.

'Oh, it just surprises me that a high elf would stoop to sleep in a barn,' Balmoth said.

'What's so special about him?' Hilly asked.

'Makron's the finest swordsman at the academy and also the son of the Seers Eloise and Marlos La Sore,' Balmoth said.

'So he has powers like the King,' Billy asked.

'Makron's a high elf like the King, yes so he should be able to use all the elements, but since his parents are siblings he was born abnormal, with no magic,' James said.

'What he's inbred like webbed toes?' Hilly joked.

'I don't know how it works, but high elves are very free when it comes to love and keeping their bloodline pure,' Lord Balmoth rolled his eyes. 'That's sick,' Mor said.

'Your people eat their young, don't they?' Balmoth quipped. 'Not anymore,' Mor muttered still drinking.

'So both his parents are Seers?' Hilly asked.

'Yeah and he's moving up the elites fast, most would already follow his orders,' James said sounding oddly proud.

'This doesn't matter. What does is what to do with the two of you? Getting you two into the academy, which shouldn't have been a problem before when it was just us and the King who knew of you, but now the Seers will want this taken to them,' Balmoth said.

'He's right, you four put on quite a show, news will soon spread of the unlikely allies of Tailor's Hope,' Landon said laughing. He'd been listening to the conversation from the bar. 'That's what I'm hoping for,' Hilly said.

'Why? If everybody knows about you, the Seer's will have to act,' James replied.

'If we were a secret, they could just do away with us whenever they wish, but now if the only human in Alidor goes missing, everyone will know who did it,' Hilly said.

'That's easier said than done. I may have the King's ear but the Seer's would be quite happy to see the rangers disbanded completely. They will use the fact I let you live against us,' Balmoth said. Then, a bright white light burst in threw the windows of the bar blinding everyone inside. As the door flung open, nearly coming off its hinges from the force, a woman wearing an orange gown walked in. Her hair matched the colour of her dress and was so long it was dragging along the floor behind her. As the light faded Hilly and Billy could see the woman making her way towards their table as Balmoth began rubbing his eyes. 'Well quite an entrance as always mistress,' Balmoth said. She ignored Balmoth and walked straight over to Hilly until she was towering over him. He looked up at her but could barely see her face past her huge breasts. 'This is the human?' the Headmistress asked.

'Yes that's him,' Balmoth replied. She moved her hand and held it above Hilly's head then her stern expression went to one of shock. 'He has two of the items how does he even have one?' she asked

'Wasiz,' Balmoth sighed.

'That damn Goblin,' she said stepping back from Hilly as her hair and dress began to turn a darker red to reflect her growing frustration. 'Place them on the table boy,' she said sternly to Hilly. 'Place what?' Hilly asked confused.

'Your dagger and the hourglass,' Balmoth said. Hilly took his dagger from his belt and the hourglass from round his neck and placed them on the table in front of him. 'Where did you get these?' the Headmistress asked.

'I got the dagger from a cart that was going through the Fang, the other Wasiz gave me. I get why'd you want to know about that but what's my dagger got to do with this?' Hilly said. 'Do you know the story of Lex Darum and the weapon he created' Balmoth enquired.

'Yer Wasiz told us just before you showed up,' Billy answered. 'Well you know what happened then, just the sword didn't go missing as everyone thinks. Even the sword couldn't control its own power so it disassembled itself and became five different items. Your dagger and the hourglass are two of them,' Balmoth said. 'Yes and the fact you can use two of the items at once is unusual, even I can only handle one,' the Headmistress said, tapping the eagle shaped hairclip that was keeping her fringe back from her face. 'What are the others?' James asked.

'My sword is another and the King has the ring,' Balmoth said. 'What a mess you've made Balmoth. We must return to the academy,' the Headmistress, said walking over to Balmoth and holding her hands out like the Princess had done to Hilly to heal his wounds. 'Thank you, I was wondering how long you'd make me wait,' Balmoth said. She ignored Balmoth again and turned to the tavern door, she tapped her hairclip then opened the door. 'Follow me,' she said, the group got up to follow her but Balmoth quickly grabbed Hilly's shoulder. 'Once you go through the door not a word out of all of you, got it. You too, James,' Balmoth said. The boys nodded and went for the door, Mor pulled himself up and followed. 'Thanks for the drink Captain,' Mor said, giving a small wave to Captain Landon who was still stood at the bar amazed by what he had just witnessed.

# The Unlikely Allies

## The Ranger's Academy
### Chapter 8

They walked through the door, but to their surprise it didn't lead them back to the market of Tailor's Hope instead, they were in the grounds of the Ranger's Academy. To the left of them lay a large training area full of young rangers training with bows and swords, alongside others in golden armour the same as Makron La Sore had worn were with them. Right before them was the castle twenty stories high, made from polished grey granite. Legends say it was built by elf masons, whose skill could only be bested by the dwarves of the Iron Hills. The castle and grounds had been built for the sole purpose of training the rangers, and the Headmistress had a say in every aspect of the build, allowing her to not only create a place to train soldiers, but to educate them as well. On the right were a set of three wooden buildings that looked like dormitories. Each of the three buildings had a plaque above the door. The furthest one from them and closest to the castle had a white rose above it. The centre one had a gold helm, and the third had a leaf. Surrounding it all were tall stone walls with four towers, one in each corner and on top of the castle itself stood a fifth, stretching high into the sky. The boys had entered the grounds through a door beside the main gate, and looked on amazed as the others followed the pair stumbling forward. Both straining their necks to try to see the top of the fifth tower, 'How are we here?' Billy asked, looking at Hilly, who was still in shock. 'It's the head's hairclip. It can open a door to wherever the holder wishes,' Lord Balmoth said as Mor closed the door behind him, and stood beside Hilly, and Billy. 'I don't like all this elf magic. it's too trippy,' Mor said.

'Quiet! They're coming,' Balmoth snapped. There was a group of people walking down the grey granite steps of the castle. Ahead of them was the Princess running towards them, trying not to trip over her long red dress as she ran. 'You're finally here. What took you so long?' She shouted as she rushed over to Hilly, and Billy, 'bird's have already shown up from Tailor's. Everyone's heard about what happened that's why father sent the Headmistress to get you. Wait why do you smell of whiskey?' The Princess asked.

'That's not us, it's him,' Hilly said, pointing at a wobbly Mor, as the group of adults approached the Headmistress. 'Well done Headmistress,' a fat, bald high elf said, 'have the elites lock this lot up 'till we can return them to the grand city.'

'My Lord Seer this is my academy not yours, it is me who gives orders here not you,' the Headmistress replied.

'How dare you, these boys are criminals and the orc cannot just be set loose upon the grounds,' the Seer said.

'Princess take the boys to my office I'll be there soon,' she ordered. The Princess grabbed Hilly's arm to lead him and Billy away. 'James, you better go too. Take Mor with you, he should probably sit down,' Balmoth said noticing how much he was wobbling. 'You cannot just do as you please because you have a title. It won't be stood for I tell you,' the Seer continued trying to regain the Headmistress's attention. 'Where is the King? It is him who will have the final say on this,' the Headmistress said. As she and Balmoth walked past the Seer, and his entourage. 'That's Seer Dune to you and that would be the case, if the other Seers weren't arriving soon,' Seer Dune spat. Balmoth stopped and turned back to him, 'all the Seers are leaving the Golden Tower for this one boy and a puppy that's unprecedented,' Balmoth said.

'No ranger what's unprecedented is the way the King allows you, and that harlot to do as you like with no consequences. Best hope that the human's head is the only one on a pike at the end of this day,' Seer Dune spat in anger. Balmoth turned back to rejoin the Headmistress and entered the castle.

They walked through the massive wooden doors into the main dining hall, with three long tables in the centre that could easily seat four hundred on each. At the far end of the hall was a fourth smaller table. In the centre of this table was a golden throne carved into the shape of a Griffin with golden wings stretched out. King Elidom sat there eating a vast range of exotic berries and fruits. 'When are they getting here?' the Headmistress shouted to the King as she stormed towards him, hair still glowing red. Balmoth keeping the human a secret from her had frustrated her, but hearing all the Seers would be coming to her academy had enraged her. 'By they I assume you mean the rest of the Seers, they should be here soon,' the King replied ignoring the anger in her voice. 'You know what they're going to want,' Balmoth said. 'Why all this effort to save these three Balmoth? If you go against the council on this your fame among the wood folk won't be enough to keep saving you,' Elidom said.

'I promised their father I'd keep them safe, but it's not just that. Before I went to Noress to find James, after fighting through those damn orcs in the Fang, guess who I ran into? An old friend of ours, he was quite manic about the pair he claimed they may be the only way to stop what's coming. True he didn't say a thing about the orc, but I believe we will need him,' Balmoth said taking a seat beside the King at the table. 'Who could know such things?' the King asked.

'It was June,' Balmoth replied. Elidom and the Headmistress looked at him, both shocked to hear his name. 'That's impossible,' the Headmistress said through gritted teeth. 'It's true he even gave me the herb I needed to save my son,' Balmoth said. 'It is possible he may have learnt foresight or stolen it from another, either way we shouldn't concern ourselves with the ramblings of the betrayer,' the King said.

'There's something else too. Hilly holds two of the five,' Balmoth said. The King looked down at the plain silver band on the middle finger of his right hand. 'He can wield two of them?'

'I believe so,' Balmoth said.

'How did he get them?' Elidom asked.

'Wasiz,' Balmoth and the Headmistress replied in unison. Then the doors of the dining room opened and Makron La Sore entered, followed by Seer Dune and the other three Seers. 'I hope you know how peeved I am to have to come all the way here to sort out your mess Balmoth,' Seer Eloise La Sore whined, as she walked in holding the arm of her husband. She was wearing a long, white silk dress with her light blonde hair tied up in a bun. The other Seers wore long white capes embroiled with a golden eye, the symbol of the Seers, over their expensive tailor made suits. 'Indeed, I see this as even more reason to do away with this pet project of yours, my King,' Seer Marlos La Sore said.

'I'm sure we can all come to an understanding on this matter,' the King said gesturing to them all to take a seat. 'There's nothing to understand my King. The law is the law we must put the human to death,' Seer Dune said sharply.

'He's just a boy. Why do you fear him so?' Balmoth wondered. 'Don't think me heartless ranger if this was just one mere human that would be one thing, but of all the races in Alidor this boy was raised by the damned wolves. If he were to find another pack and the human's hatred is allowed to fester once more it could spell the end for many. I will not allow it,' Seer Dune said. 'Their pack is dead along with their alpha, their father, with that any hope of the wolves ever rebuilding is gone, I'm sorry to say,' Lord Balmoth argued.

'What of the attack on the cove?' Seer Marlos asked.

'It was destroyed by orcs they moved on to the Fang and Noress after that. If they hadn't encountered Hilly they would have then went on to Meceller, so we have him to thank for that,' Balmoth said. 'How do you know this for sure?' Marlos asked.

'Their leader told us himself,' Balmoth replied.

'At this attack on Tailor's Hope we have just been hearing about?' Seer Marlos asked.

'Yes, I believe he wanted to see for himself if the human was real,' Balmoth said.

'And the man, who is he?' Eloise asked.

'He called himself the Dark Seer,' Balmoth said causing Eloise to look to her husband in shock. 'It can't be the same man,' Marlos sternly replied.

'Indeed, because you killed the Dark Seer yourself, didn't you my Lord, in the battle for the Ash Caves?' Balmoth said to Seer Marlos. 'Yes, this man must be an imposter, a copycat of some kind,' Marlos argued.

'Right, a copycat who can control the orcs and has shadow abilities I haven't seen since the first great war,' Balmoth replied. 'What are you trying to say ranger?' Marlos said.

'Whoever he is, he will clearly be more of a problem than the human,' Balmoth insisted.

'Maybe, but it is up to the rangers to deal with orc matters, the human is our problem,' Seer Dune declared.

'The rangers are scouts, at best a peacekeeping force. We can't fight a war with the orcs alone we need the army. The elites must march,' Balmoth said.

'The army must not be used. The elites are vital to protecting this side of the river,' Seer Dune said.

'If not now, when. Will you let all the people of the south fight and die whilst you sit idle?' Balmoth asked.

'The south side of the river is your domain ranger,' Seer Dune said in the most condescending tone he could. 'This should be discussed later when we are all of clearer minds,' Seer Avlor Tranem said. He was the only one of the Seers who had not yet spoken. 'He's right but we must decide the humans fate,' Marlos insisted. 'And what are the options as you see it my Lord Seer, you are the wisest of us all,' Elidom said to Avlor.

'The boy and the wolf, I sense the presence of them in all our futures, good or bad I cannot say. I ask we test them to see if I may then ascertain their purpose,' Avlor said.

'A test, what sort of test?' Lady La Sore asked.

'You wish them to train as rangers yes? Have them take the first years final exam,' Seer Dune said.

'With no training it would kill them, even Balmoth's own son barely passed after a year of training,' the Headmistress said. She had held her tongue and been content to stand to the side as the others spoke, but the final exam took training, the pair simply weren't capable of completing. 'Maybe, maybe not it is that or the course of action I would prefer but either way they die,' Dune said. The King stood up at his table.

'Do you all accept this, that the human and the wolf will take the final exam. If they pass they will have earned their place here and Lord Balmoth will take responsibility for them. If they fail Seer Dune will get his way,' the King announced. The Seers all raised their hands in agreement. 'Then it is agreed,' the King said. 'Good, we shall do it first thing in the morning, the sooner I leave this place the better,' Dune scoffed.

'One night, you must give them more time to prepare!' Balmoth protested. 'If you insist Balmoth I suppose we could push it back 'till, lunchtime, yes dinner and a show,' Dune laughed. 'Don't mock me Seer,' Balmoth said, doing well to not speak his true thoughts. 'Enough the matter is closed, tomorrow at noon the boys will be tested that's the end of it. Now Marlos would you join me,' the King said as he made his leave followed by Seer Marlos La Sore. 'Indeed come Richard,' the Headmistress said, making her way to a door close to where Balmoth sat, she clicked her fingers, and the door went from leading to a corridor to the Headmistress grand office at the top of the tallest tower perched on top of the castle. But as the pair made their way out, Seer Dune had one last comment. 'I shouldn't worry too much if the boys die Balmoth we can just add it to the long list of Richard Balmoth's great failures,' the fat Seer said chuckling to himself.

They walked into the office to find Hilly, Billy, and James sat on a large leather sofa. All of them were half asleep, clearly worn out from the day's adventures, and climbing the tall tower. Mor had passed out on a frost troll fur rug on the floor, he had barely made it through the door. The Princess sat in an armchair reading from a small book with a ripped brown cover. 'Wake up,' the Headmistress shouted, slamming the door once Balmoth was through. The boys jumped awake while Mor remained asleep on the rug. 'What happened?' James asked, rubbing his eyes.

'What happened Miss, you're back at school now boy,' the Headmistress snapped, 'and you should be preparing for classes go on now,' she said to Emma ushering her out of the office. 'It's not the best news but it's better than it could have been,' Balmoth said opening a cabinet and taking out a bottle of wine and two glasses. 'First the matter of your suspension, young Balmoth,' the Headmistress said with a glare to the young wood elf as she sat down behind her paper covered desk. 'What did you do?' Billy asked James.

'He was found in the girl's dorm,' the Headmistress answered for him. 'It's not like it sounds,' James whispered to Billy. 'You make it sound so bad.' Lord Balmoth chuckled as he poured himself a glass of wine. 'Quite Richard, the boy's too alike you as it is, but in light of recent events you have more than earned your place back here, although you must attend you magical orientation lessons. Miss Perry told me you only went to two in your first year,' the Headmistress said.

'Is my time not better spent training? I can't wield magic, it's just a waste of time Miss,' James said.

'You must attend all classes that's that,' the Headmistress said sternly. 'Off with you now best get on with making a new bow,' Balmoth said. James nodded stood up and went to the door. 'Now as for you two, the Seers have decided that you are going to be tested by taking the rangers exam for first years. If you pass you'll stay and train here as rangers. If you don't well we can work that out if it comes to it,' the Headmistress said. Hilly glanced over at Lord Balmoth. He didn't want to be a ranger, and doing their tests sounded like far too much work, but at the moment it was the only option he had. The only way to get closer to finding out if his mother was still alive. Billy on the other hand could hardly contain his excitement, and couldn't keep his tail from wagging uncontrollably, he wanted to find his pack as much as his brother, but he never thought he'd ever have the chance to train with wood elves or elves at that. 'What's the test?' Billy asked excitedly. 'You won't find out until you get to the testing ground tomorrow,' the Headmistress said.

'So, how do we prepare for it?' Hilly asked.

'Anyway you can, we cannot be seen to be helping you it would only give the Seers more of a reason to have their way. You will have to call on everything your father and mother have taught you to pass. I have to say this is not what I brought you here for. I brought you here to keep you safe, but we are left with little choice now the Seers have become involved. Seer Dune will do everything within his power to see you fail,' Balmoth said. 'Also you must keep in mind although Balmoth wishes you to stay here this is my academy, I do not have any ill feelings towards you, but I will also show you no favour. Every wood elf here has had to earn their place you shall be no different,' the Headmistress said sitting like a queen in her fine leather chair. Balmoth stood up placing his now empty glass down. 'Go on now, you have much to plan for, and you will need a good night's rest,' Balmoth said gesturing to the door.

'What about him?' Hilly asked, pointing to Mor still passed out on the floor. 'I'll deal with him,' Balmoth sighed.

Hilly, and Billy left the head's office. In the hallway sat at the top of the spiral staircase, the Princess was waiting for the pair, still reading from the book. 'How did it go?' she asked, closing her book. 'We have to do some test for first years,'Billy said.

'You mean the rangers test for the first years, the final exam?' she asked, worry creeping across her face.

'Yer they didn't tell us what it was though,' Hilly said.

'It's different for everyone, come on I'll tell you on the way to your dorm,' she said and led the boys down the stairs.

'So what do we do in this test?' Billy asked.

'It could be anything, sometimes they're mental tests, sometimes she summons a creature, the last time I saw the test was when James did it,' the Princess said.

'What happened to him?' Hilly asked.

'She summoned a horde of banshees, he only just passed,'
'How do you beat banshees, we've never seen them,' Hilly wondered. 'He was quick enough to dodge their talons while he made a torch to light his arrows. Banshee's hate fire. Once he had the torch he was able to scare them into submission,' the Princess said, as she led the pair back down the spiral staircase of the Headmistress's tower. Then through the castle passed painting after painting of the Headmistress, the eyes seemingly watching each of them as they went back into the courtyard. 'That's the guy who came here with you isn't it, who is he?' Emma said

pointing to an elf man excitedly jumping about a cart, as he was was unloading wooden boxes. 'His name's Leonardo, he's a professor,' Billy said.

'A professor of what? He doesn't look like any professor I've met,' Emma said as Leonardo saw the boys and waved over to them. 'Ah good boys, grab a crate,' he shouted over.

'What is all this?' Hilly asked.

'My inventions dear boy, my life's work. I say is that the daughter of Elidom there with you?' Leonardo said diving into a large wooden box. Reappearing with a metal cube with handle on the side. 'My lady I have lived many years, and traveled much of your father's lands. In this box is the sweetest song I have heard in all my travels, just turn the handle,' Leonardo claimed handing the box to her. 'You do not look much older than us Professor, how many years is it you've travelled?' Emma asked taking the box from him and turning the handle. 'Well I am merely twenty seven in actual years, but the sheer fountain of knowledge I possess surpasses that, I am sure'. As she turned the handle, the lid of the box sprung open, and the sound of a sweet, relaxing melody began to play. 'That's incredible, what sort of magic is this?' Emma wondered.

'It's making my ears feel all warm,' Billy said smiling as his little head swayed to the tune. 'There's no magic here Princess, just science and a little careful soldering,' Leonardo said, delighted at their reaction to his invention. As Emma, and Billy listened to the melody, Hilly walked over, and looked into an open crate in the packed cart. It was filled with weird looking devices and metal contraptions he'd never seen before, but one caught his eye more than the others. He reached in, and pulled out a device with a circular bronze barrel and a wooden handle with a silver trigger on the underside. At the end of the barrel was a small grappling hook. 'Be careful with that!' Leonardo said, whipping it out of Hilly's hands. 'What is it?' Hilly asked.

'I call it the super, speedy grappling hook, launching and pulling device,' the Professor said, proudly holding the device aloft. 'Long name,' Billy said.

'Well we can't all be as simple as wolves, can we?'
Leonardo snapped. 'What does it do?' Hilly asked.

'Well, I made it to help scale walls faster than having to
use a ladder, and it was very handy for cleaning the top floor
windows at my... well my now destroyed workshop. You just
fire it, and it will hook in and pull you up, could never find
anyone to buy them though,' Leonardo said.

'Why not? The rangers would love something like that,'
Emma said. 'You'd think, but the rope I use is from blind
spider's web so it's hard to get hold of, but it makes an
indestructible rope,' Leonardo said, taking out a box of
cartridges, so they could see the silky white rope. 'I'm lucky
really, as soon as the bird came with a letter saying I'd been
accepted to teach here I got so excited. I hired carriages that
night, so I had already sent my most valuable inventions and
designs ahead of me before the attack.'

'So, what is it you are here to teach?' Emma inquired,
but before she got her answer Billy saw James running over to
them. 'Hi um. So I've got bad news,' James mumbled.

'Can it get much worse?' Hilly asked.

'Well the rest of the rangers don't want you in the dorm,'
James said. 'Does that mean we have to go in a barn again?'
Billy wondered. 'No but you'll prefer a barn to the alternative,'
James sighed. 'They're not putting them out there, are they?'
Emma asked. 'There's nowhere else, go on, I'll help the
Professor,' James said as he climbed up to help Leonardo unload
his cart.

Emma led Hilly, and Billy through the grounds of the academy,
passed the other dorms. They followed the wall until they came
to a worn down, rotting, wooden shack in the corner of the
battlements. It was full of holes and both of its two windows
were broken, barely a tile was on the roof. It was completely
hidden from sunlight that gave you a ghostly chill when you
walked close. 'So this is it?' Hilly said disappointed, he'd been
looking forward to having a real roof to sleep under. 'I know it's
barely even a shed,' Emma replied. The boys walked into the tiny

shack, it only had the one room with nothing in it but broken chairs and old pots and pans. 'Well, it could be worse,' Billy said. 'I can bring some things to help make it nicer, if you like?' Emma said, turning to Hilly trying to make their bleak situation seem a little better. 'Thanks for all your help,' he said, the pair then stared at each other, both desperately trying to think of something witty to say, until the quiet was broken by a loud thud from outside the shack. Hilly looked out to see Mor laying on the grass, 'You couldn't wake him then?' Hilly laughed.

'No this orc sleeps like the dead,' Lord Balmoth said slightly out of breath from carrying the large orc. 'My lady you shouldn't be out here, head back to the main hall, dinner should have started by now,' Balmoth said.

'I'll see you two later,' the Princess smiled at the pair delaying leaving as much as she could. 'Don't worry Princess they will still be here tomorrow,' Balmoth joked as she once again gave him an angry look as she walked away. Balmoth handed a bag to Hilly. 'Here you'll need this for tomorrow, can't have you going out there in those rags,' he said as Hilly looked in to find a green ranger uniform and black boots. 'I really have to wear this?' Hilly asked.

'Yes if you want to be a ranger. There's food in there too, have something to eat and get some rest, you have a big day tomorrow,' Balmoth said leaving the boys to deal with Mor. 'What should we do with him?' Billy asked.

'Just leave him, he has to wake up eventually,' Hilly said still looking at the green uniform. 'Why do woody's like green so much?'

'It's not that bad,' Billy said.

'You're only saying that 'coz you don't have to wear one.'

The Princess made her way to the main hall and took her seat beside her father at the table at the top of the hall along with the rest of the Seers, the Headmistress, and a few of the teachers. The hall was packed with students. The home economic's girls sat on the far left table giggling and joking with each other. The rangers were much the same but the elites sat in the centre row all silently eating their meals ignoring the noise around them, until Makron turned to the rangers table behind him. 'You! Where's James Balmoth?' Makron asked a boy at the rangers table.

'That twat, he's with the Princess's pets,' the ranger shouted back making Makron turn back to his dinner. The Princess began picking at the fruit salad in front of her as the adults around laughed and drank until something Seer Dune said caught her attention. 'So what do you have planned for them tomorrow?' he asked the Headmistress.

'Don't worry yourself they will be tested fairly. I won't be going easy on them if thats what worries you,' the Headmistress said. 'Come on give us a hint, a swarm of murderous crows? A slime from the pits of the crook's hollow? Well my lady?' Dune said trying to persuade her.

'I thought it was obvious to anyone with a basic knowledge of magic what my intentions are for tomorrow. Pilgrim's ink has only one use after all,' when the Headmistress said this her eyes locked to Emma's only for a spilt second, but long enough for her to know what to do. 'Father may I be excused I'm not feeling well,' Emma said.

'Yes my dear go on, I'll check on you later,' the King replied. Emma got up and looked over to the home economic's table for Maggie. She saw her, sat alone at the end of the table. Emma waved to her handmaid, and she quickly got up and followed her out the hall to a side corridor. 'Whats going on?' Maggie asked. 'I know what Hilly and Billy are fighting tomorrow, come on we need to tell them,' she said pulling on Maggie's arm. 'We can't just go running round the place looking for them,' Maggie said hoping to calm the now very excited Princess. 'You're right someone will see us, and they'll just change the test if the Seers find out that we helped them or worse. Wait I've got a better idea come on,' Emma said. The pair ran down the corridor and into a corner tower of the castle which was filled with birds of numerous different colours and species. Maggie raised her arm and a large grey parrot flew down and landed on her. The Princess had taken a quill and paper from a small desk in the corner of the room and wrote a note, rolled it up and then handed it to Maggie. 'Are you sure? If your father or the Headmistress finds out,' Maggie said.

'Don't worry, she never would have said anything if she didn't want us to tell them. It's the only way they have a chance tomorrow,' the Princess said. Maggie reluctantly placed the note in the capsule and tied to the bird's left leg. Emma stroked the bird under his chin and whispered, 'take this to James Balmoth,' the parrot spread his wings and flew out of the open window.

The sun had already set as Mor finally woke to find himself on the grass in front of the old shack. He saw Hilly, and Billy had made a fire and the little wolf was resting beside it. 'Where's the other one?' Mor asked as he pulled himself up rubbing his aching head. 'I don't know he just said he had to get something,' Billy said. 'He shouldn't be wandering around alone,' Mor said going into the bag of food Lord Balmoth left. 'Stinking elves I'd kill for some meat right now I find it hard to believe that Balmoth lives on only leaves and bread,' Mor groaned biting into a dry piece of bread. All Lord Balmoth had left them was a loaf of elven bread which even with a fine soup is as dry as sand, along with that was only a cabbage and a few sprouts. 'This green stuff makes me sick,' Mor said looking at the sickly green cabbage leaves. Then James walked over he sat down at the fire with the others looking quite upset. 'Why you here?' Mor wondered.

'I got kicked out of my dorm,' James said shyly.

'Why, what you do?' Billy asked.

'They think I'm a traitor, said it right to my face, then told me to leave all because I helped you,' James said.

'You can't blame us if your mates are whelks, all races have fools who blind themselves to the truth of things, the reason you're here now is the same reason I was hanging from a tree,' Mor said. 'That's pretty deep for an orc and why are you staring at a cabbage?' James asked. Mor was staring at the vegetable intensely. 'It looks like brain but tastes like licking an old orcs foot,' Mor said.

'Why would they hate us so much? I don't understand it,' Billy said butting back in. 'You can answer that yourself. Look at the past of your own race. Once allied with the humans, even the great hordes couldn't contain them,' Mor said.

'Now, imagine if the orcs make an alliance with wolves, elves would be done for they don't hate you, they fear what you may do,' James said. As James spoke Hilly ran up to the others, and put the large sack he was carrying down. He also had a brand new bow flung over his shoulder. 'Good you're here,' Hilly said taking the bow from over his shoulder and handing it to James. 'Where did you get this?' James asked looking at the perfectly polished mahogany bow. 'I stopped by the elite's dorm and their armoury was basically open, I mean there were three locks, but a child could have opened them,' Hilly smirked.

'So you stole it, how did you even break the locks?' James said. 'The word is procured James. I procured them and I made some lock picks with the odd bits of cutlery from the shack. Wasiz showed me how to make them out of almost any bit of metal,' Hilly said showing him the fork he had broken and bent into a pick. 'No it's stealing Hilly. How can I use this when everyone knows only the elites have gear like this?' James said. 'Simple.' Hilly reached into his bag and pulling out a jar filled with dark black dust. 'Black dye?' Billy asked.

'Yep, we just dye the bow, and they'll never know,' Hilly said heading into the shack. He reappeared with a boiling pot which he struggled to place over the fire. Hilly filled the pot with water from the small well next to the shack and poured in the black dye leaving it to boil. Then something caught Billy's attention, it was a large grey bird, it flew down and with a huge flap of its long wings mounted itself on top of James's left shoulder. 'What's that thing?' Hilly said shocked at the size of it. There wasn't many birds in the Fang certainly not one like this. Billy however was slyly licking his lips, his instincts had kicked in as he hadn't eaten meat in days. 'Calm down, it's the Princess's messenger bird. It's a grey parrot, they're nearly extinct.' James said holding his arm out and the bird walked down from his shoulder. A small capsule was tied around its leg,

James opened it and took the note from inside. 'Why's she sending me messages?' James said, placing the parrot on the ground and unraveling the note. 'It's for you,' James leant over to hand it to Hilly. 'What's it say?' Hilly asked.

'Oh yer, the wolves didn't teach you to read did they?' James said. 'I can read most things, just tell me what it says,' Hilly scoffed. True, he could read a bit, but next to an elf of his age he would be at least ten years behind. Wolves didn't read books. They would tell their tales rather than write them down and Wasiz was not much of a teacher. Also Hilly was easily distracted and whenever Wasiz would try, Hilly never paid much attention. 'It says that the Headmistress is using pilgrim's ink in your test tomorrow and good luck,' James said. Hilly stared back at him with a blank face. 'Well, that explains why she sent me the note, you're clueless,' James laughed, then like a flash of lightening Billy shot past him. 'What are you doing?' James shouted turning to see the Princess's messenger bird halfway down Billy's throat. 'Billy, stop it, spit it out,' Hilly ordered as Billy continued to munch down on the Princess's endangered pet. After he was finished Billy turned back to the others, the few feathers around his mouth were the only thing to show there had ever been a parrot. 'I'm so sorry, I just, you know instincts,' Billy said, feeling quite ashamed but very full. 'I can't believe you did that,' Hilly said.

'You just ate the whole thing beak and all,' James said shocked. Mor however, was laughing his head off, finding the whole thing extremely amusing. 'So what's pilgrim's ink then?' Hilly asked James. 'Oh right, you use it to create golems. You draw a glyph on a bit of wood or stone anything really, and it brings it to life.' James said, still pale from shock.

'I was expecting an obstacle course, but my plan should still work though,' Hilly said, seeing the pot boiling on the fire he picked up the ranger uniform Lord Balmoth had given him and dropped it in the pot. 'Come on, we can do your bow when we get back,' Hilly said.

'Wait where we going?' Billy asked, Hilly went into the sack he had brought and pulled out tie rings with brackets attached. 'I got these from the stables. We need to sneak into the arena and put them up. It should be dark enough now. Come on, you too ranger time to pay us back for saving your life,' Hilly said throwing the sack back over his shoulder. 'I still can't believe you ate it whole,' James said, pushing himself up using his new bow.

Chapter 9
The Ranger's Exam

Students poured into the arena, filling every seat in the large
stadium outside of the battlements of the academy, built solely
for the rangers exams. Ten stories high walls and six towers
encircle the mile wide arena below. Built into the walls were
stands and balconies for spectators to watch. Not only students
filled the seats, common folk from towns and villages had
travelled from all around. Elves from the fishing village of
Muckbay, and the town of Hanerson came to see if the rumours
they had heard were true. The speed of which the Headmistress
had organised the event had not slowed the spread of gossip
among the wood folk and loose lipped elves. Many had flocked
to the academy to see the spectacle, even a group of dwarves
who were traveling from the Iron Hills to the markets of the
grand city of Duniesa, had decided they could not continue their
journey until they saw the pair with their own eyes. They were on
one of the balcony's looking down, waiting impatiently to see
what was about to unfold, the Headmistress looked down on the
crowd from her balcony looking over the arena on top of the
wall. With her was the King and the Seers, but the Princess had
chosen to sit beside Maggie in the stands hoping to get a better
view. Behind them sat Lord Balmoth with Leonardo. The
Headmistress made her way to the edge of the balcony and raised
her hand. The crowd instantly fell silent. 'Rumours spread like an
uncontainable fire, the only way to put out such fire is with truth.
All of you here heard what happened at Tailor's Hope on the
evening of the third day of nine in the month of Elidom himself,
how the town was saved by some unlikely allies. Many probably
don't believe the things you've been told. Today I tell you the
rumours you have heard are true. Tailor's hope was saved by the
son of Lord Balmoth but he was not alone, with him was a
human, a wolf and an orc. This human and wolf known as Hilly

and Billy, son's of Balvor Lord of the Fang will today they will under go the rangers end of year exam.' The Headmistress waved her hand, and with that the door of the arena flung open and Hilly, and Billy made their way in, to the shock of the crowd most of whom were now speechless. 'What has that boy done to his uniform?' Lord Balmoth said as he saw Hilly had dyed his green uniform black. 'Do you think they're going to be alright?' Emma asked Maggie. 'I'm sure they'll be fine, James made it through didn't he and he was alone,' she said.

'But he had a year of training,' the Princess mumbled looking back down to see the pair now stood in the centre of the ring. In front of them sat a huge pile of boulders. 'Looks like she was right,' Billy smiled.

'Yer just got to keep to the plan,' Hilly said. The crowd soon got over the shock and were now screaming profanities at the pair. 'They seem nice,' Billy joked.

'Don't worry they'll be cheering my name by the time we're done,' Hilly said tapping the black bag he had tied around his waist. The Headmistress looked down to them, 'are you prepared?' she shouted down.

'Do we really have to do this?' Hilly shouted back as she raised her hand. The boulder's in front of the pair began to move rising from the ground, stacking themselves on top of others until they formed two forty foot stone Golems. They both had two arms, two legs and a torso but no head. One wielding a stone shield and sword, the other had no weapon. It was soon evident why, it raised its left arm stretching apart the bolder at the end of its arm, splitting it into a hand with three fingers. Once the Golem could move its fingers they instantly began to glow green. All of a sudden a green beam of earth energy shot out at Hilly and Billy. It completely covered them, the crowd jumped from their seats thinking the pair had already met their ends, but thanks to the hourglass they were both saved from the magical beam. 'There's two of them,' Billy barked.

'I know new plan,' Hilly shouted.

'Which is?' Billy asked.

# The Unlikely Allies

'Just keep running,' Hilly said as the beam finally faded, 'go!' He bellowed as the golem prepared to fire again. Billy shot off making the Golem turn trying to target the little wolf as he ran around it. The other golem charged at Hilly swinging its sword at him, he dived to his right just missing the blow from the huge stone sword as it slammed into the ground beside him. He reached into his bag, and pulled out Leonardo's super, speedy, grappling hook launching and pulling device. He looked up and saw the tie rings they had placed on the towers around the arena the night before. He quickly armed the device, and pulled the trigger the grappling hook shot out followed by the blind spider web rope. It hooked into the tie ring and Hilly released the trigger. Instantly he was pulled off the ground and into the air with such force he felt as if his arm was being pulled from its socket. 'Where did he get that from?' Balmoth said turning to Leonardo. 'Don't look at me, I didn't give it to him he must have stolen it from my new workshop,' Leonardo said as Hilly flew up to the tie ring wrapping his arm around it. He quickly reached into his bag and pulled out another cartridge to reload his repel. Just as he clicked the cartridge into the device the Golem swung its sword at the tower, smashing it to pieces. Hilly pushed himself off trying to dodge the falling stone from the Golem's broken sword, firing the repel as he did praying it would hit something. Thankfully it did, and just as Hilly was about to hit the ground the repel swung him back into the air. He looked down at the golem and saw its earth glyph on the top of its torso, the Headmistress had draw on them to infuse the boulders with the earths magic. Billy was still running circles around the other Golem then he saw Hilly swinging through the air towards him. Hilly reached out his hand and grabbed Billy as he shot past firing the pair back into the air. 'It's on the top' Hilly shouted.

'Wait what?' Billy said as Hilly let him go. Hilly landed back on the floor in front of the shield wielding Golem, but Billy had landed on top of it. He found the glyph and licked it clean off the boulder. The magic holding the golem together faded, and it broke apart falling to the ground and breaking into pieces. Billy barely had time to leap from it into his brothers arms as the beast crumbled beneath him. 'Well that's one,' Billy said as the other Golem fired another beam of earth energy at the pair. The hourglass protected them but they were pinned against the wall of the arena and the Golem was moving closer. The creature must have known its magic was useless but it could at least use it to pin the pair in place while it got close enough to crush them with its hands. 'What do we do?' Billy asked frantically.

'Remember how dad took down the mammoth,' Hilly said reloading his repel again. 'This is the last one we can't miss.'

'Don't worry, I'll get it,' Billy said. Hilly forced himself forward, pushing back the beam just enough for Billy to run out. As soon as he did, Hilly fired the repel. Billy ran to the left to avoid the Golem's magic, then ran off after the grappling hook, which shot past the Golem, followed closely by Billy, who caught up to the hook and grabbed the rope in his mouth. The Golem hadn't noticed Billy until the little wolf began to run around his feet, binding the creature's legs. Then he stabbed the grappling hook into the ground, 'Now!' he shouted to Hilly. Hilly released the trigger, pulling the wire tight around the Golem legs, making it lose balance and fall. Its huge body slammed to the floor, making the entire arena shake, knocking Billy off his feet. The Golem noticed this and raised his hand once again and began to build up the energy to fire at Billy. Then Hilly saw the Golem's glyph on the underside of its outstretched arm. Hilly began running quickly, spitting into his right hand and taking the hourglass from around his neck with his other. Throwing it towards Billy, just as the Golem unleashed another beam of earth energy. Hilly made it to the Golem and used his spit covered hand to wipe the glyph off, making it fall to pieces like the other. Hilly looked over to his brother, but he was hidden in the dust that the Golem had kicked up. He ran into the dust and found Billy lying on the floor, motionless. 'Billy, Billy are you ok?' Hilly said, terrified he was hurt. Then Billy rolled over and opened his mouth to reveal the hourglass. 'You git. I was really worried,' Hilly said laughing as the dust cleared, and the pair looked up to the crowd staring down at them in silence. Then they cheered and clapped. The Princess and Maggie were on their feet cheering with the crowd, Leonardo turned to Lord Balmoth, 'at least I finally got my device tested,' he said, smiling. Balmoth however, had his eyes firmly fixed on the Seers to see what they would do now. The Headmistress held up her hand and once again the crowd calmed. She stepped aside and King Elidom took her place. 'Congratulations, the pair of you are now students of the Ranger's Academy.' As the King spoke, Seer Dune got up from his seat and stormed off, clearly displeased with the results, but Seer Marlos was the complete opposite. He was smiling from ear to ear as he stood beside the King to look down on the boys. 'Yes, a fine performance boys, worthy of Lord Balmoth himself and the rangers of old I dare say. You both will make fine rangers and even finer additions to this academy,' Marlos said.

'Go now rest, your lessons begin tomorrow,' the Headmistress said. The pair made their way back to the door of the arena, Hilly had begun to wave and blow kisses to the crowd. 'What are you doing?' Billy said.

'Just giving the people what they want,' Hilly said with a crooked grin as the pair left the arena triumphant.

Once outside, they found James and Mor waiting for them. 'I can't believe you survived,' James said, brimming with joy.

'How did you ever doubt us, and thanks for helping put the rings up,' Hilly said.

'I'm not the one you should thank,' James said, pointing to the grappling hook stuck in Mor's arm. 'What? How did that happen?' Billy said, shocked.

'When Hilly fell from the tower, he tried to catch it, and it got stuck in his arm,' James said.

'You saved me. Thanks, guess that's your life debt paid then,' Hilly smiled.

'I suppose so, to you at least, what happens now?' Mor grunted. 'Now we find Emma to fix your arm,' Hilly said.

'That's Princess to you, and while you're doing that I'm going to find Seer Dune. He left as soon as you two passed, I know my father noticed as well,' James said.

'So what are you going to do?' Billy asked.

'I just want to see where he stormed off too,' James replied. 'Okay, Billy get him to the Princess, I'm coming with you,' Hilly said.

'Fine, just don't steal anything else today,' James smirked.

'Princess, Princess!' Billy shouted, running to her and Maggie who were coming out of the arena. Emma had forced her way through the cheering crowd to find the brothers and celebrate their victory with them. 'You did amazingly in there Billy,' she praised the little wolf as he ran to them. 'Thanks, but I need your help again,' Billy said. He led her and Maggie to the stable where Mor was sitting beside Jenna waiting with the hook still in his arm. 'What happened to you?' Maggie said.

'I know, can you fix him?' Billy asked.

'I can try,' the Princess said. She had a look at Mor's arm, then grabbed the hook and pulled it out, Mor didn't even wince as she removed it. 'Did that not hurt?' Maggie asked.

'Orcs do not feel pain,' Mor boasted.

'That's not true, I think that's just you Mor,' Billy joked. She looked over Mor's scarred arm then over to Billy, whose fur had got tangled and greasy. 'I can't believe how much you've all been through. Wait, where's your brother?' Emma asked as her hands glowed, and she healed Mor's arm. The wound wasn't deep thanks to his thick skin. 'Him and James are umm doing something,' Billy replied.

'They're getting into trouble then,' Maggie scoffed.

'Don't worry, they just had to check something out,' Billy said. 'There you go, just go easy with it, no more catching grappling hooks,' Emma remarked, as the glow covering her hands faded. Mor looked at his arm, it was healed, not even a scar. 'That's amazing even our greatest shamans could not do such things, where does this magic come from?' Mor asked.

'My mother she was born with it, same as me,' the Princess said as Leonardo walked into the barn. 'Congratulations young ranger, but next time you want something from my workshop, just ask,' Leonardo said to Billy.

'Sorry, Hilly's not very good at asking,' Billy said.

'Well to apologise I want you to come by the workshop later. I have something the pair of you could help me with,' Leonardo said and with that he left the barn with a smile, still extremely pleased his device worked perfectly. 'He is a rather odd one isn't he?' Maggie said watching the Professor skipping away in delight, 'Now as for you,' the Princess said, looking at the mucky wolf with a menacing stare. She then walked to the horse trough just outside the stable closing her eyes and holding her hand out over it as the dirty water spun turning it clear and clean. 'There you go get in,' Emma ordered

'In there, why? and how did you do that?' Billy questioned. 'I'm able to control water. Well, small amounts anyway. It's what my father passed on to me, like my mother passed on her healing abilities. Now come on, get in,' Emma said ushering him towards the trough. Billy put his paws on it, sliding one in slowly he felt the water was warm, the Princess had not only cleaned the water but warmed it as well.

Whilst Billy was enjoying his bath, James and Hilly had made their way to the dining hall where Seer Dune was sat at the top table stuffing his face trying to eat his anger away. 'Quick down here,' Hilly whispered, the pair snuck in through a side door and quickly hid under the rangers table concealed by the green cloth draped over it. Then they heard the main doors opening, in walked the La Sore's and Seer Avlor Tranem. 'Well that was entertaining,' Eloise La Sore said sarcastically.

'It's a damn disgrace, it cannot stand!' Seer Dune said, spitting out his food. 'This was your idea Kuran, remember that,' Marlos La Sore said pulling a seat out from under the table for his wife. 'Exactly, you brought this on yourself. I told you we could handle the human and his wolf. The Thorns could have dealt with them, but now you have the masses chanting their names and singing their praises,' Eloise scoffed.

'They should have failed. They clearly had help, where in Alidor did he get that toy he had and how did they withstand the Golem's magic?' Seer Dune said.

'That was an interesting piece of equipment. As for the magic maybe there's some elf in him after all,' Marlos pondered.

'The only reason this was agreed to is because of you Avlor, did this help uncloud your vision?' Dune said with a condescending tone. 'Something or someone still blocks my sight of what is to come for the pair. A darkness covers them like I've not seen before. It disturbs me. But I would not have the Thorns spoken of, from what I have seen they are still innocent,' Avlor said, ignoring the tone of Seer Dune's voice. 'So this was a complete waste of time then?' Seer Dune spat.

'What do you mean, a darkness?' Lady La Sore asked, but before Avlor could respond, the doors opened and the King and Lord Balmoth made their way into the hall. Both in good cheer from the afternoon's events. 'Dune, I was worried you'd already left,' Balmoth said laughing.

'You will show the proper respect to me Balmoth,' Dune said with the juices of fruit running down his bloated chin. 'Let's not start this you two, the boys passed the test. They are now members of this academy that's the end of it, now there's other things that need to be discussed before we leave here,' King Elidom said. 'You're right the ranger should leave, these are matters for Seers not Woodys,' Lady la Sore snapped.

'Richard will stay, and he will be heard!' the King demanded. 'Fine then, have him speak,' Dune mumbled. Balmoth composed himself, knowing this was his last chance to convince them the orcs and Dark Seer were a real threat. 'Lord Seers, nearly eight days ago now the orcs took the city of Orashson back from King Strigs Darrum who had ruled there since his Father's Day. I don't know the full extent of the damage done or casualties but from what the orc Mor has told me I fear all forty thousand dwarves that lived there are now dead or enslaved. Once done there they attacked our outpost, the Cove. Two thousand men were defending it. It was deemed by this council a safe outpost, so their families were also with them. My own son went to the outpost to find it completely over run. When he got back to me, I was in the Fang speaking with Lord Balvor Mammoth slayer of the Fang, the Leader of the Wolves. He and his hunters fought bravely, but were also defeated by the orcs. My lords, the events at Noress were the only thing that stopped the horde from attacking Meceller. Their fear of humans has given us a chance and time we desperately need. Whoever this Dark Seer is, he will now be preparing his next move, but we must move before he does. Send the elites to Meceller, and from there we can force the orcs back to the Blood Works,' Lord Balmoth finished speaking and sat down at the table. 'You speak as if our world is ending Balmoth. I am sorry for the loss of your rangers. Good men, all I'm sure, but I will not let you turn this into an elf war. The dwarves will surely take care of the orc problem themselves, they have defeated the orcs there before they will do it again. But we should send a bird if they ask us for aid, I will consider it,' Marlos La Sore said.

'It will be too late then, the dwarves will sit in their mines as they have always done since the death of Lex Darrum, and we have no time for dealings with the dwarves they will barter and scream with us until we're blue in the face. By the time we come to an agreement with them the south will have been lost,' Balmoth said.

'I would also move to ban any ranger missions south of the river,' Seer Dune said ignoring Lord Balmoth.

'I agree there's no sense risking their lives, we should wait till we hear from the dwarves,' Lady La Sore said.

'Fine, I'll order all the rangers back to Meceller with a promise you will send Elites to help protect the city. Rangers alone cannot hold it if they do attack,' Balmoth said.

'Agreed,' Seer Marlos nodded.

'Good, now are we done here I wish to return to the tower,' Seer Dune said.

'Yes you are all free to take your leave,' the King muttered, waving his hand. 'Will you return to Duniesa with us your highness?' Lady La Sore asked the King.

'No, I will spend one more night here,' the King replied. 'Very well, we will see you on your return and Lord Balmoth it was a pleasure to see you again,' Marlos said. Then he led the rest of the Seers out of the hall to their waiting carriage. 'You best go recall your rangers,' the King told Lord Balmoth.

'I will, I gave my word, didn't I?' Balmoth said, standing up from the table. 'But?' Elidom asked.

'But I must hunt the Dark Seer if it's the real one or not, he must be found,' Balmoth declared.

'If you leave here Balmoth, if you travel over the river you will be alone. I cannot help you,' the King said.

'I know, do not worry I won't get myself killed. I'll find help,' Balmoth said. The King sat forward in his chair, 'the watchers are lost Balmoth, just the two of you remain, and he will not help you. He will mislead you, he will blind you to his true intentions they call him the betrayer for a reason,' the King said. 'Even so, he wants to stop the Dark Seer, June will prove useful in his own way,' Balmoth said and made his way to the door. The King rubbed his eyes with his hands then looked over to the ranger's table. 'You should probably go wish your father luck young Balmoth he won't be returning for quite some time,' the King said looking over at the table the two were hiding under. They crawled out and James quickly bowed to the King. 'Thank you, your highness,' James said. He gave Hilly a look as if to say, we are in so much trouble. He then hurried out the hall to find his father. Hilly turned, hoping he'd be allowed to slip away as well. 'So Hilly, you're a ranger now,' the King said, making Hilly turn back to him. 'That's what they keep saying,' Hilly muttered as the King waved his hand, gesturing for Hilly to join him at the table. 'You heard our conversation?' the King asked as Hilly sat down. 'Most of it, you're not going to send rangers to look for my pack,' Hilly said.

'I'm sad to say that the chances of your people still being out there is slim, but if they were out there they would have made it to Meceller by now,' The King said.

'Me and Billy would be better off with Balmoth, if he's going back over the river we should be with him,' Hilly said.

# The Unlikely Allies

'No, here is where you'll stay. You're both lucky to be alive as it is,' the King replied.

'Me and my brother are more helpful than you think. If Wasiz was here he'd tell you,' Hilly whined.

'Ah yes, Wasiz the goblin. I only got to meet him a couple of times. He always stank of pipe weed and wore the most unbecoming garments to put it nicely,' the King scoffed.

'All true, but do you know what he was great at?' Hilly said. 'Do tell,' the King asked.

'Getting one over on any git who came after him,' Hilly said, Elidom was taken aback by his language. 'Wasiz once told me he was known as the greatest thief Alidor has had. He had enemies on enemies, everyone but his girls and us wolves wanted him dead for one reason or another, and they tried many times. But every assassin they sent for him left the Drunken Goblin drunk in the arms of a woman or in a bag. Wasiz was always one step ahead,' he brimmed as he spoke about his old friend.

'He wasn't one step ahead of the orcs though,' the King said, knocking the wind from Hilly's sails. He took the hourglass out from under his shirt. 'Maybe you're right but then maybe not, the night the orcs attacked Balmoth found us at the Drunken Goblin, Wasiz had just told us the tale of Lex Darrum, King of the Iron Hill's. Now I have two pieces of his special sword it can't be a coincidence,' Hilly said. The King smiled then took the silver band from his middle finger. 'You may be right, but Wasiz would also know you'd be sent here and have planned for that, not off with Richard getting yourself killed or worse,' the King said. Hilly slumped down in his chair, he could be right but what good did staying here do he thought to himself. 'You know, the last time I sat with a human was a few days before oh, well never mind, you should get back to your dorm now,' the King said, his smile was now gone replaced by a gloomy look, as if he was haunted by a memory. He stared at the table as Hilly quickly made his way out of the hall to see Lord Balmoth charging through the gates of the academy on horseback.

Hilly was the first back to the shack and began to try to light a fire. 'Guess I am a ranger now then,' he muttered to himself. After a few attempts at lighting the fire he gave up and lay back on the ground closing his eyes, but he couldn't sleep, there was too much to think about. Then the fire came to life, Hilly sat up, and a face looked back at him from the fire. 'You got lucky at Tailor's boy, but your wolf won't be there next time,' the booming voice of the Dark Seer came from the face in the fire. 'So sure? Stop sending your shadows and face us for real then,' Hilly said, doing his best to hide the fear in his voice. 'You think being a ranger will help save your pack, the only person who can give back what you have lost is me,' the Dark Seer's voice crackled from the fire. Hilly remained silent. 'The darkness calls to you, your race was born from it. Join me and all our enemies will fall. I will give back all you have lost, your father, your mother, your goblin friend. I shall return it all. Only once will I offer this pact,' the Dark Seer said and the face in the fire waited for Hilly's response. Hilly pulled himself up and brushed off his ranger uniform, then he smiled and began to laugh, 'What's funny?' The Dark Seer bellowed.

'You fear me the big bad Dark Seer, scared of a fifteen year old human,' Hilly said, continuing to laugh.

'Do not jest, defy me now, and I shall destroy everything you love, everything you hold dear I will eradicate it all, and then I will pry the skin off your bones,' the Dark Seer exclaimed his frustration with the human growing by the second. 'No, you won't because I'm going to find you and stop you. No idea how but I'm going too,' Hilly said, with that the fire rose and the Dark Seer's sickening laugh crackled out of the flames. 'You? Stop me, you are nothing, nothing but a bug. One cocky human thief cannot stand before the power of the Dark Lord,' the fire bellowed out, almost burning Hilly. 'What if he has a wolf?' Billy said, walking towards Hilly and the fire. He wasn't alone. 'Whose the fastest in the world, I might add,' Billy said, standing beside his brother, he could feel the Dark Seers hatred pouring out of the flames. 'And a wood elf whose bow will be staying by their side,' James said, joining the pair readying an arrow in his new black bow. 'And an orc who is severely pissed off,' Mor said. Laughing came from the fire. 'The ranger, the hunter, the warrior, and the thief, the unlikely allies of Tailor's Hope, all of you will fall to the darkness,' the Dark Seer said and with that, the fire went out. The logs were cold, as if they'd never been burnt. 'Did you hear all that?' Hilly said.

'Most of it,' Billy replied.

'We got here about the time you told him to stick it up himself,' James said, smiling.

'If he wasn't coming for us before, he definitely is now,' Hilly said. 'And when he does we smash him to a bloody pulp,' Mor shouted. 'It's not about smashing him, we need to be a step ahead of him,' Hilly said.

'That would be easier if we knew his plan,' Billy pondered. 'Look, we've had a long day. We can sort out what to do next after lessons tomorrow. Tonight I have something for you, here,' James said. They were all too preoccupied to notice the bag James had over his shoulder. He handed it to Mor and he pulled out a bag of pipe weed and under that a huge joint of meat. 'Where'd you get this? Thought you elves didn't eat meat,' Billy said. 'We don't. I found these in the ranger's storeroom. They keep confiscated goods there sometimes,' James said.

'I'm meant to be the thief you know,' Hilly laughed, the group lit the campfire and Mor began cooking the meat while the boys passed the pipe Mary had given Hilly back and forth.

Chapter 10
Fallen Hunter

The Princess lay in her bed alone in her large dorm room. The rest of the students had to share dorms, but because of her standing she had been given her own room in the East Tower above the aviary. A lavish room filled with fine furniture, and a large four posted bed. She tossed and turned in her bed too busy thinking to sleep, feeling as if her world had been turned upside down, she had spent most of her life living in a big city surrounded by mostly elves. The only other races she had normally met were diplomats or merchants, but now she'd used her powers to heal an orc and a human, she helped a lost wolf, and she was still extremely proud that she'd done her bit to help Hilly and Billy pass their exam. She felt butterflies in her stomach as she remembered first seeing the young human and didn't understand why. Sitting up in bed her eyes locked onto a tapestry adorning the wall. It showed an elite on horseback riding away from battle with the Princess he had saved clinging to him, before she could ponder more a loud bang came from the open window of her room. Shocked she looked over to see a hook had embedded itself into the stone window frame. 'It can't be,' she said, as Hilly pulled himself onto the windowsill. 'Hi, sorry, did I wake you?' he said slightly winded from pulling himself up.

'What are you doing? What if you were to fall?' Emma said, quickly pulling up her blankets to cover her nightdress. 'I'm fine, don't worry. I didn't think the rope would make it to be honest, amazing how much Leonardo fits in this. Let's just hope he doesn't mind me borrowing it again. Had to sneak into his workshop on the way here to get more hooks too,' Hilly said.

'That still doesn't tell me why you snuck into my room in the middle of the night, how did you even know which room I was in?' Emma asked.

'I had Billy sniff you out, I wanted to give you these,' Hilly said, reaching into his bag and pulling out a variety of crumpled flowers. 'Sorry they got a bit messed up in the climb,' Hilly said as petals fell from the flowers. The Princess got her dressing gown from the end of her bed throwing it over her shoulders and walked over, taking the flowers from Hilly. 'I need to apologise too,' Hilly said.

'What for?' she asked.

'Well, Billy kind of, accidentally, very accidentally ate your bird,' Hilly said.

'You're joking, right?' Emma said, hoping he was.

'No, I'm truly sorry,' Hilly said. The Princess was clearly quite upset hearing about the demise of her parrot. 'How could you just let him eat him?' Emma asked.

'I didn't let him, it just happened so fast I couldn't stop him. I'll get you another,' Hilly said.

'That parrot was one of the rarest bird's in the whole of Alidor and you just let your dog eat it, how stupid could you be?' Emma exclaimed, her sadness had been replaced by anger. 'For the last time I didn't let him, and he's not a dog, he's a wolf. He hadn't eaten meat for days his instincts kicked in he can't help it, I really am sorry,' Hilly said trying his best to defend his brother. 'I guess I forget how different it is here compared to the Fang,' Emma said. 'Tell me about it, I'd only met one elf proper before all this,' Hilly said. Emma joined Hilly on the windowsill.

'So, are you going to tell me?' Emma asked.

'Tell you what?' Hilly wondered.

'What's going on? I see you all sneaking around. Balmoth keeps running off to who knows where. Orcs are attacking people and whenever I ask anyone, they just say not to worry and don't tell me anything,' Emma said.

'Where should I start?' Hilly muttered. He then told her about the orcs attack on the Fang and Noress, then about the Dark Seer. Finally with some hesitation he told her about King Lex Darum's weapon and the Watchers. 'Wait, so that ring my dad wears?' Emma asked.

'Yep, that's one of them,' Hilly replied.

'And the Headmistress too. I honestly thought them all quite dull. I can't believe they kept all this from me, but if these items are as strong as they say, surely they have the power between them to beat this Dark Seer,' Emma said.

'That's why he killed them. Our fathers, with the rest of the Watchers together they could have beaten down the hordes and the Dark Seer, that's why he sent the orcs to pick them off one by one. Now he even has your Seers running scared, I snuck in and heard them talking before Lord Balmoth left. They hope the dwarves of the iron mines will win the war for them, but they're wrong, they haven't seen him. They haven't stood before him and felt his intent. I'd never seen magic, not real magic anyway before meeting you, but when he shot that purple light at us, I could feel every bit of his hate towards me, but it wasn't just hate for me. It was for everything in this world not just the people, the lands, trees, rivers, even the bugs. He despises it all,' Hilly said. Then the pair heard the gates of the academy being pulled open and the ranger's shouting. 'What's going on?' Hilly asked. 'I don't know,' she said, leaning out the window to try to see, 'I can't see but look it's Billy,' Emma said. Billy was running as fast as he could to the gate. 'Come on,' Hilly said, putting his arm around the Princess's waist and leaping from the window. 'What are you doing?' she screamed, wrapping her arms round him and holding him as tight as she could as they repelled down the side of the tower, landing gently on the ground. 'I'm getting the hang of this thing,' Hilly said with a crooked grin across his face. 'Never do that again,' Emma snapped.

The pair made their way to the main gate, where Billy and a group of rangers were waiting as a horse drawn cart approached. It turned, and they saw what was in the back. 'It's Jerrest,' Billy shouted, and ran to him with Hilly and the Princess struggling to keep up. He jumped into the back of the cart before the ranger's could stop him, seeing how bad Jerrest's injuries were. He was unconscious with cuts all over his body, but worst of all, he was missing his left front leg. Billy turned back to see the Princess looking pale at the sight of him. 'Princess, please can you help him?' Billy begged. She got up into the cart and her hands began to glow. As she placed them on Jerrest but nothing happened. 'I

can't do anything, I'm so sorry. He's too badly hurt,' Emma said
with tears building in her eyes. Leonardo and the Headmistress
came running over to the cart. 'What's going on here?' the
Headmistress questioned her hair and dress yellow reflecting her
curiosity. 'He's Jerrest. He's a wolf from our pack you have to
help him,' Hilly said, but before she could do anything Leonardo
had jumped into the cart extremely excited. 'Yes, yes he's
perfect, get him to my workshop,' he said.

'Wait, what are you doing?' Hilly asked.

'Don't worry, I can help him, but he's going to die if we
don't act now,' Leonardo exclaimed. They stepped back, and the
rangers lifted the large wolf out of the cart and carried him to
Leonardo's new workshop. Hilly, Billy and Emma sat on the
floor outside as an old elf man made his way over to them. 'Hello
there, I found that there friend of yours,' the old elf smiled to the
boys. 'Where did you find him?' Hilly asked.

'He was dragging himself through a cornfield 'bout
thirty miles or so from here. Told me he was looking for a lost
pair of wolves he did, before he passed out you see and well I'd
heard about what happened at Tailor's hope so I got him 'ere.
Was hoping I was doing the right thing the whole way you
know,' the old man said.

'How did he get so far alone?' Billy wondered.

'Very determined that one is,' the old man said.

'Our father always used to say that Jerrest was the best
our pack had, that we should always follow his example,' Billy
said, then the door of Leonardo's workshop flung open, and the
Headmistress looked out. 'Princess, come here,' she ordered, the
Princess ran over, and the door slammed behind her. 'What do
you think they're up to in there?' the old man asked.

'Helping him I hope,' Hilly said.

'Thank you for bringing him I'm sorry we don't have
anything to give you for your trouble,' Billy said, looking to his
brother. 'Alright,' Hilly muttered he reached into his bag and
pulled out a purse. He opened it and took two pieces of gold out.
Then saw the disappointed look on the little wolf's face. 'Fine,'
Hilly said and handed the purse to the now brimming old man.

'There must be fifty pieces in 'ere. That's mighty good of you young lad' the old man said.

'Well you better treat yourself and thank you again,' Billy smiled to the old man as he walked back to the cart and began his journey home with his new found wealth. 'I can't believe you made me do that,' Hilly groaned.

'You stole it anyway,' Billy snapped, 'that man smelt familiar don't you think?'

'How should I know,' Hilly grumbled and the pair sat there until the morning bird calls from the aviary woke them. Emma emerged from the workshop her hands and dressing gown were red with Jerrest's blood, and she was completely exhausted. 'I'd never imagined I'd be doing things like this here,' she said, looking to the boys. 'What happened?' Billy asked, but before she could reply the Headmistress strolled out, her hair and dress had changed from yellow to a dark shade of purple. She put a hand to the Princess's shoulder. 'You did very well in there, go to your dorm get cleaned up you can start lessons tomorrow. You two come here,' the head said pointing to the boys. The Princess walked off as the boys went into the workshop. Jerrest was laying on a table in the middle of the room with what looked like iron armour where his left leg used to be. 'You're really here,' Jerrest said in a whisper to the boys. Before they could say a single word the boys began to cry. The joy of hearing an old friends voice was too much for them. 'None of that! Wolves don't whine,' Jerrest barked, 'that mother of yours made you soft.'

'Well what do you think?' Leonardo said walking over.

'What did you do?' Hilly asked wiping his eyes.

'He made me into a machine,' Jerrest said snapping at Leonardo. 'I did not! Just one part of you,' Leonardo snapped back, 'you see your friend's leg was gone, that's why their magic won't help. Their healing only works if the parts are there to fix back together so I made this. The auto mechanical leg movement device,' Leonardo continued proudly.

'So it works like a real leg?' Hilly asked.

'In theory, the hydraulics connect to the remaining muscle and' Leonardo stopped because Hilly had raised his hands as if to say I'm getting none of this. 'Basically, then yes it works like a leg, but it will take time to perfect. This is science not magic,' Leonardo said folding his arms. Billy turned back to Jerrest. 'Do you know what happened to mum?' Billy asked.

'I don't, I'm sorry. You're not asking 'bout your father is he?' Jerrest said.

'He died in the attack,' Hilly said.

'I should have been with him,' Jerrest barked.

'If you had been you'd probably be dead too. How did you get here?' Billy asked.

'I was out looking for you, your mother was worried. When I heard the drums I began to make my way back to the dens, but a group of orcs took me by surprise. They hacked my leg off and took it like a damn trophy. All I remember after that is seeing that witch looking over me, no idea how I got here,' Jerrest said looking to the Headmistress. 'Come now boys you have lessons to attend and he needs rest,' she said ushering the boys out of the room. 'We'll come back soon,' Billy said the Headmistress closed the door behind them and lead the boys back into the castle.

The first floor of the castle was taken up mostly by the large hall with only a few corridors surrounding it leading to the aviary and other towers. The other floors however, consisted of many different classrooms and winding hallways connecting them all. The Headmistress led the pair down the hallway past a room where smoke bellowed out from underneath the closed door, another they could hear students laughing on the other side and one that seem to be just a big bush. Thorns and nettles seemingly creating a doorway. They carried on until they came to a door with a line of ranger and elite recruits waiting to enter a classroom. 'Join the line and wait to be called in,' the Headmistress ordered the boys. 'I don't get it, what are we doing?' Hilly said.

'You're learning now line up!' she snapped. They stood in line beside a wood elf with thick rimmed glasses and a freckle covered face. 'Oh can't believe you're really coming to lessons,' the boy said. 'Should we not be?' Billy asked.

'No, it's not that, sorry that must have sounded rather rude. It's just I've read so many books on the wolves, I never imagine I'd ever meet one. I did read your were bigger though,' the boy said. Hilly laughed as Billy's little ears went down.

'They are I'm just small for some reason,' Billy sighed.

'I'm Ernest by the way,' he said introducing himself just as a centaur made his way out of the classroom. He wore a black vest over his white shirt, with a dark black mane tied into a ponytail on his top half with brown fur and a tail matching the colour of his mane on his bottom half. His large hooves echoed down the hall as he walked. 'Go in and take your seats and keep quiet I don't want trouble,' the Centaur ordered. The students walked in and the boys sat down at desks beside Ernest. There were four rows of ascending desks on either side of the room with a blackboard at the end. 'What is this class anyway?' Hilly asked Ernest. 'The history of Alidor and its people,' he said.

'Well that sounds extremely dull,' Hilly scoffed.

'What? How could you say that Alidor has an incredible history, this class is the only reason I'm here,' Ernest said.

'So you don't want to be a ranger?' Billy asked.

'You don't just come here to be a ranger but it's what I need to do to get the education I need,' Ernest said as he took multiple books from his rucksack. 'So you can do what? Be a tiresome old fart who reads books all day,' Hilly teased.

'No it's to become a bookkeeper at the vault of the high elves,' Ernest announced.

'A vault why do you need to know history to guard gold?' Hilly wondered.

'They don't keep gold there it's where all the knowledge of the Seers is kept. It's full of books not gold,' Ernest said.

'Sounds like a dull job,' Hilly joked.

'Stop picking fights,' Billy snapped at him as the Centaur walked over to them. 'Am I going to have trouble with you two?

# The Unlikely Allies

I don't like trouble nor troublesome students.' He said adjusting his dark blue bow tie. 'No Professor Carny I was just catching them up Sir,' Ernest said.

'Good I won't stand trouble here,' the professor said making his way to the blackboard. 'Today we will look at the year two hundred and seventy two to two hundred and seventy four. Find that year in your book.'

'Here,' Ernest said moving his book so they could all see. 'Umm. we can't read,' Billy whispered.

'Don't worry he just reads from the book just look as if you're reading along,' Ernest said.

'This is how you learn?' Hilly asked.

'Shh,' Ernest said placing his finger to his lip. The class continued and Billy listened intensely to the Professor taking in every bit of information. Hilly however was fidgeting in his chair bored of just being sat there growing ever more annoyed by Ernest tapping his shoulder to keep him awake. After what seemed like an age to Hilly but minutes to Billy a bell rang and the students began making their way out of the classroom while Professor Carny shouted. 'Quietly now I don't want trouble.' Once the boys were out Hilly began to wander off. 'Where you going?' Ernest asked.

'Are we not done?' Hilly whined.

'No that was the first of five classes.' Ernest replied.

'You're joking right?' Hilly said.

'How did you not enjoy that? It was just like Wasiz telling us a story.' Billy said.

'Yer I know, but it was just boring I'm going to go check on Jerrest,' Hilly said as he continued to walk off.

'You have to take this seriously,' Billy barked after him.

After a day of classes, Billy returned to the old shack completely worn out from the days learning. Hilly however, was laying by the fire with his pipe hanging from his mouth. 'Oh, you're back, how was it?' Hilly asked. Billy didn't say anything, he just walked over and snatched the pipe from Hilly tossing it into the fire. 'Why'd you do that?' Hilly said.

'You're coming to class tomorrow,' Billy said, staring down his brother. 'Fine, I'll go. Been a bit bored to tell the truth, maybe even more than I was in that classroom. I checked on Jerrest he was fast asleep when I left him,' Hilly said.

'I spoke to Ernest about the humans war, the things our people done to them, Hilly there's so much Wasiz didn't tell us,' Billy said, sitting next to him. 'Like what? His stories about the war were pretty gory already,' Hilly wondered.

'The Flutterlins' Billy said.

'What's that?' Hilly asked.

'A race our people wiped them out. They were little round yellow furry things not hurting anyone, but they had a power that let them control the surrounding weather, Ernest said the human King didn't like that, so they drove them into hiding in caves. When they found them, they sealed the caves and waited 'till they starved to death,' Billy sighed.

'Guess I should have listened more in class,' Hilly said, then he looked to his brother and his little ear's dropping down. 'It wasn't us though. They may hate our ancestors and the stupid stuff Lords and Kings made them do, but they have no reason to hate us, unless I steal from them that is,' Hilly said smiling at his brother, as Mor made his way to join them looking quite angry. 'Where have you been?' Hilly asked. Mor walked over to the shack and punched a hole through the old wooden wall. 'Don't do that, it will fall down,' Billy shouted.

'I have been teaching,' Mor said, anger swelling in his voice. 'What?' the boys said in unison.

'That Headmistress, I was happily sleeping in the stables, and she woke me up.' Mor said as Hilly interrupted him.

'What? How did she wake you?' he asked.

'She dropped a stinking pig on my head,' Mor spat. The boys broke out in laughter. 'That's good to know. Go on,' Billy giggled. 'She said I couldn't just sit around taking up space, made me teach a defence class for the girls. I am a great warrior of the Blood Works not a damn handmaid, I am Mor the mighty not Mor the wet nurse,' Mor shouted and complained but the boys however, were nearly in tears from laughing so hard.

## The Unlikely Allies

The next morning, Hilly did as he promised and went back to class, and over the next few weeks began to at least put a bit more effort into the lessons. Billy was still enjoying every moment of it, and after almost two months the boys had become quite fond of their new home and their new lives. They had learnt about the six types of elemental magic that many races of Alidor could wield from Miss Perry's magical orientation class. Water, air, earth, fire, the light and the shadows. Miss Perry's knowledge of shadow magic however, was extremely limited. Mostly due to the fact all known books on the subject had been locked away in the vault of the high elves. Hilly and Billy had become fitter too. Billy was getting faster by the day and Hilly had become quite fond of sparing in the training ring, even winning a duel against Makron using just his dagger. He did cheat to do so, but it was only after the duel that Makron noticed Hilly had blunted his blade beforehand, but the whereabouts of their mother was still in the forefront of their minds.

In the city of Orashon things were not as tranquil. In the halls of the dwarf kings, the grand throne room of the city. Built from the iron and copper that once filled the ash mountains, a resource that made the previous ruler of Orashon ridiculous wealthy. Now the Dark Seers shadow sat on the iron throne, but he had not taken the city for its wealth alone, he looked down from his throne to the chained orc before him. Ore Ash War chief of the orcs of the Blood Works. He had his hands bound by chains. Ore looked to the guards scattered around the room, to his surprise they were not orcs. They wore dark purple heavy armour which covered every bit of their skin, Ore wasn't even able to see their faces beneath their helms. 'You did well in winning this city war chief, so why would you betray me now?' the Dark Seer said.

'I have not betrayed you, my master,' Ore said.

'Oh have you not. Then why is Meceller still standing? Why did your forces return here? Why is your brother now at the RANGERS ACADEMY?' the Dark Seer shouted jumping up from his throne. Then a door opened and Oshan the executioner

116

walked in leading three young orcs in chains. Ore recognised the boys, they were his sons. He turned back to the Dark Seer. 'My master, they have done nothing wrong,' Ore begged.

'You orcs have proven what I have long suspected,' the Dark Seer said. With a wave of his hand, Oshan took out his knife and slit the throat of the eldest boy. 'My master, please give me a chance to redeem my honour,' Ore cried as his son's body fell to the ground. 'You are weak, it is time for a new race to inherit this world,' the Dark Seer continued. He spoke as if the pair were sat at a table together as old friends. With another wave of his hand the second of Ore's sons had his throat cut. Oshan moved to Ore's final son. 'Wait,' the Dark Seer said as he walked over to the boy. Ore looked up, hoping he would spare his youngest son. The Dark Seer took a vial of purple liquid and with Oshan's help forced the boy to drink it. 'See now war chief. See what will soon rule all we see,' the Dark Seer proclaimed as the boy fell to the ground in pain. His green skin had begun to turn purple, his ears grew long like an elf and his face changed to look like one too. 'Look war chief, your son is now one of thousands who share the same face, the same skin created from broken races and turned into something new and powerful. Stronger than orcs, smarter than elves, and able to be controlled only by me. This war chief, this is the beginning of a new age. The age of the Dark Elf begins.' Ore's youngest son stood back up he was no longer an orc. Another dark elf emerged out of the darkness. It's face was a perfect copy of the other they were completely identical what was Ore's son was lead away by the other. The Dark Seers shadow walked to Ore and began to stroke the top of his head. 'Soon war chief, soon my new army will move, the Lavender Lake will be crossed something your own race never managed but to do so requires more bodies, two thirds of your people will drink. The rest you will take back to the Cove, wait there for my orders. This is the only way you will ever walk with those who fought before you, the only way to redeem your horde and yourself,' the Dark Seer said looking to his servant. 'Yes my master I will do as you command,' Ore said knowing there was nothing he could do to avoid his fate. Oshan released him from his chains and he walked out of the throne room to look over the city as he heard screams from orcs young and old. It had already begun. Dark Elves marched down the streets with vials of the purple potion and orc after orc were being forced to drink. Oshan joined Ore carrying a new black suit of steel armour. 'This is how it must be, the strong will be spared the weak will drink,' Oshan said. 'Will you leave for the Cove with me?' Ore asked.

'No, our lord has other plans for me,' Oshan said and with that Ore made his way to find what orcs he could and head for the Cove.

## Chapter 11
## Hanerson

The boys studying and training continued at great pace, and they were both now quite capable of reading and writing. Billy had become very fond of the botany class. If this was down to a new found love of flowers or just the fact the teacher Miss Jando smelt wonderful he would not say. Hilly was still complaining most of the time, but it had become well known, and the other students would giggle or ignore him as he normally says something witty within his sarcastic whining such as not even dwarves do this much work or to wake the dead would be easier than this bull. They had also put a lot of work into the old shack. Leonardo had made them new windows and a door that he claimed had an unpickable lock, whilst Mor had repaired most of the holes in the walls and put new tiles on the roof. Inside there was now a bunk bed to the left of the door, the rest of the small room was taken up by two fine leather chairs and a sofa placed by the yet to be fixed fireplace the origin of which no one but Hilly knew. That was until Master Cunningham the metal work teacher put posters around the castle inquiring about the whereabouts of two armchairs and a sofa missing from his office. But after more than three months there was still no news of their mother or of Lord Balmoth, both of whom were still at the forefront of their minds as they made their way to the grand hall for breakfast. 'Do you think Balmoth's ever coming back?' Hilly asked his brother. 'James said he always comes back eventually we just have to wait,' Billy said.

'We have been waiting, it's been months now,' Hilly whined. The boys made their way into the hall to see it was empty apart from Ernest sat at the end of the ranger's table surrounded by books and scrolls. 'Where is everyone?' Hilly asked. 'Did you not hear most of the students are going to Hanerson for the day? You better hurry if you want to join them the coaches will leave soon,' Ernest said.

'Are you not going?' Billy asked.

'Oh no, I'm much happier here with my books,' Ernest said. 'You two won't be going either, the Headmistress has said so herself,' Professor Carny declared, trotting into the hall carrying even more books to add to Ernest's pile. Hilly went back to the door and saw the Princess's carriage waiting to leave. Makron and other elite recruits were guarding the gate checking the students as they passed through. Billy walked up beside his brother. 'What are you thinking?' Billy said, but before Hilly replied, he ran off with Billy following close behind.

James pulled himself up onto the driver's side of the Princess's carriage, he would much rather have taken Jenna but had been roped into being the Princess's chauffeur. Jenna was still stood beside them, not wanting to be left behind and perfectly happy to trot along side them. 'Are you ready to leave down there?' James shouted down to the Princess and Maggie who were sat inside both eager to leave. 'Yes, ready when you are little brother,' Maggie replied, and he went to whip his reins. Then Hilly suddenly jumped onto the carriage beside him. He was wearing an old brown cloak that covered him from his shoulders to his feet. On his head was a worn straw hat, and covering his face was what James assumed was the lining of a fur jacket Hilly had pulled out and fashioned into a very unconvincing beard. 'Oh hello there young fellow, mind if I get a ride to town?' Hilly said, trying his best to speak with the accent of a west lander. 'What are you doing?' James asked.

'We want to see Hanerson,' Billy said, poking his head out from under the brown cloak where he'd been hiding. 'And you think this was how to do it,' James said, staring at them both in disbelief. 'Oh now don't chat and whine. Go now, we shall see what golden boy thinks,' Hilly said keeping up the pretence. James sighed knowing Makron would never buy his terrible disguise, but it may at least be worth a laugh for them both. He pulled the carriage up to the gate and Makron walked over and looked up at Hilly. 'What are you doing human?' Makron asked.

'Huuuuman where boy? Where be this human?' Hilly said, looking around. 'Was this your idea?' Makron asked, smiling at James. 'Do you really think I'd come up with this?' he replied, laughing. Makron turned back to Hilly. 'The Headmistress has left strict orders. You're not to leave or you Billy,' Makron smirked lifting up the cloak to reveal Billy's bushy tail hanging out, Hilly grabbed it and quickly covered him back up. 'It's okay, go. I'll tell the head you must have snuck out or something just keep an eye on them,' Makron said looking sternly at James. 'Don't worry I'll keep an eye, and I'll come find you when we get back, I wanted to speak with you,' James said with a glint in his eye as he took the carriage through the gate and onto the road following the others.

Once away from the elites at the gate, Hilly turned to James. 'You two speak differently these days you and Makron,' Hilly said, finally dropping his terrible accent and removing the fake beard and straw hat. 'Do we? I don't see how,' James said, trying to look straight ahead at the road. 'I feel like you're keeping something from us young Balmoth,' Hilly said with a smile.

'I notice it too,' Billy said, poking his head back out, 'plus Makron's heart was beating so hard when you spoke James it nearly deafened me.' Billy continued, hopping onto the seat between them. 'I don't know what the pair of you are on about,' James said trying his best to ignore them, but for the whole two mile journey the boys paid no attention to the idyllic countryside that they passed as they were far more interested in grilling their friend. But James remained silent on the matter until Hilly and Billy's attention turned to Hanerson. The carriage left the dusty road and came onto a stone path with many different colours going along it, in long colourful lines leading into the town. The buildings looked like any other elf town with long steep wicker roofs and grey brick walls. The main difference was that the doors on many of the houses corresponded with the colours on the paved floor. 'I've never seen somewhere painted in colours like this,' Billy said, his little eyes growing wider.

## The Unlikely Allies

'This is the most popular market town on this side of the river,' James said. 'There's so many shops here, they painted the roads to make it easier to find what you're looking for'. He pulled the carriage over, beside the others that had come from the academy. They dismounted and Hilly ran to open the door. He did so and held out his hand as the Princess looked at him shocked. 'May I? My lady,' Hilly said, smiling to her. She took his hand, still shocked he was there. 'I heard James talking, but I never thought it was you two. Did the Headmistress not make you stay behind?' Maggie asked, following the Princess out of the carriage. 'She did, but my cunning plan meant we were able to sneak out,' Hilly said as James and Billy sighed.

'Well, never mind that now. Come on I have something you can help me with,' Emma said taking Hilly's arm and pulling him away down the street.

The pair of them walked along the road arm in arm, following a light orange line on the ground. 'Where are we going?' Hilly asked. 'To the wings of afar,' Emma replied.

'And that is?' He wondered.

'It's a messenger bird shop. I do need a new one, don't I?' She said, raising an eyebrow 'and you should really have one too,' they met the door that matched the light orange line on the floor. Above the door hung a sign with two white doves on and the words wings of afar written below them. She opened the door, and the pair walked in with Hilly quickly closing it behind him when he realised the birds were all out of their cages and flying around the small shop. There were so many different species that Hilly had no idea what most were. Then a loud thud came from the top floor, and an old elf man appeared and hurried down the steps to them. He was bald apart from a small tuft of grey hair above his ears, wearing a tunic and trousers that matched the colour of his door. 'Oh my, a customer, how wonderful,' he said walking towards them, almost hopping. Then he removed the small round glasses he wore and rubbed his eyes, 'And a young Princess at that,' he said smiling then turning to

Hilly, 'and you would be that human the fools of this town have been going on about I'd say.'

'Guess I am,' Hilly scoffed.

'Well, not a great fan of your people I am, but as long as you mean no harm to the beasts and birds of this world, well you're okay by me and my birds will follow your commands as they do an elf's. Oh, I say all this excitement. I completely forgot to introduce myself. I am Edward Crowfoot master of the birds,' he said, taking Hilly and Emma's hands in turn and shaking them vigorously. 'What brings the daughter of Elidom to my humble little shop?' he asked.

'I need a new messenger bird, my last one, well, I need a new one,' she said, not wanting to tell him why, 'and he will need one too.'

'Well for you my lady, I have the perfect bird in mind.' He made a quiet whistle and a large bright green bird flew down from a hole in the roof and landed on Edward's shoulder. 'This is Juliet. She's a green phoenix not as rare as the red yes, but if you ask me they're much more beautiful, the perfect bird for a Princess,' Edward said. Emma held out her arm and Juliet hopped on and made her way to Emma's shoulder. The feathers of her tail were so long they stretched down the Princess's back making it look like she was wearing a bright green scarf with an orange beak and light green eyes. 'She's wonderful,' the Princess said, stroking the bird's chin who seemed as fond of Emma as she was of her. 'As for you, well, I think I may have something for you,' Edward said and then went back upstairs. After some banging and quite a lot of shouting, he reemerged holding a small, fat grey pigeon in his hands. It looked sickly and only had one eye. 'He may not look all that, but he's quite a capable bird, when he wants to be,' Edward said handing him to Hilly. The bird sat in his hand like he was frozen, with his one black eye staring at Hilly. 'Well, he's nice, I guess,' Hilly said, slightly displeased he didn't get a phoenix. 'His name's Bob, I called him that because he likes to bob his little head up and down when he's happy,' Edward said with a smirk. 'And since you seem to be the perfect fit for each other, I shall let you have him for nothing but words of thanks and a smile.'

'That's so kind of Master Crowfoot, don't you think so, Hilly?' Emma said, tugging on his arm, not wanting him to be rude. 'Yeah, thank you, I'm very grateful I think?' Hilly said, still looking at Bob. Hilly had now noticed that he not only looked odd, but also smelled it too. The Princess and Edward had made their way to the till, after she was done paying for her bird Edward closed the till, and he turned to look at the pair. 'You know seeing the pair of you reminds me of the old days we used to get many humans here back when I was young. The people today remember your lot as one thing,' he said pointing his long boney finger at Hilly, 'but me I remember them as they truly were, and a fine people many of them were indeed. Alas, they are gone now but glad I am to see a kindly human face once more before I pass,' Master Crowfoot said. Hilly had still been looking at Bob until Edward said about passing. 'Passing, but you're an elf, ain't you? You won't have to worry about that I feel Master,' Hilly said. 'Everything dies young human, even us elves. One day we will pass on as well, but now do not worry yourself. I promise I shall still be here the next time you come to town,' Edward said. Then with a few more warm words, they left his shop with the promise the birds would be sent to the aviary at the academy.

As the pair left the shop and began walking down the road to find the others, Hilly began to get an odd feeling. He turned to see two elf men wearing grey cloaks. The same men had been watching them since they had arrived in Hanerson, but Hilly and the Princess had both been too distracted with each other to notice. Now Hilly had, he put his arm around Emma and pulled her close as a carriage pulled to a sudden holt in front of them. Hilly went to pull out his dagger, but before he could he felt something hit him on the head, and he fell to the floor. One of the elves had struck him and the other was now binding Emma's hands as she screamed, unable to use her abilities without the use of her hands. They forced her into the carriage whipping the reins and charging off, as Hilly pulled himself back up. 'Shit! Shit! Shit! Get back here you gits,' he yelled as he ran after the carriage, but he was too slow. He ran down the street after them until he saw James, Billy, and Maggie at the market across the road, he called over to them 'Billy! The Princess, the Princess!' He cried, pointing to the carriage leaving the town as he did. Without saying a word Billy shot off after the carriage.

Inside, the Princess was struggling with her captors trying to unbind her hands, but one of the elves held them firmly shut. 'This one's trouble,' the elf said, 'she's not doing as she's told like the other.' The carriage had now left Hanerson and was now in the Wayondays woods with its bumpy ground that slowed the carriage. Then something hit the side of the door with a bang. The elf not holding Emma still opened the window and as soon as his head poked out, he was pulled from the carriage and fell to the ground, snapping his neck in the fall. Billy came flying in through the open window, sharp fangs poised. The elf quickly reached up and grabbed the wolf. As soon as he let go of the Princess's hands, she waved them and using the pack of water that was in the carriage, instantly encased his arms in ice. Then the carriage came to a sudden stop. James had called Jenna, and the pair had caught up to the carriage and James had used his bow to shoot the driver. 'Come on, we should get you back,' Billy suggested. 'No wait,' she said, turning to the elf still stuck in ice, 'what did you mean by the other one?'

'Go stuff yourself, high elf hussy, I ain't telling you shit,' the elf said, with that Billy bit down hard on his leg. 'Don't be rude to my Princess,' Billy growled at the man screaming in pain as James rode up to the window. 'Tell her,' Billy ordered.

'In the woods, North West of here they have the other one there I'm sorry. Don't kill me, I didn't believe the stories, but I do now. Please Princess have your pets spare me,' the man begged and the Princess and Billy got out of the carriage. James dismounted and lent in dragging the elf out as Hilly ran down the road extremely out of breath. He had refused to get on Jenna with

James, something he now regretted. 'What happened?' Hilly said, panting hard. 'You need to stop smoking, that's what!' Billy said.

'Seem's like a kidnapping attempt. I knew you should have stayed behind. You must have given her away, not many girls about with a human on their arm,' James said.

'It wasn't just me. They took someone else too tell them,' Emma said, kicking the elf who was now sat on the floor beside the carriage. 'The other we took a month or so back don't know her name just that the boss wanted her,' the elf reluctantly said.

'And who's the boss?' Billy asked.

'Don't know his name, names ain't really needed in our work, but he wore black with bandages covering his face, weird one he was,' the elf was quite chatty now, still hoping he would be spared. 'It's him,' Billy growled.

'Right, so we tell the guard back at Hanerson and let them handle it,' James insisted.

'They will have moved on by the time they get there, you know that,' Emma said. As they argued, Billy sniffed the air.

'I can smell them. They're not far and there's a smell similar to the Princess.'

'Wait, we're not meant to be here anyway, and we can't take him on by ourselves. We have to head back,' Hilly said but his brother and the Princess had made up their minds, and she was already following Billy deeper into the woods.

The four of them walked through the woods for almost half an hour, James and Hilly had put the elf on Jenna still encased in ice, and sent her back to town to warn the guard. They continued walking until they saw a group of elves camped in front of an opening to a cave. In front of the cave was a large willow tree with a young girl tied to it. Her face was covered with a brown bag. Wearing a fine white dress, she seemed well kept and unharmed. The group began to decide their next move but when the Dark Seer's shadow walked out of the cave they all fell silent. The boys had known what to expect but the Princess could hardy believe the feelings of dread and despair washing over her as she first set eyes on him. He walked out to stand beside the girl and pulled the bag from her head. 'That's Vanessa La Sore daughter of Marlos and Eloise La Sore, Makron's sister,' James whispered then the Dark Seer turned to the elves with him. 'Well, where are they?' he asked.

'They'll be back soon boss, must have just been delayed,' an elf replied.

'No. No, that's not it. They have been killed or captured. Is that not right unlikely allies of Tailor's Hope?' He said looking out to the woods. 'He knows we're here,' Hilly muttered, placing his hand to his dagger and getting it ready, James did the same with his bow. 'If he finds us, we can't hold back all of them,' James whispered. 'You came here for her, did you?' the Dark Seer said, pointing to the girl. 'Still wish to hide? Well maybe I can think of something to make you show yourselves.' He stroked Vanessa's face, her eyes were filled with fear and tears. Then with a click of his fingers shadows built behind her eye's until they poured from her eye sockets, leaving nothing behind but a cold lifeless body. Before the Princess knew what she was doing, she stood up in full view of the Dark Seer, she used the water on the leaves around her and created a spear of ice, that flew through the air to the Dark Seer. 'There you are my dear,' he said with a flick of his finger. The spear shattered as a purple glow covered his hands. Before he could retaliate, an arrow struck him in the chest and his shadow faded. Then with a cry, a group of rangers came running through the woods. Jenna had made it to Hanerson and found help. Emma and the others stayed in cover as the rangers fought off the remaining elf rogues in the camp. Many had already run, but only when the battle was over did the rangers noticed the young high elf dead, at the bottom of the tree. As the rangers wrapped the body in cloth from their packs, what looked like the captain walked towards them. 'What in Alidor are you playing at Balmoth?' The man said, looking at James, but he was speechless. They all were. They just watched as the rangers pulled Vanessa's body onto Jenna until the man shook James. 'Snap out of it boy. What has happened here?' the Captain asked. James looked up and finally recognised the face looking at him, 'Captain Roian what are you doing here?' James said. 'Answer me first what happened to her?' Roian asked.

'They tried to kidnap the Princess, and we stopped them. One of them told us there was another, so we came looking,' James answered. 'And almost killed yourself and the Princess too. Come we must get back to town just as well your father sent me when he did,' Roian said.

'Wait, you've been with Balmoth where is he? What's he doing?' Billy asked, his little ears had pricked up hearing Lord Balmoth mentioned. 'Later! We must get back to safety first,' Roian said, leading them back to the road into town.

As they approached, James saw Makron and other elites waiting. They had heard there was trouble and rode down to escort students back to the academy. James ran ahead of the others to him. 'You promised you'd watch them. What trouble have they gotten in to?' Makron said smiling to James, but his smile vanished and turned to worry when he saw the grief on his friend's face. 'What's happened?' Makron asked, then he saw the body covered up on Jenna's back, 'who's that?'

'Makron I... I'm so sorry there was nothing we could do an...' James stopped speaking as Makron pushed past him and went to Jenna. He pulled back the cover to reveal his sister's cold face looking back at him, he quickly covered her again, 'How? How is she here? How could he, why I don't understand,' he muttered to himself his head in his hands. 'I'm sorry Makron I'm so sorry' James said placing a hand on his shoulder, Makron did not speak again as he watched his younger sister's body placed in a coffin, covered and slid onto the back of a carriage.

In the grand hall that night the students and teachers sat at their tables in silence eating quietly. The death of the young lady had turned the normal vibrant group of students into mourners. That was until Miss Jando stood up. With every movement she made she seemed to waft sweet smelling calming fragrance over the hall. 'It is far too quiet in this hall tonight, for even in the darkest caves light may still be found. Master Cunningham a song perhaps, it is said that dwarf song can cheer even the most gloomy of caves,' she said. Cunningham stood up and went around the table his long platted beard dragging along the floor. 'A song of my people let me think,' he muttered, then began to sing. 'For once, there was a dwarf so bold, he could stomp on the floor to tame the ground and so, he would use his hand to beat the rocks, until the great Orashon was born. Through blood and toil and broken bones, the great Orashon was born, soon she stood as grand as she could oh mighty Orashon mighty and grand. Old dwarves they did created our world, through stone and iron and blood and bone.' Master Cunningham stopped singing then looked at the weary faces of the students. 'Maybe songs of my people are not right for this day. Alas a new song we need. What of the wolves? They must have songs that even the old do not know,' he said looking down to where Billy sat.

'My people don't sing songs sir we...' before Billy could reply, Hilly had stood up. He was sitting beside Billy but was now walking to the end of the ranger's table. 'Our people may not have songs Sir, wolves don't tend to have great voices for song like dwarves seem to Sir, but we do have tales. I'd tell you one if you would hear it,' Hilly said looking to the Headmistress she nodded, and he continued. 'This is the tale of the meeting of my parents, the great Balvor Mammoth slayer and Salene the white light of the Fang. This is the tale of how they won their names.' Hilly continued to walk up and down the table. 'Many years ago, when the Fang was still truly wild, as the old wolves say. A time when mammoths and even greater beasts would roam our forest. On the first day of summer, my father went out on his first hunt to prove himself to the pack. He was determined to win, and he stalked the Fang until he found his pray, a great mammoth known as Broken Tusk to wolves. He had killed many, and even after the rest of his kind left the Fang for the west, he remained. My father did not sneak and strike the beast, he walked into the clearing where he dwelled and there they fought a duel lasting from the rising sun to its setting. 'till finally by binding the beast's legs with strong vines he lay before my father, defeat showing in his large eyes. Father prepared his jaws to end the beast, but he and all wolves have something in them. Something I never truly understood back then anyway. Looking at Broken Tusk, my father no longer saw a foe but an old worn out hunter. Balvor untied the beast, cutting the vines with his sharp teeth. Then they stood there silently as the forest groaned about them. Before either of them had said a word, they were both surrounded by a pack of sabertooth's that had been roaming the Plains of Nore. They had heard the battle of Balvor and Broken Tusk and with great speed they had made their way to the clearing. For killing a descendent of Barramore would bring them all great fame among their kind. They attacked my father and even with Broken Tusk beside him they were failing. Both worn out from their own duel, as saber after saber charged to them, their end seemed inevitable. Then a howl rang out. It was the most beautiful sound my father or any wolf of the Fang had ever heard, and there she stood. My mother Salene, and here she would earn her name. The sabertooth's had not only been a bane to the Fang but also to the pack she belonged to, the whitepeak wolfs, known for there beautiful white coats. They had attacked them as they made their way to join the wolves of the Fang, after the attack the only wolf that remained was her. She had not been idle, she had licked her wounds clean and pursued the sabers 'till finally she had caught up to them. With a great white flash she shot across the clearing, sabers fell to the ground as she did and together, her, Balvor and Broken Tusk fought on 'till the sabers were defeated and scattering. After the battle my father finally spoke, "Such beauty I'd never imagined and such rage I have never seen," with that the pair were bonded. Her eyes met his and from that moment they would never care to look away again.' Hilly finished his story. He was now on top of the rangers table putting on quite the show as he concluded claps and cheers came from all the tables. Good cheer and laughter had crept back into the hall. Whatever fear the Dark Seer had placed into their hearts was broken.

The Princess had remained in her dorm since their return, not wanting to be pestered and questioned by the other girls. She looked out of her window to see a half moon shining down, illuminating most of the ground save for the old shack where she could see the fire burning outside and shadows moving around. Maybe I should speak to them, better than just sitting here wallowing, she thought to herself. She turned and went to leave her room when a loud familiar bang came from her window. 'Hey,' Hilly said, pulling himself up.

'You can't keep doing that,' Emma said, trying desperately hard to stop herself smiling. 'I just wanted to make sure you were okay, I didn't see you at dinner,' Hilly said as she joined him on the window sill. Their late night talks had become a regular thing, they would sit there just talking nonsense most of the time. Hilly had never looked at a girl like he how looked at her, finding any reason to spend even a second alone with her. Tonight, however, their moods were different from normal, without saying a word Emma lay her head on his shoulder and the pair sat there. Silently looking at the moon as it moved over the sky until she spoke, 'I was told high elves were the strongest beings that had ever been. Vanessa was a high elf, I'm half one, but that man he can just click his fingers and she was dead. Her heritage didn't help her. We're never going to be strong enough to stop him. All I can think is he will click his fingers, and I'll be next,' tears ran down her face and her eyes became blood red. 'That won't happen. I won't let him. This git think's he's winning right now he's feeding off us, feeding off our fear, the despair we all feel now. Wasiz told me that wars are not only won with swords and numbers, if you can break your enemy before your army even leaves your halls then you lose nothing, but gain it all. The Dark Seer think's he can win that way, so when he comes all will fear him and none would dare stand against him, instead they would bow to him, serve him. Fear is a far greater weapon than any sword or magic hourglass,' Hilly said, fiddling with the hourglass around his neck. 'Did your mentor tell you how to stop it?' Emma asked.

'Yep, fairly simple really. Don't fear him and put your trust in me,' Hilly said with a crooked grin.

## The Unlikely Allies

'Great, the world's going to war and I have a cheeky human thief who was raised by wolves of the wilds as my champion. You know most Princess's get a valiant knight or elemental mage,' she said, smiling back at him wiping tears from her rosey cheeks. Hilly hooked the end of his repel on the brick and lent out. 'Valiant knight?' he replied sarcastically, 'ha overrated, now a lovable rogue with companions like mine, in times like these, my dear Princess we are exactly the champions you need,' with that he leapt off the wall and flew down to the ground.

## Chapter 12
## Defence of Aceonse

The next couple of weeks passed slowly, after Makron had left
with his sister's body and returned to the grand city of Duniesa
for her burial. A month of mourning had been decreed by the
Seers and Seer Dune had once again called for the Princess's pets
to be imprisoned, but the King had firmly condemned this,
publicly praising the group for rescuing his daughter. Captain
Roian and his group of rangers had remained at the academy
following the orders of Lord Balmoth and after a few days of
pestering, he finally spoke to the boys of the Lord's whereabouts.
'A bird came to the Undercroft a couple of months back now,'
Roian said, 'there I saw Lord Balmoth's hand ordering us to
withdraw and go to Meceller, so we did, leaving the Undercoft
undefended. I couldn't understand it. We had held that fort for
almost an age holding back every orc raiding party and the
monsters that dwell to the West. Now we were just leaving it to
them, anyway we began our journey home when almost half way,
who do I see on the road ahead of us but your father,' Roian said
pointing at James. Himself, James, Hilly and Billy were sat in the
grand hall listening intently to Roian's story. 'Anyhow he told
me not to go to Meceller but to come here and watch over you. I
had been quite displeased to be truthful. My skills are better used
elsewhere, I said to myself at the time but Lord Balmoth was
right,' Roian lent in so others around could not hear and spoke in
a whisper. 'I didn't believe him when he said the Dark Lord had
returned, but now I've seen him as you have,' Roian said, staring
deeply into the cup of water in his hand. Suddenly the doors of
the hall were swung open and in ran a ranger covered in mud.
He'd clearly be traveling continuously. 'A message! A message!'
he cried, running to the head table where the Headmistress sat.
To her left, Mor and Master Cunningham were drinking and
laughing. The pair had become close friends. Master
Cunningham was a huge fan of recalling battles of dwarves of

old and Mor was happy to listen, especially when a bottle of dwarf's whiskey normally joined the old stories. To her right was Miss Jando, who was chatting the head's ear off about flowers and seeds. The messenger ran up and handed an envelope to her, she opened it and began to read as the messenger turned and shouted, 'I have another message, for the unlikely allies of Tailor's Hope,' he said looking around the hall until Roian said. 'Over here lad, this be them.' The ranger ran over and handed a crumpled mud stained envelope to James. 'I must go now. I have more to deliver,' and before any could offer him food or drink he ran from the hall and back to the gate. He had no steed waiting and just kept running. James opened it, looking to the head as he did who had already read hers. The hall fell into an eerie silence as students and teachers watched James open the letter and read it aloud. 'It is from Captain Landon of the Tailor's Hope guard he says the West gate is under attack, not from orcs but a new enemy with armour that's as thick as dragon scales and who show no fear. We have held them on the bridge, but we are failing, we need help I'm sending messages to all who I hope would aid us especially to you my unlikely allies. I must once again ask for your aid,' James spoke and waited for the head to respond, but before she did Billy jumped up. 'We need to help them, are these gates not hugely important to the elves?'

'He's right, the gates are the one thing stopping whatever's happening in the South from spreading here,' Ernest shouted from the other end of the table. 'Quiet!' The Headmistress said, 'none of you will be going anywhere Captain Roian prepare your rangers to ride for the West Gate.'

'My lady, I have barely thirty rangers. We shall ride, but I fear we would not be enough alone,' Roian said then Hilly leapt to his feet and quickly walked to the head's table. 'Miss, please send us as well we can help, Landon's our friend,' he said walking around to stand close to the Headmistress, moving his hand to her shoulder. 'Please Miss, we can do this, we can help them,' he said as the Headmistress gave him a stare that would stun the faint hearted. 'Remove your hand boy before I turn you into the cocky crow you act as,' she snapped. Hilly backed off and went back to his friends as Roian joined the Headmistress to discuss their plan Hilly and the others began to leave the hall.

'Mor come with me would you I need to show you something,' Master Cunningham said. The pair left the hall and Cunningham led Mor to his office on the second floor. They walked in, and the old dwarf continued to an iron chest in the corner of the room that had once been hidden by a sofa. He opened it and took out what looked like a small builder's hammer. 'Many legends are told of how ancient dwarves would forge weapons that could slay the gods themselves. Many legends turn out to be only fables but a few are true,' he handed over the hammer to Mor. 'This is Anersham forged in the hills of Orealas by a great smith of old,' Cunningham said. Then Mor felt an of rush of energy flow through his arm from the hammer. Then with a bright golden light it transformed into a huge two handed war hammer cast in a bright silver metal Mor had never seen before and with bright blue gems and green sapphires running along the four foot shaft. One side of the hammer was flat, the other had a sharp dagger blade, but the war hammer didn't get heavier it still weighed the same as when it was a small workman's hammer. 'Yes, yes I knew she would choose you, she sees the good in that heart of yours my grumpy looking friend,' Cunningham said. 'Why give me such a grand gift?' Mor asked.

'Because dear orc, you know as I the call of battle. I feel it calling now, I know you do too, as do those you have vowed to protect. I would be fighting with her myself if I weren't so damn old now. Three hundred and three I am now, a fine age and strong my mind is but weak this old body feels. Alas, in your hands Anersham will sing I am sure of that,' Cunningham said.

'If this is the Dark Seer then I would happily meet him in battle with Anersham in hand, though the Headmistress seems to not want our aid,' Mor said.

'Will that stop you? Will that stop them?' Cunningham said. 'No, no it shall not,' Mor said and the hammer transformed back to normal and he placed it in his belt.

'We have to do something,' Billy barked as they walked into the courtyard. 'What can we do?' Hilly said.

'We can help. We can't just ignore Landon, I'm fed up with sitting while people die,' Billy said.

'Your serious about this?' Hilly asked, 'back in the Fang if we knew all the people we know now and asked for their aid, do you think they would have helped us?'

'That doesn't matter, our friend is calling for our help I will answer,' Billy proclaimed.

'We can't just go running every time someone cries for help,' Hilly said. 'Why?' Billy asked sharply.

'Why? 'Because we can't, that's why.' Hilly scoffed.

'Back in the Fang, no, we couldn't, But now we can. No one came running to save our family you're right, but that won't stop me running to others,' Billy barked.

'I knew you'd get like this,' Hilly reached into his pocket and pulling out the Headmistress's hair clip, but in his hands it had transformed into the shape of a key. 'How did you get that?' James said, shocked. 'You really think that show back there was for my own good. I was honestly terrified of her turning me into a crow,' Hilly said then he turned to his brother who was now vigorously wagging his tail, so impressed by what he had done. 'We meet back at the stable in fifteen minutes, there we can use this to open a door to the West gate, then we just save Landon and whoever else is left and get back. We are not fighting a battle,' Hilly said, then Emma came running over.

'What are you planning?' she yelled to them.

'Nothing, what do you want?' Hilly said, trying to hide the Headmistress hair clip in his hand. 'That's hers, isn't it, you stole it from her, you're going to the West gate aren't you?' She said getting more frantic as she spoke. 'We have to, we can't just sit here and wait anymore,' Billy said then courage and confidence filled her 'Well,' she said, snatching the hair clip from Hilly's hand, 'you have no idea how to use this do you? But I should be able to work it out.' In her hands the hair clip turned into a bright white star. 'You're not coming with us,' Hilly said.

'Without me you're not going anywhere and these are my people you know. If anyone should be going it's me, now where are we doing it?' she snapped.

'The stable fifteen minutes,' Hilly muttered, she was right he didn't know how to use a magic hair clip. The four of them ran off to prepare and Hilly ran for Leonardo's workshop. He opened the door and ran in as Jerrest pulled himself from his bed in the corner of the room. 'What are you doing?' he barked as Hilly began rummaging through box's and drawers. 'Just looking for stuff that will help,' Hilly said. 'Help? Help with what?' Jerrest asked.

'Umm. You know never mind how's the leg?' Hilly said trying to change the subject. 'I'm walking on it well, be able to run as fast as I...' Jerrest was interrupted by Hilly filling his pockets with odd looking things and running out the room shouting, 'okay Jerrest thanks bye.'
'What's he up to?' the curious wolf said to himself, getting up and walking to the door.

James was in the ranger's armoury filling his quiver with arrows, he turned back to the door to leave only to find Captain Roian blocking his way. He stroked the perfectly groomed moustache below his nose and spoke softy, 'What are you doing?'

'Just going to practice shooting Sir,' James lied.

'Then why not use training arrows those are green leaf arrows best us rangers have. Don't waste them on target dummy's,' Roian said knowing exactly what he was up to, he then stood aside for James to pass. A few minutes later, James made his way to the stable, where the others were waiting and Mor had joined them. 'How did you know what we were doing?' Billy asked him. 'I am a clever orc little wolf, you cannot pull wool over my head,' Mor said.

'It's eyes, wool over your eyes,' James said joining them and then seeing Maggie with the Princess, sword and shield in hand wearing a mail shirt over an old leather tunic and trousers. 'No don't even think about it,' James ordered.

'We already tried don't bother,' Hilly said.

## The Unlikely Allies

'I should be able to help same as you, plus Master Ash has been training us. I can fight just as well as any of you,' Maggie said. 'The girl speaks true, a true warrior dwells within that one,' Mor said.

'Have you worked it out yet? She must be onto us by now,' Hilly asked the Princess as she fiddled with the hair clip. 'I'm trying, just give me a minute,' she said struggling to work out how to make it work. Then Jerrest approached them with Captain Roian and his rangers beside him. 'Oh no,' Hilly said.

'The Headmistress would like her hair clip back young thief,' Roian said walking towards them, 'but she didn't say when she wanted it back,' he said holding his bow ready.

'And I should like to get revenge for our pack just as much as you. I will not be left behind!' Jerrest barked.
'But your leg, are you sure?' Billy asked.

'My leg is as good as one of flesh, it will not slow me and I will not hinder you,' Jerrest said.

'Wait, wait,' a voice cried out. Leonardo was running to them carrying a small black shoulder bag, 'You ransacked my workshop and didn't even look in the right drawers,' he grumbled taking the old pack from around Hilly's waist and looking in. 'Don't steal things that you don't understand. All you have here is junk,' then he handed the other bag to him. Hilly looked in to see there was a slot for his repel and three cartridges. On the other side were six throwing stars with four razor sharp points. Normally, they have a hole in the centre, but these had silver marbles instead. 'Just make sure you're a good distance away when you throw them,' Leonardo said. Before Hilly could ask more, a shout came from the Princess 'I've got it,' she cried and the stable door in front of the group lit up with a bright white light. Mor walked forward and opened the door, with that the Princess, her handmaid, the rangers of the undercoft, the last hunter of the Fang and the unlikely allies of Tailor's Hope walked through, leaving Leonardo alone.

The Princess was the last to walk through the door, as she did she fell to her knees sweat dripping from her forehead. 'Are you okay?' Maggie said, coming to her aid.

'Yes, I just need to rest. That took a lot more out of me than I expected,' she said, cursing herself in her head for feeling so weak. 'It's okay just rest. You done your part well. Now it is for us to do ours,' Mor said. The party were in the hall of an old tower carved into the rocks of the Karrom Mountains. Emma had remembered it from a trip long ago with her father. Many tunnels and opening had been made by the dwarfs, now it housed the people of Aceonse. It was easy to hold the tower and caves, but there was also no way out. Other than one door leading to a courtyard where the inner wall encircled the tower with one gate which was now in pieces on the floor. The bridge had been lost, and now Captain Landon was rallying his men and holding the enemy at the gate. The party pushed their way through the mass of civilians hiding terrified. As they ran to the door they heard cries of despair coming from them. 'No don't go out. There's demon's out there,' an elf shouted as Mor opened the door and the party looked down on the gate. Landon had been pulled away from his line and was now in the mist of the enemy, surrounded by purple armour, but Landon did not falter. Since the events at Tailor's Hope he been training hard, with sword and shield and his skill now shone out from him for all to see. 'Look to him,' Mor cried, running down the steps of the tower and charging to the front line. 'Look to him Captain Landon of the guard, I name you here, I name you Landon the Defender,' Mor shouted pulling the hammer from his belt, transforming it into the mighty war hammer Anersham and pushing through the front lines. With one swing of his hammer the enemy were thrown into the air and Mor stood beside Landon. 'It is good to see you my friend, I knew you would come, but I did not expect you to come from within my own keep,' he said as he thrust his sword into a purple clad soldier. A hail of arrows followed, clearing the front lines giving much needed relief to the solders, if for only a short time. 'What are these things?' Hilly said looking at the face of the enemy, they had purple skin and elf like faces, but their eyes were blood-red. 'Their leader called them dark elves. They attacked us at dawn, we tried to hold the bridge but had to fall back. These men here are all I have left. My forces were divided, half went to the barracks to the east. There's a large group of civilians there also, but I fear they may be lost,' Landon said, as Billy sniffed the air. 'No, they're still there. I can smell them,' Billy said. 'I am Captain Roian of the rangers we must take back the bridge. I will move my men to the roofs of the buildings along this street and we will give as much cover as we can, you must move your line as we do.'

'The bridge is lost. I even sent men to destroy it, but they fell. With them all the black powder we have,' Landon said as they argued about their next move. Billy saw another group of eighty or so dark elves marching toward them. 'We don't have time for this,' he muttered then his brother looked down to him. 'Can you smell that black powder stuff?' Hilly said. Billy sniffed the air and he could smell it, an odd ashy smell. 'I can I think, why?' Billy asked then Hilly turned back to the arguing captains. 'James,' Hilly shouted making the others go silent, 'get to a view point where you can see the bridge, Billy will get the black powder there. Just wait 'till he's off to light it, the rest of you form line and draw as many from Billy and James as you can. If we can destroy the bridge the dark elves here will have no choice but to surrender.' They all stood there looking to the young human giving them orders. 'Well,' Mor said, 'what are you waiting for let us find our glory!' with that he ran towards the oncoming dark elves and with a cry of Anersham he slammed the hammer down upon them. 'To the orc,' Landon cried and the rest charged with him, the rangers were quickly on the flat roofs of the dwarven town houses firing arrows down on there enemies with pinpoint accuracy. Jerrest was now by Mor's side his iron leg deflecting the dark elve's swords and using his powerful jaw's to rip through their armour like it was made of butter. 'Go, now you have to be quick,' Hilly said.

'What are you going to do?' Billy asked.

'I'll get the rest of Landon's men back here. These dark elves should be pretty distracted now,' he said looking at Mor tossing another handful of dark elves into the air. 'Don't you dare die!' Billy said.

'You too, now go quick,' Hilly shouted and Billy shot off to find the black powder.

Hilly ran down a street to the East in search of the barracks. Most of the dark elves had moved to the front line as he had hoped. Turning a corner he then saw the barracks was now just a pile of rubble and bodies. Standing above the wreck was a thirty eight foot monster. It's skin looked to be sewn on and large metal clamps held its arms and legs to its body, it had no eyes, ears, or nose just a huge mouth with sharp rows of bloodied teeth. *What in Alidor is that?* Hilly thought to himself. As he did the beast looked up and bellowed out running forward. Hilly quickly pulled his repel and used it to reach the rooftops as the monster slammed his patchwork hand to the ground where he had been standing. Hilly reached back into his bag and pulled out a throwing star, he threw it, sticking it into the beast's shoulder and after a second it exploded. Sending rotting flesh flying and breaking the clamp holding its putrid arm to its body, leaving it hanging by a thread. 'Damn it Leo I could blow myself up jumping around with these,' Hilly said to himself looking into his bag. There were still five left and two cartridges for his repel, he loaded one and fired just as the beast smashed into the building causing it to collapse. He flew through the air, but then came to a sudden halt. The beast had grabbed the line and shook it, throwing Hilly to the ground, making his bag fly off his shoulder and slamming down to the other side of the street. Then after a second it exploded, the thud was enough to activate the throwing stars. *Maybe Leonardo was trying to punish me for stealing from him* Hilly thought as the beast's hand bared down on him. He pulled his dagger out the only weapon he had left. 'Great. Balmoth's lightening sword, that fancy ring, all I have is an old dagger and a hourglass that stops mag... magic!' He shouted aloud as the beast swept him up in it's remaining hand. Hilly quickly wrapped the chain of the hourglass around his dagger and as the beast opened it's jaw's to eat him whole he threw his dagger into the opening. It embedded itself in the back of the monster's throat. Then the hourglass began to glow and with a groan the beast began to fall apart, dropping Hilly back to the ground. He pulled himself out of the grotesque lifeless hand looking over the body seeing a glyph of three skulls as he did. One above the others, it was drawn on the inside of the beast's stomach and was now exposed as it fell apart into many pieces. He ran over and used his hand to wipe it off. After, he began rummaging through the flesh and bones of the beast until he found his dagger and the hourglass. Then a noise came from the barracks like someone was banging. He walked over and saw a piece of broken stone, that was once a wall covering a cellar door, where the banging was coming from. He used a broken wooden beam from the floor to move the stone off. It was heavy, but he was able to lever it up enough to kick another stone under and create a space big enough for the cellar door to open and someone to crawl through, 'Can you hear me?' Hilly shouted, going to his knees and looking under. The door opened, and a young guard appeared. 'Thank the gods. I thought that beast would have us all, is it gone?' He asked crawling out.

'Yes, how many are left?'

'We were able to get the innocents underground before they attacked. My guard did not fair as well I'm afraid,' he said as they helped the others out. 'You must take them to the keep, then join the front line Captain Landon needs you,' Hilly said.

'Who are you ordering me around you're but a younglin. Wait, those ears,' he said noticing Hilly's human ears, 'you're the human, Landon's ally am I right?'

'Yep, that's me and I'm not the only one who answered his call. Now round everyone up. We must go before more of these purple gits get here,' Hilly said as he helped pull people from the cellar.

James quickly made his way to the tile roofs of the town with the other rangers, raining down arrows on the oncoming dark elves, but he soon left them behind following Billy on the ground as best he could. The little wolf was charging down the street dodging dark elves. Many of whom barely saw him speed past them. The ones that did were soon cut down by an arrow from James's bow. Billy sniffed the air again then he saw the bodies of two members of the guard, one of whom had a pack on his back. 'That must be it,' he said running to it and taking the pack in his mouth, pulling it from the back of the dead guard. He turned back to the bridge and there was another regiment of dark elves making their way across. He looked around and saw some wooden stairs leading to a deck beneath the bridge. He ran for it, James realised this and moved around the roofs to find somewhere he could shoot from, using a rag to ready an arrow as he did. Billy made his way under and placed the pack to the left of the centre so James could get a good shot, he went to run back, but a dark figure appeared blocking his return. 'So this is the new Lord of the Fang' the dark figure hissed. Then the shadows faded, and he emerged wearing a smooth black trench coat that covered his whole body, trailing along the floor, making it look as if he was floating. His skin was as white as snow, and he was totally bald with two holes in the side of his head instead of ears and to two slits in the centre of his face instead of a nose, black lips like a corpse and his eyes had been sewn shut, but somehow he was still able to see. 'What are you?' Billy said.

'I am one of the five great general's of the Dark Lord. We are his hand, I am his Necromancer, creator of life eternal and you dog have been a bane to my master for long enough now,' with that the familiar purple glow covered his hands, but before he could cast any spell James let off three arrows in quick succession. They flew through the air towards the Necromancer perfectly aimed heading right for their target, but the Necromancer saw and with a turn of his head the arrows stopped and fell. 'The ranger won't save you dog,' he spat. Then out of nowhere Bob the pigeon swooped down and began pecking at the Necromancer's face. He had been sleeping above the door of the barn when the others went through and had followed them keeping watch from the sky. 'What is this thing?' the Necromancer cried flaying his arms about as Bob pecked away like a bird possessed. Billy quickly got over his shock and leapt up. He grabbed Bob in his mouth and planted his four paws on the Necromancer's chest, he pushed himself off and sent the Necromancer tumbling over the railing down into the chasm below falling with a sickening scream as he went. Billy let go of Bob, and the pair sped from the bridge and back up the wooden stairs. As soon as they were clear, James let loose a flaming arrow it stuck in the pack and ignited the black powder. A tremendous explosion rang out ripping through the bridge. It shuddered, then wobbled and then began to crumble and the west bridge over the Lavender Lake fell into the waters below, taking the dark elves crossing with it.

Mor was still fighting hard, to his left was Captain Landon to his right Jerrest of the Fang. Together with the rangers and the town's guard, they beat down their enemy. Never before had such a sight been seen even by the very old. Song's would be sung of the orc, the elf and wolf who fought as one against a mighty foe, whose valiant deeds would go before them as they go, but the dark elves were still many and the ranger's quivers were running low. Then Hilly reappeared with the remaining guard from the barracks, bringing a renewed hope to the soldiers. As Hilly ran to the front to stand with Mor picking up a sword in his left hand, and holding his dagger in the other. Billy was soon back by his side, and together they fought. Mor flung his hammer wildly until he saw a spear wielding dark elf running at Landon. 'Look out Captain,' he roared Landon span, but before he could react Maggie leapt down and slammed her shield into the face of the dark elf, stabbing him in the neck as he fell to the floor. Landon looked at her, her light brown hair shone like diamond's in his eyes and for a second he had forgotten about the horror's around them. 'What are you looking at? Fight on Captain!' she shouted to him. 'There are still too many,' Hilly yelled to Mor as water appeared around their feet. It then made its way beneath the dark elves, with a flash the water shot up impaling them on long sharp icicles. The Princess had used the remainder of her strength and easily halved the dark elves numbers. She fell back on the door of the tower unable to move, but this was enough. The dark elves who weren't impaled were soon beaten down by Mor's hammer, but they still would not yield, they still fought like they had a hope of winning. Not until the sun began to set was the last dark elf slain by Jerrest's jaws and silence covered the town save for the crying and whimpering of the injured and grieving. Landon quickly began moving the innocents from the tower and prepared them to evacuate. They had won the battle but Aceonse was lost. Most of the town was now rubble and what wasn't stone was burning. Hilly made his way to the bridge and looked over. There he saw a man in black looking back, the dark seers shadows had been watching. Billy joined his brother 'I see him too, why do you think he didn't get involved?' Billy said.

'He's been watching us seeing how we fight,' Hilly said.

'And we have shown him,' Mor roared behind them. 'Do you hear man in black, the free people of this world don't fear you! Fight us wherever you please, and we shall smash everything you send,' Mor shouted across the gorge. A few seconds passed then a voice came as if the wind had brought it, 'You should fear warrior of the Blood Work's you should fear me,' the Dark Seer's voice echoed and all in the town heard, then he vanished. Mor then heard a wounded dark elf crawling along the floor his leg had been hacked off, and he left a trail of purple blood on the ground as he dragged himself towards a sword. Mor raised his hammer, but Hilly stopped him 'Wait!' He said going to the side of the dark elf 'What's your name?' He asked, but the dark elf didn't reply, 'Where do you come from?' He said kicking the sword the dark elf wanted further away. The dark elf's face didn't change and still remained silent 'Speak scum!' Mor shouted kicking the dark elf onto his back, but all he did was try to get back on his front, to get the sword his eyes were fixed on. Then Hilly took his dagger and stabbed it through the dark elf's arm, but he didn't make a sound he just kept trying to get the sword. 'Do you not even feel pain?' Then still trying to crawl the dark elf died of blood loss.

Aceonse was quickly evacuated and a carriage and horses were found for the Princess's party. She was still too weak to use the hair clip again, her and Hilly sat beside each other fast asleep for most of the journey back to the academy. When they finally returned in the dead of night a day and a half later the Headmistress and Leonardo waited at the gate. After a long talk with Captain Roian she turned her attention to the others. 'My hair clip,' she said holding out her hand, the Princess took it from her pocket and gave it to her it turned back into an eagle and she placed it into her now red hair. 'I am not happy or wish to endorse this sort of thing, but I am proud, as I'm sure your father's and mother's would be too, but this cannot happen again. It may already be too late when the Seers learn of what you did. Well, let us hope they are proud also, now go wash the battle from yourselves and find some food,' the others walked off but Mor remained. 'What do you suppose they will do?' Mor asked.

'You are wise for an orc Mor, you know as well as I what they fear,' she replied.

'Fear. I'm fed up of hearing this word fear, for it is an elf word, one my people don't use, today they fought bravely, and I am proud to have stood beside them and if your leaders fear that then they are fools. If people as different as us can stand together why not us all.' Mor said with that he walked away.

'That is not the world we are in, good simple orc,' she muttered to herself as her hair turned white. Then she used her hair clip and walked through a door. She went from the grounds of the academy to the Seers great golden tower in the city of Duniesa.

She stood in the bedroom of King Elidom Godborn, he turned in the chair he sat in. 'You're too late they have heard,' the King said anger covering his face. 'And news that my daughter was with them'.

'They had all left before I could stop them,' the Headmistress said. 'Balderdash,' the King shouted, leaping from his chair throwing the golden cup he held to the wall. 'You would never let that clip off your head without knowing, same as I would never remove my ring. You let the human take it, you let them go!' Elidom said, trying to contain his anger.

'Yes I did,' the Headmistress said looking into the King's deep blue eyes. 'The town is lost. Yes, but it's people are saved if I had not let them go it would all be gone now and these dark elves would now be marching here.'

'I did not send my daughter to you to send her to battle,' the King shouted. 'You must remember your daughter is not just yours. She had a mother once and more of her lives on in that young girl than you will see. She will not sit in a tower watching as the world falls down around her as you do,' she said shyly turning back to the door. 'I feel myself getting weaker, I must return. Truthfully, I only came to tell you she was safe, and you should be proud.' She cast a spell on the door once again as the King sat back in his chair. 'I will do my best to quell the Seers, but if it comes to it, I shall do what I can to warn you,' he said as she left the room. Elidom raised his hand and another golden cup appeared. 'What would you say I wonder if you could see her now? Who is it that would suffer your anger her for going, or me for wanting to stop her?'

As Billy and the others made their way back to the shack they saw Ernest by the stables looking quite upset. With him were few other recruits they all had bags with them as if they were going somewhere. 'Ernest what's going on,' Billy said running over to him. 'You're back I'm so glad you're all ok,' Ernest said.

'We're fine, don't worry about us, but why are you out here this late?' Billy asked.

'The Countess Elander of Accultian came this morning shes been testing students all day,' Ernest said.

'Testing you for what?' Hilly asked, joining his brother.

'To see which of us can wield magic. She makes your drink this tea, once your done she reads the tea leaves. They show her if you're able to control elemental magic,' Ernest said.

'And you can?' Hilly said, shocked.

'Yes according to the Countess I can, she said with training I could be able to control fire and perform basic spells,' Ernest said. 'Then why do you look so worried?' Billy asked as another voice called out to them. 'It's about time the scum returned. Come here, the both of you,' the voice bellowed. The boys turned to see an elf woman wearing a bright purple dress with a fascinator on her head, covered in purple feathers and her face was heavily painted with make up. They began to make their way over to her but Professor Carny blocked their path. 'You have no right to put these two through your tests, they are here under Lord Balmoth's protection,' Carny said as frustration covered the Countess' face. 'How dare you? I have the right to whoever I please, now take your abhorrent self out of my path,' the countess shouted. 'I shall not and if it was in my power I would not let you take the others,' the Professor said.

'You have no power here horse, they will be tested if I say so,' the Countess demanded. 'If you insist upon it, we shall wait for the Headmistress, and you can take this up with her,' Carny said standing his ground and not letting her comments get to him, knowing the last thing that Countess Elander wanted was to deal with the Headmistress. She gave a dirty look past Carny to Hilly, and Billy. 'She protects these two as she does the Princess, so be it the rest of you get into the coach, it is time we were out of here and back to a real place of learning,' with that she raised her hand and a large purple carriage came out of the stables pulled by pitch black shire horses that were far larger then Meceller horses. Billy could think of no other words to describe then but evil looking. The students began to board. 'I guess that means me too,' Ernest said sadly.

'I am sorry, if there was anything I could do I would,' Carny said. 'It's alright I knew this could happen coming here, thank you for all you have taught me Sir,' Ernest said turning back to Hilly and Billy. 'If you don't want to go just stay we won't let her take you against your will' Billy said.

'No, it's not as simple as that and you two will have enough to deal with in the days to come, do not worry about me I will be okay, but I will miss you both,' Ernest said trying to convince the little wolf he would be fine as he patted Billy's head, then with a wave and a forced smile he boarded the coach. The Countess slammed the door behind him as he got in, she climbed up beside the driver as the carriage pulled out of the academy. Leaving Professor Carny and the brothers to watch Ernest get taken away to a fate only Professor Carny truly knew, for Accultian was no place of learning.

## Chapter 13
### Secrets of a King

Two weeks after the dark elves attack, life at the academy had changed. An uneasy fear covered the old castle. When the Princess's party returned the mood was joyous, but once stories of the dark elves spread fear gripped them. Most worrying of all the stories, were rumours that all the dark elves shared the same face. As the end of the school year loomed preparations were already being made for the graduation ceremony. The Princess opened the door of her room to leave for class but to her surprise her father blocked her way. They had not spoken since long before the dark elves attack. She had written him letters but he had not written back. She looked at her father and for the first time she saw him as old, his long golden hair had the slightest hint of silver and he looked like she had never seen before. 'Sit down we must speak,' Elidom said, and she sat down on the end of her bed and waited for him to say something. 'Do not think I'm not proud, impressed even, to do the things you have done at your age. Well it would have been beyond even me, but this must end. You may stay until graduation but after that you will return home, and stay home,' the King said sternly.
'But why? You said yourself you're impressed what will locking me away again achieve?' She asked.
      'Speaking of being locked up, you're to remain in this room until the Seers have been and taken the human, wolf, and orc away.'
      'No! You can't, you said they could stay here you can't just hand them over,' she begged.
      'I do not have a say in the matter anymore thanks to you and your actions. I am a figure of ridicule. His daughter and her human pets do what the King and Seers cannot. That is what they say in the city you have left us no other choice. Believe me when I say daughter that this is for the best.' Emma stood up from her bed and ran to the door. She opened it but four elites stood in the

hall. She went to leave but they blocked her way not letting her passed. 'Tell them to let me go,' she snapped to her father.

'I can't, they are here under Seer Dune's orders not mine,' the King said. She ran back to the window as the King left the room 'I am sorry,' he said closing the door. Emma lent out trying desperately to see someone. Then she saw Maggie who was coming to get her since she hadn't shown up to class 'Maggie, Maggie,' she cried, but she didn't hear, Emma grabbed a glass of water from her bedside, with a wave of her hand the water flew out and turned into a ball of ice that she tossed down from the tower. Falling close to Maggie she looked up to see the Princess. What's she doing now? She thought to herself as she heard the Princess cry down. 'They're coming for them the Seer's they're going to take them,' instantly Maggie knew who she meant but why would she not warn them herself. Then she saw the King walking towards her. Maggie dropped the books she was carrying and quickly sprinted off to try and find the Princess's pets when suddenly, she froze and the King's voice came from behind her 'Where are you off to with such speed young Balmoth?' He asked, Maggie felt her body become hers again and she shyly turned to face him 'I was just coming to get the Princess for class my Lord,' she said as her lip began to wobble. 'She won't be coming to class for a day or two. I did expect her to try to help her pets but to have done it before I even leave the stairs to her dorm,' the King giggled a little under his breath, 'Please don't think me cruel as my daughter does what happens next was not my wish. Now go.' Maggie nodded to the King and went to find the boys.

Billy and the others were just getting up when Maggie came running over panting with a red panicky face. 'They're coming for you,' she mumbled, breathing hard.

'What's going on?' James asked the only one who was fully awake. 'The Seer's the King's already here, Seer Dune can't be far behind come on we need to get you out of here,' Maggie said shaking Hilly awake.'They can't just come and take them,' James said.

## The Unlikely Allies

'Really? Why what's going to stop them? Even the Headmistress can't stand against all of them, now get up,' she said in true drillmaster fashion as she kicked Mor's side until he woke. 'Wait? Leave just like that?' Hilly said sitting up.

'But we've done good things here why now?' Billy asked. 'Some see what you do as good Billy, but others don't.' Then she went quiet and stared off. The boys looked and saw the Headmistress was making her way over to them. 'I assume you have heard,' the Headmistress said. Mor then stood before them all and reached for the hammer on his belt. 'Do not Mor. I'm not fighting you, not here anyway,' she said, in her hand was a new black bag. It was the same as the one Leonardo had given Hilly before. Hilly took it and looked in, to see a repel and the throwing stars still with the exploding marbles in the centre. With an extra slot sewn in with a variety of different coloured metal marbles inside. 'Leonardo said he remade them. They're less unpredictable now, that's what he says anyway,' the Headmistress said, 'Billy come here I had him help me with this also,' she reached up her sleeve and pulled out a black collar with three shining stones embedded into it. 'Allow me to put this on you,' she said kneeling before him, but Mor didn't like this. 'Don't, they're for slaves, that is the black collar of the crows of the wilds. Evil elves who made their money from selling others, many of mine have been in them,' Mor said.

'It is, I chose it because it is the best made I could find but it has been toughened even more by my magic and Leonardo's science. Each of the three gems will give you much needed aid, with the green gem the blessing of wood folk will follow even if no trees can be seen. The blue gem is the blessing of wisdom so the path before you may seem more clear, and the white gem is my own blessing I will watch and do what I can,' the Headmistress said. Billy lent in, and she placed the collar around his neck. It fitted perfectly and went well with his brown fur. As soon as the clip was tied Billy felt a rush of energy, his eyes opened wide to look on the world anew. He could hear every sound around and his senses were greatly increased. 'Now Jerrest is already preparing, and a horse has been made ready for

Mor. Come we must get you away'. She then walked to the door of the shack and it burst into light. Maggie then noticed her brother getting ready to leave also. 'It's them that have to go, not you,' she said trying to grab his quiver out of his hand before he put it on. 'Will you really ask me to stay?' James said.

'We're not asking you to go,' Billy said, seeing the worry in Maggie's eyes and not wanting to drag James off on yet another quest that may end in death. 'You don't have to Billy, nor does Hilly or Mor we started this together in the Fang that day. I won't stay here while my friends run for their lives,' James said.

'Hilly,' the Headmistress then shouted, they all looked around for him, but he had gone.

The Princess paced back and forth in her room, she was trying to think of something she could do to help. She went back to the window and looked out, then began to smile as she saw Hilly aiming his repel. She stood back and in a few seconds he was there before her, she threw her arms around him. Then the panic set in. Speaking low so the elites outside could not hear she said 'What are you doing? You have to run they'll be here soon'.

'I had to see you before, I had to know if you'll be okay,' Hilly said. 'I'll be fine. They just won't let me leave until you've gone, the Seers think I'll try and help you,' she said.

'Really? You'd never do such a thing,' Hilly joked.

'How can you make light of this?' Emma asked.

'Don't worry, the Heads already spoken to us. She's going to help. I should get back to them I just had to say goodbye,' Hilly said.

'Do you think...'Emma said stopping when she realised what she was about to ask, then Hilly placed his hand to the side of her head pulled her close and said. 'I will find you again, I promise, my Princess,' he lent in to kiss her, but that second horns sounded from the gates. The pair ran to the window the gates were opening and in walked Seer Dune, with him fifty elite solders with long golden spears and golden heavy armour. 'Search the grounds find the villains and bring them to me,' Seer Dune ordered as the Headmistress ran over her hair bright red with her dress, her anger plain for all to see. 'Do not dare,' she bellowed, and the elites remained still. 'You no longer have the right, not that you did before now hand them over,' Dune ordered.

'Guess that means the head can't help us now,' Hilly said jumping up onto the window sill. 'Don't they'll see,' Emma said.

'That's the point,' Hilly said smiling he hooked his repel back on the window then he shouted down to Seer Dune. 'I see you with a big, fat, old high elf down there Miss he looks pretty irate or does his face always look that bloated and deformed,' the Seer and Headmistress looked up to see Hilly stood in the window of the tall tower. 'How dare you!' Dune spat, 'I will throw your body from the battlements of the great city and that wolf with you'.

'Will you now?' Hilly said giving a whistle, 'and how shall you do that Seer, you would have to catch me first and your large self could never keep up with me,' then the door to Emma's room opened and the elites guarding it rushed in. With a wink to the Princess Hilly leapt from the window, 'Go! Get him when he lands, kill him if you must just bring him to me,' Seer Dune screamed with all his might. The elites rushed off, but before they got far a blood chilling howl ran out. Then they saw what all elves of old dreaded, as Hilly had glided to the ground he had been swept up and was now sat in a black leather saddle, tailor made for the rider and steed with gold thread and an emblem of a white wolf emblazoned on the left side. For a second Hilly thought he'd been swept up by a horse, but he quickly realised he wasn't feeling sick, and then he saw the soft fur and missing left ear of Jerrest. He turned his head to see James and Mor had mounted their horses and were speeding towards the gate with Billy. Jerrest turned to the oncoming elites and with another mighty howl they froze in place. With a click of Jerrest's iron leg he leapt over them all and ran for the gate. 'No you don't,' Seer Dune said raising his hand a ball of white light appeared, but he hadn't noticed the others, Dune was far too fixated on Hilly. 'Look out!' Billy shouted as he jumped up onto Seer Dune and sent him tumbling to the floor, causing a considerable thud as his huge arse hit the ground. Students had began to pour out of the hall hearing the commotion outside. As they did they saw the Princess's pets ride through the gates as Seer Dune rolled around on the floor desperately trying to get up. Emma ran from her tower, her guard had gone and joined the others who were now running after her pets, with no hope of catching them. This was her only chance to follow, she began to make her way to the stable but was soon intercepted by the remaining elite guard who were searching the grounds who, to her surprise took her to Seer Dune who was now being pulled up by another elite. 'Where would they go girl?' He snapped. 'Girl, how dare you I'm...' Seer Dune quickly struck her across the face. 'I am not playing girl. Your games end here where would they go?' He raised his hand to strike her again as her cheek began to swell suddenly a huge pain overcame his hand and he could feel his blood freeze. He looked up to see it completely covered in ice. 'Come here Princess,' the Headmistress ordered and she quickly went to her side as Dune writhed in pain. 'Fix this, fix this now,' he cried.

'Certainly my Lord,' the Headmistress said with that she took his ice cover hand and the hair clip from her head acting as if she was about to heal him with it somehow. She then slammed the clip into his hand smashing it into a thousand pieces. Seer Dune's cries became ever more frantic and shock had overcome the Princess. 'You will die from blood loss at this rate all that crying won't help, did you really expect another fate than this for raising a hand to her, the King's daughter,' she said with an odd grin through the mist of screams. The whole academy could hear the Seer begging for his life, then finally Emma spoke, 'You can't just let him die.'

'He raised a hand to royalty, death is the punishment I am no healer anyway,' she lied, 'you could save him though if you wished,' the Headmistress continued. She could save him. She knew exactly what to do, but even if she did there was no guarantee he would stop hunting the others and leave them be. Seer Dune then passed out, his body beginning to go cold, before thinking Emma ran forward hand's alight and sealed the Seer's wound. The Headmistress walked over and placed a hand on

## The Unlikely Allies

Emma's shoulder 'Well done, I knew I could count on you,' she said.

King Elidom sat in the Headmistress's office until he heard the shouting from outside. He looked to the window to see the Princess's pets charging through the open gates, then to the Headmistress who seemed too preoccupied to have aided them. Then he watched as Seer Dune walked over to his daughter and struck her across the face, before thinking his fingers snapped and froze the offending hand solid. 'Ha nicely done I say, although I would have frozen him solid just leaving the head exposed,' a voice laughed. A voice Elidom had not heard in more than an age. He turned, and sat in the Headmistress's leather desk chair was the Wizard June. A ball of bright gold appeared in the King's hand 'Get out!' He ordered.

'Don't be like that my ancient friend, I would not have come if there was any other way.' He was a short chubby dwarf man with a long grey beard and hair, both platted to match, wearing an old red robe that was stained and tattered showing its age. 'How did you even get in here the Headmistress's power should stop you from being able to enter,' the King said hands still ablaze. 'You must go to them Elidom and tell them of your greatest woe and greatest lie,' as June spoke the light in the King's hand faded 'You knew this day would come. Yes, I didn't expect to ask you to tell your tale to them, but they must hear it,' June continued. 'Why? What good would it serve, you show up when all is being lost and once again expect me to heed your words with nothing but a riddle to guide me. I won't be lead blind by you again, Balmoth may have fallen for whatever plan or scheme's you have, but I washed my hands of you long ago,' the King said looking as if he had grown taller as he spoke and his demeanour grew darker. 'Balmoth yes, Balmoth went past my sight many months ago now. I don't know where he is or if he still lives. You are right I have not always told you what you have needed to hear. I shall do so now in hope it makes you understand what I say to you and why they need to know,' June said standing up and making his way to stand in front of Elidom.

He held out his hand to perform a spell so old that only the pair knew of it. Elidom placed his hand on top and in a second he knew all he needed and much more. June's memories shot into his head and when they both opened their eyes tears filled the King's, 'How? How could you not say sooner? Oh my dear I'm sorry, I'm so sorry' he said falling to his knees before him and throwing his arms around June's waist. 'Look at what I've become, you would never have understood but it's alright dear King. She is safe and well, and I believe in love, which is why we must act now. I don't know who is behind this. Still, I won't stop and nor should you. Tell them your tale, it will give them the push they need and without it I fear they won't return to her. It is not just her I worry for, their small alliance has already saved so many of our people, with them gone the hearts of the elves will fall to fear.'

The party had hardly gotten four miles before Billy started insisting on going back, worried about all he might be missing. They carried on regardless until night fell, finding a spot just off the road to Tailor's Hope, hidden from the road and covered by trees it made the perfect camping spot. James and Mor got about starting a fire, whilst Billy and Hilly went further into the trees to do something they hadn't done since back in the Fang. They were going for a hunt, neither knew what they might find in the mist of tightly woven trees and sharp holly bushes, a small field mouse would do. Billy sniffed the air and a familiar scent came into his nose and worry crept over him he turned to see a dark figure standing behind Hilly, in a dark grey hooded cloak. 'Hilly look out,' he barked and leapt at the figure as Hilly span pulling out his dagger. The figure raised their hand and both boys froze in place. Billy was floating in midair waiting to fall. 'How do you not recognise me with just a simple change of attire,' the figure said pulling his hood down to reveal his long high elf ears and golden hair. James and Mor came running hearing Billy's cry to see King Elidom stood before them. James and Mor reached for their weapons, but before they could the King quickly spoke

# The Unlikely Allies

'Don't, I'm not here to fight or to take you to the Seer's I'm simply here to talk,' he said.

'How can we be sure you're word seems to mean little?' Mor spat. 'Because I am here alone and with great effort I have to say, now may we speak?' The King said as Billy floated back to the ground. They led him to the fire James had started. With a click of the King's fingers five mounds in the shape of chairs sprang up out of the ground around the light. They sat down and remained silent for awhile as the King fiddled with his ring until he spoke. 'I must tell you all something. A secret I have been keeping for so long that even the lies now feel like truths, I do not wish to tell you, but I know I now must,' he let out a large exhale of breath then his hand began to shake, he grabbed it with the other. 'I must, I must tell them,' he said to himself under his breath. James got up and took a canteen of water from Jenna's saddle bag and handed it to the King. 'It's just water I'm afraid my King, we had not time to grab wine before leaving,' James said Elidom took a swig. 'Thank you young Balmoth, do not fret over wine, such things are not needed I am just buying myself time you could say,' he handed the canteen back and looked into the fire. With a wave the fire came to life and the King's tale began. 'After myself and June created your people. The humans, I mean. I became rather close to one of them, Galivn Emra was his name we met on the field of battle,' as Elidom spoke the figures in the fire acted out his history. 'I had led my forces to do battle with the orc Menace. We met our adversary on the slope of Mount Kanshala. I had hoped to get behind their lines and end the war in one fell swoop but they were waiting. Orc's of those hills called themselves the frostbitten, living on the tops of the mountains had given these orcs tougher skin, and they are far taller then others of the Blood Works.' Mor grunted at this, not believing a word. 'Anyway, they cut us off. It would have been my new army's first great defeat if not for him. As I fought the orc's on the narrow slopes I thought myself soon to die, then a cry came from above me, it was him. With a swing of his sword the orcs around me fell. He lent down to me thinking I was just an elf like the others fighting with them, then he spoke to me in a way even then I was not used to. He pulled me to my feet by my hair and shouted at me, "Stand now elfie there's fighting to do stay to my back and I shall stay to you we will live this day I tell you," and we did. We fought on together rounding up our soldiers and securing the pass until reinforcements arrived. After he found out who I was, he came to my tent begging forgiveness for his harsh treatment of my hair. Then and there, I made him the human's King, and we were together. Not in public though, hidden away like a dirty secret. Years passed, and our love grew but the human council insisted on heir's as mortals tend to do, so Galivn took a wife. One who knew of our bond, and had three children by him. Then suddenly, he died. Leaving me the curse of mortal life. I mourned until Balmoth sent word he had someone sneak into the King's room while his body still lay there, he tested his blood and found he had been poisoned. Not even subtly done so obvious, they used fungus root a simple poison it would only take a small amount of knowledge to find and cure. Me and Balmoth were both sure that his own family were behind his murder. Once I knew this myself and five others left for the Crown City my plan was to kill the human's royal family.' A sense of shock shot around the group. 'And we did two of Galivn's sons died in their sleep along with their mother, but the oldest Harold, wasn't there and as we rode away we were set upon by him and his men. The rest of my party died as we ran. I only just made it away. The next day the human's purge began, not down to them being demons or hatred of all magical life, it was all because of me.' Elidom placed his head in his hands. 'You know what comes next. Great War, many dead and all down to me but yet the tale does not end there. Year's later my own people started to insist on me marrying and having a heir. That is when I met the Princess's mother Bethany Leaflin. She was the greatest most kind, caring woman you could ever meet and that lives on in her daughter along with her healing powers. Few have abilities like that these days, but she was a master of her art. We were married and news of Emma's imminent arrival soon followed, but when the night of her birth came Bethany passed away during the delivery, and once again my love was taken from me. After blood was taken and to my horror the poison that killed King Galivn was in her blood also. I was wrong it was never his sons but someone else. I had been tricked and now they were mocking me. But this time, this time I did not act, not scared for what might happen, but scared all the same and my only thought was of guarding my new daughter. With that I hid in my tower in Duniesa and did nothing. It seems I acted when I should not have and remained seated when I should have moved.'

The King ended his tale and looked to the faces staring at him a gasp, none of them knew what to say until Hilly spoke 'Why tell us all this? Why now? Why not weeks ago?'

'Because weeks ago I did not want you to know, and now you do, but that is not the sole reason,' Elidom said locking eyes with Hilly. 'I see you how you look at her, it is how I looked to him, and when I looked to him I saw the years ahead of us like a great book I would never put down, but mortals are not bond to the same fate as elves. I watched as the man I loved grow old and whither. I do not want my daughter to go through this. Putting all her hope in a love that can never be forever with you. She may smile now but one day whether from age or sickness you will die, nothing you can do will change that fate and I shall save my daughter from this pain.' Elidom said standing from his seat 'I tell you now Hilly of the Fang you will never again see her, you will never again seek her out, you will not send a bird. You will not try any tricks this is ended and in her long life that's to come you will become nothing but a fable,' Elidom turned and whistled. A great dark brown griffin came soaring down from the sky landing without a sound. It had a bright white undersides to its long wings and body with huge back paws even bigger then Jerrest's and long sharp talons on his front, before he could pull himself up Hilly was by his side. 'What do you think I'll do now? Just leave, turn my head and never think of her again.'

'I expect you to do the smart thing, find somewhere to hide and stay there 'till the war to come has passed and hope you're still alive after,' said the King pulling himself up. With a silent flap of the beast's wings he was away. 'I can't believe the humans war was all because of him,' James said, still staring into the now dwindling fire. 'It changes nothing if we're all still standing together to help stop the war before it starts,' Billy said.

'Did you not hear a word of what he said, they don't want our help Billy. They want us gone, they've wanted us gone since the beginning. We tried to help, we fought to save these elves and woodys, and now we're the ones on the run being hunted like game by their elites.' Hilly shouted he was fed up of constantly being told what to do, trying his hardest to fit in just to be cast out. 'I'm done I've had it, let them all be taken over by the Dark Seer see if I care.'

'You don't mean that,' Billy muttered as his brother's mood grew worse. 'I do Billy, I do, we tried running whenever they cried for help and look where it got us,' Hilly said laying on the ground beside the fire. 'In the morning we ride for the bridge. We're going back to the Fang and staying there 'till all this is over,' with that he closed his eyes but didn't sleep. None of them did that night, causing them all to feel rather drowsy the next day. As the sun rose none of them spoke, they just silently packed their things and began to ride for the river.

The Unlikely Allies

Chapter 14
Ranger's Quest

Lord Balmoth walked quickly along a small path in the Red
Water Woods, named after the lake that runs through it. Once
after a great battle it ran red with the blood of dwarves of
Orashon and goblins from the tunnels beneath the woods, a place
they call Vallabom. It's close to impossible to translate goblin
speech to the common tongue and the closest meaning for the
name that can be found is putrid one. The true meaning of the
name however would never be known for all who possessed this
knowledge had passed long ago. The dwarves of Orashon
mounted a campaign to take the at the time unnamed woods for
their own, not knowing of the goblins that dwelled beneath the
soil. The bloody battle that ensued led to the death of hundreds.
Their blood mixed and stained the waters of the woods making a
lake of blood that still flowed to this day. Behind Lord Balmoth
his steed Caspian followed, the father of Jenna sharing her bright
white coat that shone out in the darkness of the woods. His coat
however had speckles of silver, showing the great steeds age and
a silver tail and mane. He made a slight groan making Balmoth
turn to him. 'Do not fear my friend the woods will not harm us
'long as we tread lightly it will remain sleeping and let us pass. I
know you never liked this place, but we will be gone from here
soon,' They walked on passed the old dying trees all around
them, the scent of blood flowing from the lake dulled all their
other senses and made their eyes burn. In the darkness sounds
could be heard in the distance the screeches and groans echoed
through the woods from the monsters that dwell there. The pair
could hear the rumble of trolls and the thrashing of viper wings
in the air. Lord Balmoth's ranger uniform and cape showed the
time he spent traveling. He'd been on the road four months now,
and he had made his way back to the south side of the river. After
a quick stop at Meceller to order his rangers back there he'd been
in the saddle ever since. Visiting friend's old and new, but none

had any information or advice to share and the Wizard June had yet to show himself again. Forcing him to travel to the Red Water woods a place he hoped never to return, to seek out an old ally who he had hoped to never lay eyes on again. Soon they came upon a large mud hut. Lights beamed out from the round windows where singing and drinking could be heard. Small green figures could be seen through them. Outside was a wooden stick with a sign hanging on it that read Goblin's Stump. The mud hut looked to be the only place where light shone in the entire woods. 'Here we are,' Balmoth reached over and took his bow from Caspian's saddle, he wrote a note and tied it to the end of a small dart like arrow and then fired it into the side of the hut. 'Come on. It shouldn't take him long to see it lets hope he doesn't dislike me as he used to,' the pair walked off to a small opening in the trees. In the centre were the ruins of a fire and around it logs were placed to sit on. As Balmoth sat down a voice came from behind, 'clever woody, not coming in pub,' a goblin said walking up with Balmoth's arrow in his hand he wore an old black tunic and ripped old trousers to match. Almost two sizes too big for him, so he had tied a length of rope around his waist to keep them up. 'That was quick,' Balmoth said not standing to greet him. 'Caniz does not like you to visit, Woody makes Caniz look bad if seen with woodys, where cousin? Where big boss? Why you here and he not?' Caniz asked, he had never been fond of Lord Balmoth. They had met many times and worked together during the humans war and Caniz was the one who had introduced Balmoth to Wasiz. Caniz however was not a lover of elves or their things like most of his people he still lived like the old days, under ground and hidden. The Goblin's were so few after the human's war that their great mines never reopened and now they were nothing but mere scavengers. They placed the disintegration of their people solely at the feet of the wood elves, for it was them who turned their backs, the day the humans, and wolves marched through the Red Water Woods to the mines of Grashesa killing all they came across, making the lake run red with the blood of goblins yet again. 'You have not heard?' Balmoth asked. 'Heard? Heard what woody? Speak? Speak?'

Caniz ordered. 'I am sorry to tell you the big boss Wasiz he was murdered,' Balmoth said.

'Mmurrrrdered' Caniz screamed, 'murrrdered by who, woody must tell Caniz Who? Who?'

'An orc called Oshan the Executioner of the Blood Works,' hearing this Caniz face changed.

'Orcy? Not orcy with wolf hat?' he said.

'Yes, how did you know that?' Balmoth asked.

'Orcy was here, if Caniz had known orcy would be dead now, Caniz would boil his head if Caniz know, but I not know orcy came with gold paid us he did, to use them old mines under my pub.'

'Your mines? What for?' Balmoth asked.

'I not know they guard it now no one gets in, but I still have a way. Yes a secret way but too scared Caniz was to go alone,'

'Wait, they're still there?' Balmoth asked

'Yes, yes many still there Caniz say that. Listen woody, orcy not here but others still down there now strange looking elfie's. They're tall with painted skin and red eyes like the beasties themselves.'

'Can you get me in to see what they're doing?' Balmoth asked Caniz rubbed his chin and then said, 'Yes woody I not like you, but for cousin I get you in, but I warn you woody them elfies ain't nice, if they scare Caniz they should scare woody too,' Caniz said ready to lead Balmoth off.

'Stay here if I'm not back in an hour run home and tell the Headmistress what we found,' Balmoth said to Caspian as he followed the goblin.

They made their way around the pub to an old drain hole leading into the mine beneath them. 'That's the only way in?' Balmoth asked. 'Yes woody come, come we must be quick,' Caniz said crawling into the hole, Balmoth soon followed behind, and after a few minutes of crawling through wet sticky mud it lead them out into a mine tunnel. To their left they saw lights flickering and could hear sounds of hammers hitting steel and felt the heat of forges. They walked down the hall looking into one of the side rooms as they did. In there dwarfs were chained to bellows and anvil's forging weapons and armour. The room was bigger than Lord Balmoth had expected. More than a hundred dwarfs were there to his eyes, all clearly exhausted and underfed, never had Balmoth seen dwarfs so malnourished. Further down the mine shaft he could see more doors and assumed they all housed dwarves or other races being forced to work. They went on walking deeper as they came to the top of a staircase that overlooked the hall of the founders, built by the goblins that came before. The great hall was now full of row after row of what looked like purple elves most were already wearing shining new purple armour and helms, long steel swords hung from their belts and on their back were kite shields with a red dragon emblem on them. Each of them held a black spear with a purple tassel tied before the sharp blade. They're faces, covered by a steel mesh hanging down from their helms. The ones at the back of the line were having their armour and weapons placed on them by other purple elves. Once it was on they stood there still and silent. 'Purple elfies, Caniz not like this woody lot more than Caniz had seen, so many,' Caniz said he had spied the purple elves, but he thought they had just painted their pale skin, but now he saw it was their skin. 'How many do you suppose there are?' Balmoth asked in a whisper.

'Stories say eighty thousand gobs used to be here never going up there, and this, the back of the hall goes far back that way, a gob could die just going to the end,' Caniz said pointing down. There were so many rows that they went on into the darkness so Balmoth could not see their true numbers. 'Come we must get out of here and warn the others,' Balmoth said then they heard a goblin's cry. They looked down into the hall to see a goblin pinned down, being forced to drink purple liquid from a vial, he rolled around in pain then stopped. His skin then changed to match the others along with every other part of his body, he rolled around on the ground. Arms and legs twisting until he stood up, he was a perfect copy of the rest. 'Mad, tots mad turning gobs into elfies,' Caniz said as Balmoth dragged him away. Caniz didn't want to look, but he couldn't stop himself. They went to make their leave and find the hole they had crawled in through. 'Other's? What others woody?' Caniz said now fearful. 'My friends, they're across the river, but now hopefully this will be enough to get the Seer's to act and have the elites March,' Lord Balmoth said. Then he stopped in his tracks, a shadowy figure was stood before them. With a blast of black shadows there stood the Dark Seer's shadow. 'There you are my Lord. I have been looking so hard for you but now here you are, what do you think old ranger of my dark elves?' The Dark Seer said. Without a word Balmoth pulled his sword as the Dark's Seer's hands began to glow. 'Stay close,' he shouted to Caniz as his sword started to spark. A huge beam of lightning stuck down on the ground above their heads creating a large hole, causing rubble to begin to fall burying the Dark Seer's shadow as the pair clambered out of the hole. Caspian ran over to Balmoth's side, he jumped up onto him. 'Quickly, we must ride!' He said, holding out a hand to Caniz. 'No, I find my lot tell them, you go, Caniz be fine woody.'

'You can't stay here they'll find you, come you must leave with me if you like me or not,' Balmoth ordered.

'No woody. I stay find rest of my lot not many gobs left don't want them made nasty elfies, but you come back woody for big boss you come back with others,' Caniz said. Then footsteps echoed from the hole Balmoth's sword had made. The dark elves had begun to March. 'I don't think you realise what staying behind means for you, this is not the time for bravery, running is all we have now,' Balmoth said as a group of dark elves made there way out of the hole. 'Go, run woody,' Caniz cried as he picked up a rock from the ground and tossed it at a dark elf sending him falling back into the hole, knocking the rest down as he went. Caniz then turned to Balmoth and with a nod to each other Caspian sped away, as if his hooves were alight.

Once out of the woods, the sound of marching footsteps faded, but Caspian's pace did not. Leaving the Red Water Woods and Caniz behind they came onto a dirt road. To the East the city of

Orashon could be seen far away. The towering walls casted huge shadows on the ground below giving the city a eerie darkness before it. Looking to the City, Balmoth saw a sight that at first filled him with hope that someone else had taken back the city from the orcs, but then dread and a feeling of doom instantly replaced this. As he watched an enormous red dragon fly down from the sky landing on the battlements. Balmoth's keen wood elf eyes could see the dragon clearly from such a distance, but he was too far to make out the shadowy figures on the wall greeting the dragon. He did however see the dragon clearly enough to tell who it was. Amunden the great destroyer, burner of the humans, bane of the wood elves. A terror for all, and the most feared being in Alidor. Caspian grunted as Balmoth made him slow to watch, and with that the dragon's head rose, and a thunderous roar rang out. So powerfully loud his roar was even elves across the river would hear, but few knew the true horrors of what this sound brings. This was the first time a dragon had been seen since the end of the human's war. With a mighty flap of his enormous wings he flew back up into the clouds above and Balmoth could see more red shapes and suddenly fire began to bellow out turning the sky red. 'Dark elves, dragons, orcs who else do you suppose the Dark Seer has aiding him and why do they do so? Dragons would never follow him out of fear alone,' he turned to Caspian 'Do you believe this is worth it old friend, so many seem to wish the death of elves, maybe it is time for our fall,' Balmoth said as the shapes in the sky moved away, off to the Blood Works. Caspian gave a light neigh as if to say would you not fight? so in tuned Balmoth was with his steed he knew exactly what he wanted to say, 'Yes you are right. I could not be idle, and I fear neither could you,' with a shake of Caspian's mane he agreed, and they rode on.

Balmoth had to stop to rest, he was spent as was his steed. Caspian panted hard as the pair stopped on top of a small hill, surrounded by small white flowers called little wisps by the wood elves. They were a good sign he had passed into the lands of the wood folk of Meceller. From the hill he could make out the tall trees of his home to the north stretching out into the sky. So tall were the trees of the wooden city, tales were told that the first woods elves climbed down from them, out of the clouds to care for the roots of the massive trees. 'Yes this will do for the night and there see Caspian, a small stream come on we both need a drink and a wash,' he said looking at his muddy mount. With a jolly neigh, the horse jumped into the shallow stream and began to drink his fill. Balmoth knelt at the side and filled his hands with water and threw it over his face, as he wiped the water from his tired eyes he became aware of a person on the other side of the stream watching him. He slowly reached for his sword, but before he could Caspian ran to the side of the stranger seemingly greeting an old friend. The figure pulled back the hood of the ragged brown cape he wore, and Balmoth saw a face he would never forget. The long crooked ears, the broken tooth, the scheming eyes. 'Wa... Wasiz am I dreaming, or have I passed on?' Balmoth whispered hardly able to speak.

'No good friend no this is no dream, and you are still very much among the living unlike myself if you are seeing this, I am sad to say,' Wasiz said sitting opposite Balmoth with the stream of water flowing between them. 'How are you here then? This sort of magic is so far beyond you, that's what I thought anyway?' Balmoth then laughed and smiled to Wasiz, 'Or have you tricked me again goblin, don't tell me you're some all powerful being?'

'No, nothing like that, what I have done here is no more than a message in a bottle. A message in time that would come to you when things seemed lost and darkness covered the world once again, I hoped this would never come but here we are,' Wasiz said taking a pipe from under his cape and lighting it with a candle that seemed to appear from nowhere. 'There's only one thing that's even capable of doing such a thing. Wasiz tell me, did you find it?' Balmoth said. There was only one thing that could cast such a spell, something the watchers had searched for but never found. 'I can only answer what I imagined you'd say, you have to ask the right questions,' Wasiz replied.

'Wasiz did you find the stone of seeds?' Balmoth said, speaking the name as quietly as he could. 'Oh Balmoth, do you really think I'd keep that from you?' Wasiz said, with a glint in his dark green eyes. 'In truth I would not want it even if you had, it would break this world faster than it is already,' Balmoth said.

'I agree, so it is good no one is yet to find it,' Wasiz said, 'but that is not why I am here, I am here to give you what you need to know'.

'Problem is Wasiz you seem to think I needed to know little? Before coming to Noress that day I had believed you. You had your farm and your pub and that was enough for you, but your meddling never stopped, and I still wait to see if any is for good or not,' Balmoth said. 'I was wrong to keep the fact I was training them from you. I know I was meant to just watch and make sure the wolf held his word, but then one day the two of them came to Noress. I saw them sneaking around and I said to myself, Wasiz look to them hiding in the shadows terrified of what could happen to them outside their forest, but their curiosity was still too great to keep them there. Whatever happens they will leave one day, through their own ambition or force I said to myself. After speaking with their mother and father who agreed seeing the same as myself. I began to train them unbeknownst to them that is, Hilly learnt more from me than Billy, but guarding my fields was great for the young wolf's agility, and Hilly quickly got the hang of lock picking and other skills a great thief like myself could teach,' Wasiz said.

'How did you get Bale to send you his dagger?' Balmoth asked. A question he'd wanted answering for a while now. 'Was simple really, I wrote to him told him I was you and that you needed it, and as expected the loyal dwarf sent it straight to me, said he'd just been using it to open letter's if you could believe such a thing. Then it was just a matter of letting slip to Hilly about a cart that was carrying some interesting items through the Fang,' Wasiz said giggling to himself.

'You do realise if he had it, he could still be here now?' Balmoth said. 'I don't know what your reply to that was Richard but if I left it with him it would now be lost. As I speak now

## The Unlikely Allies

Orashon still stands strong, but I believe it would be the first to fall,' Wasiz said.

'And you'd be right, but I still don't know why you gave it to Hilly,' Balmoth said. 'The same reason I gave them my hourglass they are the ones who have need of them now. Our tale Richard...' Wasiz suddenly stopped, sighed and lent back with his pipe hanging from his mouth. 'Our tale grows old, so very old now and soon the baton must be passed to the next, something we hoped to never do, but we now must, but we speak too long. Time runs short, I must tell you this one more thing before I go.' The old goblin lent forward with intense eyes. 'I am the greatest story teller to have ever lived Balmoth. I gave the items away. I schemed, I planned, and I have created the greatest tale there is and by telling this tale Alidor maybe, just maybe be saved. You play your part well but now as in all tales help is needed. If I am right Balmoth and my tale is being told you shall know if you wake when the moon is brightest, and look West of your home you will see what you need and if I am right Richard, you must stay your path. You must not waver, whatever comes you must play your part my bravest friend,' and with that Wasiz faded into the air and nothing of him remained. 'Wait Wasiz you must tell me more,' Balmoth begged, but it was too late he turned to Caspian and said, 'He tells us where to look but not what to look for, always that goblin gives me riddles and hopes I will do as he thinks,' he stood up walking to his steed and taking the bedroll from his saddle, laying it under the tree and laying down. 'You are lucky I am a fan of your tales old fool,' he said closing his eyes.

Lord Balmoth was woken by Caspian nudging him with his nose 'I'm awake buddy I'm up,' he said looking to the full moon that was high in the sky, looking as bright as the sun, turning his gaze to Meceller then to the West. There illuminated by the moon, he saw rows and rows of golden armour marching in perfect formation carrying white banners with golden griffins emblazoned on them. 'Yes! They sent the elites. If they wish to take Meceller now they will truly have to fight for it,' Balmoth said as hope filled his heart, but it quickly faded once again as he watched them march on passed Meceller. 'Wait where are they going?' Balmoth said quickly throwing his bedroll onto his saddle. 'Come on let's go speak with their commander,' Balmoth said to Caspian as the pair rode off. After a few miles they were behind the marching ranks of golden armour, but he was quickly stopped before he was close enough for them to see him. Caspian had reared up to avoid crashing into a figure dressed in black before him. The figure quickly held their hands up and shouted, 'Stop Balmoth if you go on they will see, and I know you believe them friends, but they are not,' Balmoth recognised the stranger's voice, but was still surprised when she looked up to him and he recognised her face. 'Calenir,' Balmoth said looking to her, trying to hide his growing grin. Calenir wore a black leather jacket and trousers, with her shoulder length black hair tied up, to keep it from her blood red eyes. Her skin was pale like she had never seen the sun. 'Your cold face, I never thought I'd see it again but the last time we met my dear Princess we were enemies, is that still so?' Balmoth smiled to her.

'We were never enemies Balmoth, the rest of my people however would still love to bleed you. But that is not why I found you,' Calenir raised her hand another figure walked out the shadows. The man was tall, far taller than a normal elf of these lands, with dark skin like that of the elves that went west long ago, but still pale like Calenir's and bright red eyes to match. 'This is Aycon, he is the head general of my fathers army and my right hand,' Calenir said.

'His general? Are you finally here to declare war against the wood folk?' Balmoth joked to Aycon.

'Yes,' he replied taking the grin from Balmoth's face, 'and no I don't want to fight elves none of our people do, the deals we made with you and your watchers still stand, but the Dark Seer has come before my Lord and he now acts as his puppet.'

'The grey count follows another, this can't be true,' Balmoth said in shock. 'It is Balmoth, terribly true. My father fears the end of us, we have changed so much to fit into this world to pull our kind away from the darkness, but fear nows pulls us back, fear of becoming one of them,' Calenir said.

'You mean the Dark elves, I saw how he made them in the Red Water Woods. He had already turned hundreds. I watched as a goblin was changed, a sight that would fill any with fear,' Balmoth bowed his head as he recalled the sight. 'And with the Dark Seer's promise that if we stand with him our people will be spared my father had little other choice. He says he believes this promise, but I did not, nor does Aycon,' Calenir said.

'So the lady and I began to watch the roads and had our eyes in the night watching all they can, these elites you follow march for La Sore castle that's the fourth group this month. Almost four thousand in all we believe,' Aycon told him.

'So they must be planning an attack on Orashon, to retake the city?' Balmoth asked.

'No they enter but are never seen again. Once in they don't come out, and theres no signs of any readying for battle. I believe the Dark Seer rule's there now,' Aycon said.

'That's impossible the Seer's castle is not so easily taken. I will have to go there, see this for myself,' Balmoth declared as he turned Caspian to head for La Sore castle. 'If we are right, you cannot just walk up to the gate, we have heard about the others that used to ride with you. I hoped them just fables, but now I see them not to be. I mourn them too but killing yourself does not help. I can get you in without being seen and maybe we can both find the answers we seek,' Calenir said, standing before Caspian. 'I hate doing that,' Balmoth muttered then with a sigh he got down from his steed and stood beside Calenir. She opened her mouth and two razor sharp teeth grew out of her top row of teeth. She bit into her thumb and a small amount of bright red blood began to ooze out sending a familiar chill down Balmoth's spine, 'I always hated this.'

'Quiet Balmoth, you always liked what used to happen after,' Calenir teased in a whisper as she drew a line of blood over his forehead and spoke words of her own people. The pair began to be consumed by shadows and with a flash of blood red the shadows screamed. They were gone leaving two black bats flying up into the night sky.

The bats flew on and soon looked down on La Sore castle. Six spire towers and battlements surrounded the fortress keep on the inside. They flew into the open window of the tallest spire, leading them into an attic and with a flash of shadows, Lord Balmoth and Princess Calenir stood there as themselves. 'I hate that,' Balmoth grumbled.

'Just like old times,' Calenir said, they quickly made their way down the stairs until suddenly Calenir grabbed Balmoth's arm. 'I can smell high elf blood in there,' she said pointing to the open door a little further down the stairs, Balmoth moved quickly and looked in. He saw Lady Eloise La Sore laying on a huge lavish bed crying as if she had been for days. 'Wait, don't,' Calenir said as Balmoth walked in.

'My lady why do you cry?' he asked in a sweet voice like he was about to sing, as he did Calenir vanished into the shadows. 'Bal...Balmoth, why are you here?' she snapped through tears. 'I had ill news of goings on here. I had come hoping to speak with you,'

'Ill news, ill news, you dare come here to break my heart more Balmoth.'

'I'm sorry my lady I have been travelling, what has happened?' Balmoth asked. She pointed to the other end of the room, there on another bed lay the body of her daughter Vanessa La Sore, cold and still, surrounded by flowers. Around the bed were books and vials, many herbs and pots. 'I have tried everything, they say she's dead, but I know she's not, she's just waiting, yes she's just waiting to wake,' Lady La Sore began muttering to herself. Balmoth walked to the girl's body, and she was clearly dead, long passed on, her body had even began to rot. 'What happened to her my lady tell me I shall aid you?' Balmoth said going back to Lady La Sore. 'Marlos says she's gone, but she's not. Like the Dark Seer, he said he killed him too, but didn't though, did he. Yes, wrong about that and this, I won't stop, I'll bring her back Balmoth. He's not taking her. She's just sleeping that's all, just waiting to wake,' Eloise said. Then Calenir appeared from the shadows. 'She doesn't even see us Balmoth, grief has taken her, high elves have so much power but their minds are weak she's no use to us,' Calenir said.

'Come my lady please the elites that have been coming here where are they? What are they doing?' he asked, but she only continued to ramble. 'Wake her, Yes I'll wake her up, he was wrong, and I'll wake her,' then they heard the iron gates of the battlements open. The elites Balmoth had been following had arrived, they moved to the window and watched as they marched in and once the gates closed behind them the new ruler of La Sore castle made himself known. A cry came down from the tower opposite them, on a balcony stood Oshan in black heavy armour and a black wolf helm. 'Elf scum, you drink or you die,' he cried down then out of the castle and towers poured dark elves, without a word they charged into the now panicking elites who one by one were pinned down and forced to drink the purple liquid. Each dark elf had the vial's strapped to their belts, the ones that could not be held down were soon dead on the floor, too weary to fight after their long march. In minutes it was over. 'My father may be right, we have no hope but to bow to the Dark Seer,' Calenir said.

'I shall not bow to him or that whelk of an orc,' Balmoth gritted his teeth in anger, 'come we must go, I must get back to the academy,'

'Is there really any hope left there, look,' Calenir said forcing him to look back to the swarm of dark elves now forming below them. 'Yes I will still fight and others will to,' Balmoth said. He would not let himself fear these dark elves. 'My father will fight with you, but only if you show him you can win Balmoth, and even I do not think you can win this one, not now, but you're right we should leave,' Calenir said biting her thumb once again Balmoth quickly turned to Lady La Sore. 'Come my lady we must leave, it is not safe here,' but she ignored him, and walked to her daughter and began brushing her hair which was coming out in clumps as she did. 'Why do you think he left her?' Calenir asked.

'The La Sore family never normally come here, it's just been elites here for ages. The Dark Seer must have known killing Lady La Sore's daughter would have broken her and driven her here to try and save her and be safe from watching eyes. Forcing the elites to cut their numbers so rumours of her leaving the city didn't spread. With a lax guard this place would be easy to take. It's too large to be held by a small force, as for why he has left her here still. I don't know maybe he just enjoys watching her suffer,' Balmoth replied. Then the blood was placed on his forehead and the shadows surrounded them once again.

## Chapter 15
## Orcs of the Blood Works

The party rode on, with Hilly, and Jerrest leading the way. Hilly had not spoken a word since the night before not even to his brother. James suggestion that Tailor's Hope or Meceller would be the best place to flee too had fallen on deaf ears, and the others were not in the mood to get caught in the middle of an argument between the pair. Billy was happy that they would return to The Fang, but he also didn't see the point, there was nothing there but corpses now. All Hilly wanted to do was get as far away from elves as he could, Elidom's lies were the reason for the elves hatred, not him nor the human's that came before him. Mulling over these thoughts in his head, his anger growing and growing as they got closer to the East gate. As they approached a young elf came running to them, 'You're here already thank the lady, we didn't expect you so soon, we only sent birds for aid a day ago. Captain Landon has taken charge but others have yet to show,' the young elf shouted up to them.

'No birds found us, we're riding for the gate to cross the river,' James said to the young elf. 'Wait you haven't heard orcs are there,' the elf said as a chill shot up the spines of all in the group apart from the mighty Mor. 'Orc's? Why are orcs there?' Hilly asked. 'I don't know they showed up a day ago. They made camp about half a mile from the bridge they now stand in line just waiting. They have not attacked yet or even fired their bows, so the guard formed a line also following Captain Landon's orders. He and his guard were here to pick up new horses from the stable master when they arrived,' he said.

'Well I'd hate to be you today, guess we will go to Tailor's and wait for you lot to work this out,' Hilly said.

'Wait we're not going to the bridge? We can try and help,' Billy barked.

'If the elf speaks true and my people wait there, fighting may not be what they're here for. If I can speak to my brother we may learn much,' Mor said sounding very wise.

'Did you not hear me last night elf problems are not ours not anymore come on,' Hilly ordered and Jerrest reluctantly turned to walk away to the west for Tailor's Hope. 'No,' Billy said sternly. 'This is not a debate Billy,' Hilly yelled anger swelling inside him plain to hear in his voice. 'No we are going to the bridge they asked for aid and we will go. I don't care what the King did, I don't care what human's or wolves or orc's did. I care about saving the people that need us now and fighting for what's right. Walk away now and you become as bad as Elidom. Come or don't come do as you want,' Billy said with that he followed the young elf with Mor and James close behind, leaving Hilly going the other way.

Jerrest carried on down the road until he sniffed the air and stopped. 'Don't stop Jerrest,' Hilly snapped.

'It's that bird, I can smell its stink,' Jerrest said. They looked and saw Bob fluttering down to them and landing on Jerrest's head. The ugly little bird had a capsule tied to his leg, Hilly reached over to take it, but Bob pecked his hand as he did. 'Hey what's that for?' Hilly asked. They little pigeon then began to squawk at Hilly clearly quite upset. 'Oh, I get it, I'm sorry we left you behind okay, there was a lot going on,' Hilly said. More upset squawks came from Bob. 'Okay I swear on the Fang, I will never leave you behind again,' Hilly said placing his hand to his heart. Bob calmed and bobbed his little head in agreement and let Hilly take the note from his leg. 'This bird clearly sees you as a friend, and I'm sure your promise is true, but what of your other friends, our other friends and the promises we made to them,' Jerrest said as Hilly read the note. There was only one person it could be from. 'I will never forget you and I always wait for you, even if we fail I will wait for you.' Hilly rolled the note up and placed it in his bag. 'Billy was right you know if we walk away now this curse the King made will carry on, nothing changes,' Jerrest said. He would follow Hilly wherever he asked, something in him made him not want to say no to the human, but this may also be his only chance to drive his jaw's into the orcs who attacked The Fang. Then a voice came from the trees around them. 'It all seems pretty hopeless sometimes doesn't it?' the voice said Hilly span in his saddle to see a figure in a tatty brown cloak. 'It can't be,' Hilly said in disbelief as he got down from Jerrest. 'Yes, I know how you feel boy but times like these are few, and even the darkest caves have some light,' Wasiz said. Hilly just stood there, not knowing whether to smile or cry until he heard another voice. 'Wasiz, Wasiz I done it look,' another figure appeared from the mist, it was him but when he was young, barely six or seven holding an open box with a smooth red stone inside. 'I remember, I found a box hidden in the pub, he said I'd never get it open, and I should leave it be, but I picked the lock in three minutes,' he said turning back to Jerrest and Bob. 'We don't see anything,' Jerrest said.

'Well done,' Wasiz said taking the stone out of the box, 'I shall have to find a better place to hide this then,' Wasiz said turning back to a bewildered Hilly. 'Why is it whenever you're told to do something you do just the opposite? I wonder if you will always be like that,' Wasiz said, then looked back to Hilly's younger self, placed his hand on his shoulder and said. 'I will ask you to remember many things over the years. Many fables and tales, plans and schemes but this is the first thing I want you to remember. We are thieves. If someone tells us there is something we can't have we take it, we smile wave and put on a good show and at the same time empty their pockets and fill our own. For once a thief has procured something be it a stone, gold, a sword, or a heart once it is yours we do not let it go,' Wasiz said, then the pair faded and Hilly was just staring into the woods. 'What happened?' Jerrest asked.

'Not too sure,' Hilly said wiping his eyes, but then he smiled to his steed and said 'Walk on Jerrest. I know what we have to do, I think that maybe it's time I started growing up, just a little bit mind you, but just enough.'

The party rode over the bridge and on the other side, just after the barn they had spent the night in was a line of town guards men's. Across the field a group of around six hundred or so orcs all with gloomy looking faces stood quietly. 'This is odd,' Mor said as he looked to them. 'How so?' James asked.

'If they were here for battle, drums would sound, and they would cry out, not just stand there like well behaved elves. They do not even look well prepared,' Mor said. Billy had run off to find Captain Landon. He was with his soldiers looking to the orcs. 'There you are,' he said seeing Billy running at him, 'and the others too, but I don't see your brother where is he?' He asked. 'Don't worry about him, he's busy,' Billy said not wanting to tell Landon about their fight. 'Do you have any idea what to do?' Landon said to Mor.

'How many are you?'

'I have two hundred men. They let me recruit twice our number after what happened at the west gate, but the guard here is barely fifty. They out number us by many. Our best bet as I see it is to hold them at the gate,' he said.

'Yes, you are right but I don't understand what they are doing here, they know this great gate. They know they will not pass here, even with their numbers,' Mor said. Then a huge blur of brown fur and a figure on top in black darted passed leaping over the line of elves and began running for the orc line. 'It's Hilly and Jerrest,' James cried as Jenna jumped the elves also to join him. Billy and Mor followed, but Mor had already dismounted and chose to run shouting to Landon as he did. 'Hold here, do not move without my word,' as they rode and ran across the field. Horses could be heard coming over the bridge, it was Captain Roian and his rangers. 'We got your letter, we were forced out to patrol for the fugitives. Glad I was your bird found me to drag me away,' he stopped speaking as he saw Landon's allies heading to the orcs. 'You let them pass?' He shouted down to Landon from his steed. 'Could you have stopped them?' He replied.

# The Unlikely Allies

Hilly was the first to reach the orc line as he did he could feel their eyes on him, feeling like each was burning into his skin. He shrugged off this feeling as Jerrest stood tall before the horde. Then Hilly spoke, 'I have had it with dealing with orcs and elves and now,' as he spoke Jerrest began to walk up and down the orc line drooling as he looked to them. His rage building as the orcs tried their hardest to avoid his glare. He had missed his chance to fight in The Fang but even if he was outnumbered he would rip into them without hesitation. 'Now I have no patience left, so I give you orcs, you worms of the Blood Works, the ones who throw their honour away to follow the Dark Seer. I give you one option,' the others approached from behind Hilly, 'that is to crawl back to your shitty little holes and make sure I never lay eyes on you scum ever again,' Hilly said spitting as rage overcame him. The orcs before him shuddered and murmured with one another and Jerrest grew ever more impatient, as he and Hilly were both feeding off one and others rage. 'Speak now or my jaws will feast on orcs flesh once again,' he growled and bared his large razor sharp teeth to the orcs until one finally spoke. Ore ash the war chief walked to the front to stand before them. 'We are here not by choice, and now it is as if a warrior of old has come to stand for the elves and ensure our doom,' he spoke and looked to his brother, 'I did not think it would come to this brother. I believed when I had them imprison you I was in the right, but I am sorry I did not listen that day, but now here we stand and all I ask is you can take me from this world brother, in the hope it may save me some honour,' Ore said.

'Do not look to him for your salvation my friend's fangs are all you shall get war chief,' Hilly said as Jerrest moved in.

'Stop this all of you, no one's fighting here, not today,' Billy said sternly. 'Battle is what orcs are here for, and it is what must be,' Ore said.

'Why? If you truly come to fight then why wait, you stand here with sword and mace in hand but wait. I feel you want to talk mighty chief,' Billy said. Mor had yet to speak he just looked over the orcs before him, he once used to call friend's and family. The way they looked to him now had changed, but what they saw in him he could not tell, but could hold his tongue no longer, but his words had to be right. 'Brother so long I have wanted to see your face again and that of your sons, but the young Lord of the Fang is right,' he said and Ore looked to Hilly and Jerrest. 'That is not the Lord of The Fang brother,' Billy then walked forward, 'He is the Lord of the Fang, Son of Balvor mammoth slayer and Salene the white light of The Fang. He is known as the fastest in all Alidor, it is his words I heed, I believe you do wish to speak and maybe words can win you this battle instead of the blade just for once,' Mor said joining Billy.

'You stand with wolves, with humans, your words are like that of elves, and I find you changed brother but for worse or better I cannot see, but looking to you now and those around you. Four I count, so small a number but so much you have done, the Dark Seer's punishment of those who fail him is brutal, and you here have caused him to inflict much punishment,' he turned to the orcs listening to them speaking. 'Warrior's, blood for once is not what the horde crave, but today we must for the Dark Seer orders us to die before their walls. He tells me today must be the day, the only way to reclaim any honour we have left is here he says,' Ore shouted to the horde and seemed to be readying them to attack. Then something clicked in Hilly's head, his rage vanished as he saw Landon and Roian waiting at the elf lines. Roian seemed to have brought all his rangers from the academy and if the orcs attacked even if they were caught up trying to get back to the wall they would still lose. They had no hope of crossing the bridge. The elves on the other side would simply raise it the second it looked like they would he thought 'Shit Shit Shit!' He cried louder and louder 'The Dark Seer said today it had to be today right?' he said jumping down from Jerrest and running to Ore his anger had gone and been replaced by fear 'Um, yes he was very adamant that we wait till the eighth day of nine in the month of the lady,' Ore said taken back by the look in the human's eyes. 'And what else happens today?' Hilly snapped, turning to James it took a second and then James shouted as it also came together in his head, 'graduation.'

## The Unlikely Allies

'Right, and now Captain's Landon and Roian are here to fend off an orc attack that has no hope,'

'Is your human broken?' Ore said interrupting Hilly and looking to Mor. 'The Dark Seer doesn't care what happens here, pay attention orc. He sent you here to die to get rid of you. Just to get us and them out of the way he wants us to be too busy fighting and killing each other to stop him,' Hilly said.

'Wait, I'm not following why would he want us all here,' Billy asked interrupting again. 'Coz he's already over the river, he may have been this whole time, he's going to attack the Rangers Academy,' Hilly said. Billy's eyes went wide with disbelief. 'What? But why, there's only students there?' James said. 'And the King, the Head, the Seers, and with Roian and his rangers here it will just be them against who knows how many dark elves and the Dark Seer's shadow won't be far off,' Hilly said.

'If you're right we need to get back, we need to stop him,' Billy said. 'It's too late we fell for it. The attack on the West gate he did that to draw us out, make it so the King and Seers had no choice but to make us leave, and now the only other guard the place had is here too. None of us will get back there in time,' Hilly said as his brothers ears fell.

'But our friends, how could we be so stupid, but I can try I'll run as fast as I can,' Billy said as his brother patted him on the head and said. 'It's too late we would never get there in time for all we know it's already happened.' Then Ore spoke,

'We have someone who may help, bring him!' And with a few grunts and moans a wood elf was pushed to the front of the horde. 'Ernest!' Billy exclaimed jumping up to him, it was him, but he was dirty and looked as if he needed a good meal. 'How are you with them?' Hilly asked.

'He was with a group of elfies that were given to the Dark Seer to be turned. I took him because he said he knew my brother, and he stays because I make good use of his clever head,' Ore said shaking Ernest's head.

'It was that Countess she sold me and the rest of the students she took, we got in that carriage next thing we knew we were over the river and surrounded by the dark elves, Ore here took me just as they were making the others drink and turning them,' Ernest said.

'Wait drink? Drink what?' James asked.

'And turned to what?' Hilly said.

'The dark elves, that's how he makes them, he just takes anyone young or old makes you drink this purple liquid then you become one,' Ernest said.

'That's how he made his army with others?' Mor said.

'Yes brother and my youngest son Bor is one also,' Ore said. 'It's worse than I thought if he's there and makes them drink, but we're still stuck here,' Hilly said.

'Maybe not Ore has been good to me, and he was smart to take books from Orashson before leaving. He let me read them and I know a spell that may send you back there, but I can only send three, even that will be nearly enough to kill me, I think if I read it right. Dwarf's writing is hard to read,' Ernest said as a female orc handed the book to him from a pack on her back. 'Wait what happens if you read it wrong?' James said.

'Even if you go back what will you do?' Ore asked Hilly turned to the orcs as Ernest found the right page in his book. 'Well war chief if Ernest can get us there, without killing us doing so, we will find the Dark Seer and we will end this, that bastard's not taking another home from us,' Hilly declared standing right before the Orc towering down over him, 'Why, lucky you got before going against the Dark Seer. Just three of you would not stand against his true power. Even the greatest orcs would not dare stand against him,' Ore said.

'Your brother does, and so do we and why you ask, I asked myself that a lot to, nearly everyday since you git's attacked our home, but I know why now,' Hilly said turning to his brother, 'It's because they're mine and no ones taking them from me,' he smiled to his brother and Ernest read aloud from the book, a great orange glow came over his hands opening a portal. 'This should put you right before the main door to the hall, go quickly I don't know how long I can hold this,' he cried as sweat began running down his face. Mor went to be the first through then a voice came to him brought by the wind and for only his ears words spoke and he stopped. 'I must stay I must speak with my brother,' Mor said.

'I did think we were about to fight about whose going,' James said as the four stood before the portal. 'Go now, I will find you boys again once this is done. I swear this to all three of you,' Mor said.

'It's okay Mor,' Hilly said.

'You done your job better than any could and we are the way we are now thanks to you guarding us, thank you,' Billy said leaping up at him. 'You are all the bravest most honoured I will ever know,' Mor said. 'Quickly!' Ernest cried and the hunter, the ranger and the thief walked through. As Hilly did he looked back to Mor. 'You're the one with all the honour you ugly old orc,' he said as they vanished through the portal. With a spark of orange light the portal was gone and Ernest lay on the floor passed out. Orc's quickly tended to him, they had become quite fond of the young wood elf, 'Why did you stay and why do you leak?' Ore asked, tears rolled down Mor's face as he turned to his younger brother, 'I leak for the passing of a friend and I did not go because I must be here brother,' Mor said.

'For what, is there still to be battle between us?' Ore asked. 'No brother, not us or the elves here. But the horde will do battle this day,' Mor said looking to the horde. 'Do you hear me orcs of the blood works, your honour is lost but it can be given back! Ready yourselves for battle, it will be upon us soon and there we must fight like true orcs of old for victory,' Mor shouted to the horde. 'What do you know that I don't?' Jerrest asked.

'Just wait friend, I have spoken to the mighty and we will have our part to play. Go speak with the Captains and have them make ready,' Mor ordered and looked back to his brother. 'Well brother, my War Chief will you stand at my side and rush into battle once again?'

'You do not just ask us to stand with you, you ask us to stand with elves, wolves, and even the human, you would have orc fight beside them,' Ore said.

'I would not have you just fight beside them, we fight with them to free ourselves of the invisible shackles we wear, to free ourselves of the Dark Seer's hold over our people, shun me now then fine so be it, but know if you do so all here will have to remain and the Dark Seer wins. Stand with me now and the shackles of the Dark Seer will be broken and orc's will for once stand tall and free,' Mor said.

# The Unlikely Allies

## Chapter 16
## A New Age

The Headmistress sat at her desk sorting papers and wondering how the Princess's pets were doing and if she had done the right thing allowing them to go. She knew there was little she could have done. Their exploits had given the Seers no other choice. Seer Dune was still recovering in the infirmary and even though most of the academy had seen the boys leave the elites had still insisted on searching the whole academy, for Hilly, Billy, and Mor. Surprisingly they also carried orders to arrest James Balmoth. The reason why none would say other than It's what the Seers order. As she stared at her papers, her long hair and dress began to turn dark black reflecting the glum mood that was overcoming her. Even Roian had been roped into searching along the borders, leaving her no one to express her true feeling's to, and all on the graduation week when the whole school was already a hive of activity. She continued pondering more as the door to her office opened, and she was surprised when Seer Marlos La Sore walked in with his hands concealed under his white Seer's cloak. 'I wasn't expecting you Lord Seer. I didn't expect you to be here until the celebrations later today,' the Headmistress said. 'Yes, well I was hoping to see you before all that. You warned them of Dune's coming I assume?' Marlos said walking over to look out of the round window behind the Headmistress as she continued making her way through her paperwork. 'Yes did you really expect I'd just hand them over,' she asked eyes still locked to her papers. 'Oh heavens no, you have me wrong I quite enjoyed hearing about that pig's hand also,' Marlos said chuckling, 'no to be honest it's exactly what I expected you to do, this way that damn dog and his disgusting human are out of the way. Even taken Balmoth's boy with them. It makes all of this a lot easier for me you see,' he said.

'All of what?' she asked, surprised at his language.

'We have been playing this game of ours for what feels like an eternity. It makes me almost sad that today the winner of our long played game will finally be crowned,' Marlos said still looking out the window as the Headmistress head began to turn he continued to speak. 'You know I took great pleasure in the deaths of your friends. You watchers have caused me so much strife for as long as I can remember and these damn items you hold, how scum like the five of you could tame such power in the first place makes no sense to me, but now it is just you and that blasted Balmoth left,' Marlos said.

'Wait what are y...' But before she could finish Marlos made his move and quickly locked a metal collar he'd been hiding under his cloak around the Headmistress's neck. As soon as the lock closed she felt her power begin to drain. 'What? What is this Marlos?' She said as she began gasping for air.

'Don't fight it my dear it will only make the pain worse, amazing contraption, that Leonardo really is a genius. Told him I needed something that would dispel all the magic in one's body, he didn't even ask what they were for. The fool just happily set about making them for me,' Marlos said with a smile that was growing by the second as he found the Headmistress's attempts to stand quite amusing. 'It was you all, this time, it was you,' she said as she fell to the floor. Marlos walked over and towered over her. 'You see on a normal elf the collar would just leave them unable to use whatever abilities they may possess, but with you my dear because you used almost every spell and enchantment there is to maintain your good looks, once the magic fades from your blood I don't think there will be anything left of you, do you?' Marlos asked, he was right she could feel her heart begin to fail, she didn't even have the strength to move anymore. She only had a few seconds, 'killing me. Killing my friends. It changes nothing. Me, Balmoth, the others. We are just pawns playing parts in a tale. Told by the greatest storyteller there is.' She choked on her words barely able to speak, her skin had began to turn to ash, her legs were already evaporating into the air. 'I have won, my victory is guaranteed, none can now stand against me,' Marlos said, grinding his teeth holding himself back from ending her, but the fear that was in her eyes had gone and she began to laugh, 'you will not. All because of a stoned goblin. He gave them all they need to end your madness,' she mustered all her might to speak a few last words 'I'll...I'll be watching you dark Seer,' with a cackling laugh that ripped through Marlos, sending chills down his spine. The rest of her body dissolved to dust leaving nothing behind but her clothes, the collar that was around her neck and her hair clip. 'I'm amazed you were able to last that long,' Marlos said to himself as he reached down to take the hair clip from the ground, it instantly began to change shape to suit its new owner. After a few seconds it chose to become a solid black square. He placed it in his pocket and left the room to join the graduation ceremony.

Makron looked up to the towers of the academy as he led a cart filled with barrels to the dorms, desperately trying to keep his mind on what he had to do, then he heard someone calling his name. 'Makron, your back, oh I have missed you. I was hoping you'd be back for graduation,' Franklin said running up to him. He was an elite recruit who Makron had known since they were young. 'Yes the Headmistress said I could still graduate even after leaving and everything else that has happened,' Makron said. 'Don't worry about that I'm going to make sure you have the best day of your life today, even a night out in the Golden City will look like a boring dinner with your parents after you see what I have planned,' Franklin said, Makron smiled remembering how excitable Franklin could become. 'That sounds great, but first my father sent me with a gift for the elites,' he said gesturing to the barrels in the cart. 'Is that wine?' Franklin asked.

'Yes some sort of tradition. I'll take it to the dorm can you round everyone up?' Makron asked.

'Will do, most are already there getting ready I'll get the others from the hall,' Franklin said, running off to get the rest of the elites. Makron got the cart to the dorm and with the help of the rest of the students got the barrels into the dorm and began to fill their glass and clay cups. 'Don't drink yet we all need to be here make sure we have enough glasses,' Makron ordered as they all crowded around filling their cups and once Makron was happy they all had a full cup, and Franklin had returned with the rest he stood on top a chair and raised his glass, 'This gift comes from my father the one who will soon be your general and mine. He sent us this wine so we could toast the ones who came before us, it is what has been done since elites first began training here, join me now and raise you glass to the old guard.'

'To the guard,' the voices rang out, and they all flung back their drinks and for a second they enjoyed the taste of the wine, but then a sickly bitter taste filled their mouths, and they felt their bodies begin to go numb. Franklin looked to Makron whose glass was still in his hand full. Tears now streamed down his face. 'I am so sorry, but this was the only way,' Makron said as Franklin fell to his knees. He could feel his insides moving around and reorganising themselves and his skin had began to turn purple. 'What have you done Makron why would you do this?' he asked but before Makron could try to explain he was gone. His friends face had been replaced and now just a pair of red eyes looked back at him, he looked around the dorm and most had now been turned, the rest would soon follow.

Lord Balmoth arrived at the academy just as the graduation ceremony was about to start, it had taken him a lot longer to return than he had hoped. After reaching the West gate and finding the once unbreakable great gate ripped from its hinges and the bridge spanning the gorge gone. Forcing him to leave Caspian and make a zip line to get across. Sending his steed on roads only beasts can take to cross the lavender lake. After a six day hike he had finally arrived, but he was surprised when he got closer to the walls of the academy and saw elites at the gates instead of Captain Roain's rangers. 'You men, where are the rangers who should be at this post?' Balmoth asked the elite looked up to him and Balmoth could see they were wearing new helmets still gold like the rest of their armour, but these one's had masks completely covering the face of the person wearing it. 'We were ordered here, the rangers left,' the elite said in a strangely deep voice for an elf. 'Left where?' Balmoth said the elite simply shrugged back and didn't say a word. 'Lot of good you are,' Balmoth said making his way through the grounds it was quiet, eerie even, Balmoth had a familiar feeling, one he had felt many times before, then a chill shot up his spine like a cold blade had run along every bone in his body. Looking up to the Headmistress's tower then back to the guard at the gate who were now advancing on him. Other's had also begun making their way to the Lord drawing swords from their belts as they did.

In the hall the King had just taken his seat at the head table beside his daughter. The extreme admiration he had for her was now overshadowed by recent events. He looked at the gloomy face of his daughter and wondered if following June's advice was right and if her pets would do as he hoped, the uneasy tension between the pair increased as the hall began to fill. There wasn't a seat spare at any of the tables, and all the students sat calmly as they waited for the last two seats to be taken at the head table. The only ones missing were Seer Marlos La Sore and the Headmistress. The elite recruits were all wearing the new helms that covered their faces much to the bewilderment of the rangers and the girls. All apart from Makron who sat at the head table beside the empty seat of his father. Then Marlos entered through a side door and made his way past the other teachers and his son to approach the King. 'My friend terrible news the dear lady's been taken ill, she asked that I might say a few words in her stead,' Marlos said.

'The Headmistress ill, I've never heard of such a thing. I shall check on her,' the King said.

'I know my King but we all succumb to the odd cold now and again, come now let it not spoil this day,' Marlos said persuading the King to remain seated. 'Well yes I suppose, but this is most unlike her,' the King said as Marlos made his way to stand before the crowd. 'Good students of the academy of the rangers. Once this was just a place for the wood folk to train to help guard elf lands and our people, but now it trains my elites and our women, and a fine education you will have got. It would put all your futures in good stead in the age of the elves, such a shame it's all meaningless,' Marlos said to the crowd, he took a quick look back to see the King's reaction. He had sat forward in his chair wondering where the Seer was going with this. 'For so long now you elves and woodys have failed. You let this world fall into ruin, you let this world be consumed by the darkness of the humans and orcs, you have left me no other choice for today. Today a new age begins,' Marlos continued as Lord Balmoth burst through a door from a side corridor at the far end of the hall, locking eyes with Marlos as he entered, the purple blood of the guards who had tried to hinder him dripping from his sword. 'Today begins the age of the dark elf!' Marlos said and with a flick of his fingers shadows span around his hand creating a magical black shadow blade. He turned and thrust it through Elidom's chest before he or his daughter could do a thing. All she was able to do was scream as the shadow blade pierced her father's chest. Then she felt a hand grab her and lock a collar around her neck. She turned to see it was Makron. He pulled her from the chair and dragged her away from the table, she desperately tried to get away but the collar stopped her using her abilities. Marlos then thrust his arms out firing a dark purple beam of shadows along both sides of the head table, killing all the teachers sat there, but one. Master Cunningham's small frame was the only reason he still lived. With that the elites at the centre table stood up and drew short swords and knives that were hidden underneath their table. They turned, and without hesitation began hacking away at the students on either side. Balmoth quickly raised his sword but he was soon surrounded, he swung his sword knocking the helm from one a elites head, to reveal a purple face and red eyes. 'Marlos stop this madness, they're innocent,' the King begged as blood squirted from his chest and poured from his mouth. Marlos had struck him with such force the sword had gone through the back of the King's golden chair and impaled him there. 'There's no stopping this now old friend, this is the end for you and your people I will end their lives as I did with your lover and your Queen,' Marlos said as he took the King's ring from his finger. 'That's impossible,' the King said. 'No, it was very easy all it took was the right herb

191

in their drink but you won't be going in such a peaceful way as they did,' Marlos said pulling his sword from the King's chest. 'Please stop,' the Princess begged through tears then with one hard swing Marlos hewed the King's head clean off his shoulders, and it fell to the floor. Marlos looked over Elidom's corpse then turned to the Princess, 'she's next, do it now!' Marlos ordered his son. 'Killing the King wasn't the plan or her. That wasn't the plan, she has the collar on she can't do anything,' Makron said. As they argued Balmoth still had enemies on all sides, his skill and powerful sword were the only thing keeping him alive. He did his best to lure the dark elves away from the students, but many had already been killed. Whilst some were managing to fight back Professor Cunningham was doing all he could to protect them, but there were just too many dark elf's for his fists to make a difference. All of a sudden the hall doors flung open with such force it almost broke the hinges holding them. 'Where's my Princess!' Hilly screamed as he, Billy and James ran into the madness that was unfolding in the main hall. They saw Balmoth fighting the dark elves then the King's headless body with Marlos beside it and Makron holding the Princess's arm. As soon as Makron saw them he began dragging her off through a side door. The boys didn't even have to say a word, they all knew what they had to do. Billy shot off as fast as he could to the door Makron had ran through, a dark elf moved to block him but before he could James fired an arrow through its neck, letting Billy give chase, as James joined his father. Hilly however only had one target he jumped onto the centre table and ran straight for Marlos reaching for his repel, Marlos quickly raised his hand firing a beam of purple shadows at Hilly, as the hook of the repel flew towards him. Marlos turned to dodge it letting it embed itself into the wall behind. Looking back, Marlos saw Hilly being pulled through the air, protected from the dark magic by the hourglass. Marlos moved to defend himself but wasn't quick enough, before he could lower his hand Hilly sliced at Marlos cutting off his three middle fingers on his left hand. 'Argh you disgusting little human,' Marlos screamed as he did he saw that Lord Balmoth along with his son and daughter were

rallying the remaining students. Master Cunningham's old age
had not dampened his vigour running at enemies more then twice
his size and beating them down with his fists alone. The girls had
picked up what weapons they could find, Mor's training was
paying off and they were now pushing back his dark elves. The
Dark Seer raised his sword to strike down the human, but he was
too slow as he did Hilly struck again, this time slicing a huge
gash into his right arm causing the blade he was wielding to
vanish, sending him to his knees. 'You killed my friends, you
killed my family now you pay for it all you git,' Hilly shouted he
aimed his blade for the Dark Seer's throat but before he could an
explosion of light came off the Dark Seer completely blinding
Hilly. Marlos quickly got to his feet and ran for a door, opened it
and slammed it behind him. Hilly ran to the door desperate to
stop him getting away, but it was too late, he was gone, he had
used the Headmistress hair clip. Hilly turned to see the three
Balmoth's, students and one remaining teacher had bested the
dark elves, but the cost was great. He could hardly see the floor
through the bodies of students and teachers, purple and red blood
covered the rest.

'Stop this madness Makron. Please just let me go you can't do
this,' Emma pleaded with Makron as he dragged her down the
hall to a waiting carriage. 'It's either come with me or die here.
You're not even that stupid are you?' Makron said.
　　'You know they're here now. They'll never let you leave
here with me just let me go and they won't hurt you,' Emma said.
　　'Your pets can't save you now Princess,' Makron
snapped. He opened a door to the courtyard where a carriage was
waiting, but the sight that greeted them was not what Makron had
expected. 'You sure about that?' Billy growled sat in front of the
carriage next to him were the body's of the two dark elves that
were guarding it. 'You're slow Makron. She's right though take
that thing off her and walk away, you were nice to us when we
got here I don't want to kill you,' Billy said, he was stern and
sounded like a true alpha. 'You kill me I'd like to see you try
little dog,' Makron said pulling his sword but as he did Billy

leapt up and used his claws to scratch Makron's face, catching his left eye. Makron fell to the ground with blood pouring from his eye socket. 'You're lucky it was me Hilly would have killed you and made a joke of it, come on Princess,' Billy said and the pair made their escape running back to the main hall leaving Makron rolling in pain on the floor. They got almost halfway to the hall before Emma fell to the floor and broke down. 'Come we need to get back they're gonna need your magic,' Billy said.

'Why did they do this? My dad's dead he chopped his head off why's Makron helping him?' she said crying so hard her face had gone bright red and her eyes were completely bloodshot. Billy saw the lock on the collar and bit into it snapping the collar in two. 'I know this sucks, this really sucks, but we have to keep going we can both cry for our dads later, right now we have to make sure there's someone left to remember them,' Billy said.

'You're right, come on we need to hurry,' Emma said she felt her strength return as soon as the collar was removed. They got back to the hall and the pair could see the true extent of the damage, then Hilly ran up to her and threw his arms round her. 'You're okay,' Hilly said.

'I'm fine, but they're not,' Emma said, pushing him away and quickly going to the aid of the injured. 'So what now?' James said. 'Balmoth! Balmoth!' A voice shouted from the courtyard they looked through the windows to see a regiment of dark elves in the courtyard, lead by Oshan the executioner. 'Come out you coward Balmoth! My master demands your head there's no escaping this time Balmoth!' He yelled.

'That's a lot of bad guys' Hilly said looking out of the window. The Dark Seer had been preparing for this day, long had his true force been hidden beneath there noses. Lord Balmoth made his way to the door. 'Where are you going?' Maggie said.

'If I can distract him it may give you all a chance to get out. Use the old gate, it's welded shut, but if you call Caspian he should be able to break it down, he should be close by now,' Balmoth said taking a small silver whistle out of his pocket and handing it to Maggie. 'And what about the ones that can't run?'

194

Emma said. 'Leave them. This is your only chance to live past this day,' Balmoth said. 'No we can't just leave them. We all need to make it out of here,' Emma insisted.

'She's right and there's no point going out there just to die we can think of something,' Maggie said Billy looked up to his brother who was still staring out the window like someone was speaking to him. A light voice had been speaking to him, words that were given to the wind to be brought to them 'Hilly,' Billy said. 'I know what you're gonna say and you're right it has to be us,' he said with a smile.

'You've got a plan?' Billy asked.

'Yer I do. It's not my plan though you don't have to go along with it,' Hilly said.

'No but I'm going too,' Billy replied the pair of them walked to the door as the others argued. 'What you doing?' James said he was the only one still keeping an eye on them. 'Don't worry we got this one,' Hilly said as he reached for the door handle but before he could reach for the other James had already placed his hand on it. 'You should stay here,' Billy said,

'You really think I'm going to,' James asked.

'You don't have to do this ranger,' Hilly said.

'Yes I do, have you not noticed yet the three of us together no one can stop us, not even the Dark Seer, be helpful to have the orc too though,' James joked.

'Don't worry he's coming,' Hilly smiled as the pair pushed open the doors. The three of them walked out quickly closing it behind them as shouts came from the others. James quickly got a spear from the ground and used it to bar the doors so the others couldn't follow. 'What are they doing they'll be killed?' Balmoth said running over to try and open the doors. 'James come back here open this door,' he ordered the boys could hear him on the other side, but then he suddenly stopped shouting as the voice that had spoken to Hilly whispered to him and Lord Balmoth began to laugh. 'What's wrong with you open the door,' Maggie ordered. 'They will open just wait the Headmistress still watch's over us,' Balmoth said.

## The Unlikely Allies

'Are you still sure about this?' James said as they stood on the steps of the academy looking down at the army of purple faces in front of them.

Chapter 17
The Dark Seer


'You are not the Balmoth I wanted,' Oshan said.

'Well, I'm the Balmoth you get,' James replied.

'Do you feel proud executioner, standing there beside these purple gits? They used to be orcs you know,' Hilly said.

'I know what they used to be. They used to be weak, now they are strong, standing at the head of the new age,' the executioner scoffed back. 'They're not all orcs you know,' Marlos shouted down from the battlements standing beside Makron. He had healed his fingers and the cut on his arm and had just finished healing Makron's eye. 'The orcs weren't the first to taste my elixir. Tell me have you worked out who the first was yet? What race I used to birth the new rulers of this world,' Marlos said. 'Yes,' Hilly replied.

'Really. Do tell?' Marlos said in his most condescending tone. 'Sixteen years ago, you broke the King's wall that caged the humans. You to went to the Crown City, and you used them as your test subjects. Whilst I was safe with the wolves, you were turning them all into these monsters,' Hilly said.

'Yes, well done. Your kind were so weak when I found them, starving to death on that island, now your broken race is fixed. You truly are the only human left in this world and what your eyes have had the privilege of seeing is but a handful of the power I hold. As we speak my army's move to conquer this world and all in it. We will be one army, one race we will spread the darkness to every living thing and the world will then finally be at peace,' Marlos announced waving his arms around as if he was conducting a symphony. 'Well before all that happens I have a message for you,' Hilly said.

'A message? Who from?' Marlos wondered, but he hadn't noticed what Makron had. The glint in the boy's eyes, the same one he had when they used to train and spar. That look told Makron Hilly had a plan, but what was it? His father's plan was perfect, there was no way for them to get away. True he hadn't anticipated Hilly and the others being able to return but now they had they were trapped. 'Father wait,' Makron said, but he was ignored. 'The message is simple from someone called Jhona,' Hilly said. 'What's the message?' Marlos snarled getting more frustrated he knew that name, but the name was long dead and she was dead now too, dead in her tower. Did she speak to him, how? And her name how did he know her name? A name that even she was meant to forget, Marlos thought to himself as Hilly continued to speak. 'The message is as follows,' Hilly said stretching this out as long as he could. Then he felt it, magical energy began to build behind the three of them. James quickly turned to see the door of the academy starting to glow. He pulled the spear from the door so it could open. 'She says we have everything we need now, and you won't win, you may think you stand as one by making everyone the same and taking away any free will, but to me, I look to your new race and I see just one stood alone. Now look to me Dark Seer,' Hilly said throwing his arm out, 'Do I? Hilly of the Fang, the Princess's pet, the unlikely ally and the last human to live, do I look like one standing alone?' with that the doors of the hall burst into light and the sound of war drums began to echo from behind. Marlos looked into his pocket the hair clip had turned back to an eagle and was glowing brighter than it ever had. 'This can't be, that woman, I killed her,' Marlos spat grinding his teeth looking back to the now opening door. Behind the door there was now a portal to Lonas and the one pushing open the heavy old doors was Mor Ash the mighty. 'The winds say you need an army,' Mor said Anersham in hand. 'I don't know about an army brother, but the horde will do some damage this day!' Ore ash screamed charging through the doorway, he now wore the blood red heavy armour of the orcs of old as did Mor. The boys barely had a second to look to each other. 'This is it,' James said.

'For Alidor,' Hilly suggested.

'No. For The Fang!' Billy roared as the three of them lead the charge.

The dark elves lowered their spears and made a shield wall but what they weren't expecting was the hail of arrows from Captain Roain's rangers. Thinning their wall allowing the orcs to push through into their ranks dividing them. Not just orcs were in the charge. Captain Landon and his guard stood with them. Jerrest leapt from the hall door and landed on the dark elves like a rock sending them flying. The orcs had not forgotten him, always they had wondered how it would feel to fight beside such mighty beasts and had clad Jerrest in whatever armour they could find to fit him. He now wore a mail coat over most of his body and iron plates on his shoulders. The orcs watched on enthralled as the great wolf made his name. Hilly ran up to a dark elf and plunged his dagger into its neck quickly taking the sword from the dark elf's belt, Billy was right beside him. Every enemy in his path was brought down by his jaw's that had gotten so powerful. He was even biting threw the dark elf's heavy armour. Marlos turned to his son. 'I'm leaving now you clean up this mess,' Marlos said.

'But father the orcs, Captain Roian what do I do? Balmoth still lives,' Makron said in a panic.

'You have been nothing but a burden, just a constant failure since the day you were born. If you wish to redeem yourself in any way take this and bring me the human's head,' Marlos said, handing him the King's ring. 'Yes father.'

James had kept an eye on Oshan, and now he had a shot. He was running up the stairs of the battlement's. He aimed and took his shot the arrow got Oshan in the leg, but that wasn't enough to stop him. James ran up the stairs after him, but Oshan was waiting hidden behind the tower wall, he surprised James punching him across his face sending him flying to the floor and throwing his bow off the edge. He reached for the sword on his belt, but before he could Oshan stamped his foot down hard on James chest and continued to push down harder. He could feel his ribs getting ready to snap like matchsticks as Mor looked up to see him pinned to the ground. 'The ranger! Get to the ranger!' He cried, trying to force his way through the crowd to get to him. 'At least I get the little Balmoth's head to mount on my wall,'

# The Unlikely Allies

Oshan grunted raising his axe. James couldn't help but close his eyes as the axe came slamming down, but it was blocked. He opened his eyes to see a beam of lightening holding back the battle axe then it exploded throwing Oshan back and making him drop his weapon. 'Good work son, get to the others now,' Lord Balmoth said grabbing his son by the shoulder and pulling him to his feet. 'No I'll fight with you,' James said. Lord Balmoth looked over the edge of the battlements. 'Not today son,' he said and pushed James off the battlement's sending him falling into a hay cart below. Oshan picked his axe back off the ground. 'You dare face me,' Oshan said.

'You're the one who keeps running from me orc,' Balmoth joked readying himself. Maggie ran over to her brother grabbing a bow from the floor as she ran. James pulled himself from the cart and Maggie threw the bow to him. 'Where's father?' she asked taking the sword from her belt and shield from her back. 'Fighting Oshan come on, he's going to need us,' James said as the pair began to make their way back to the stairs to aid their father but they were soon cut off by dark elves.

Hilly and Billy were still in the mist of the battle. Fighting beside the orcs of the blood works they were pushing back the dark elves until a ball of fire fell from the battlements. Hilly quickly grabbed Billy's tail pulling him close and the hourglass saved them, but the orcs around him were instantly burnt to death. They looked up and saw the fire had come from Makron still stood on the battlements, he had used the King's ring. 'So this is what true power feels like,' Makron said looking to the ring on his index finger. Hilly quickly pulled his repel from his bag and fired it, using it to fling himself onto the battlements beside Makron. 'You'll pay for this Makron! For all the lives you and your git of a father have ruined. I'll make you pay for them all,' Hilly shouted his words full of rage as he swung his sword at Makron. 'You and your brother, you both should have just laid down and died in that forest with the rest of your kind. Letting you live this long is one of the only mistakes my father has made. I'll set that right,' Makron said opening his hand and creating another ball of fire in it. Before Hilly could react he shot a continuous beam of fire at Hilly, he was saved by the hourglass but the strength of the blast held him in place. Makron drew his sword and began to advance. 'I'm his only mistake? You remember your sister don't you? She's dead because of him,' Hilly shouted through the flames. 'Useless human scum, it had to be, it just had to,' Makron said. Hilly was using all his energy to remain standing. The hourglass held back the fire but the heat it was creating was overwhelming. He never thought his hourglass could be broken but if anything could do it, it would be the King's ring. His sword even became red hot burning his hand forcing him to drop it as he wondered if the hourglass could hold out. Then he felt a sharp pain in his stomach. Makron had thrust his sword through the fire and stabbed him, he stumbled back and fell as the fire subsided. 'You've lost Hilly, everything you've done amounts to nothing, you're alone now,' Makron said then he noticed the crooked grin across Hilly's face. 'You twat Makron,' Hilly said clutching the wound in his chest, 'I'm never alone,' Makron knew what was coming he quickly turned, but he was too late Billy had snuck up on him and was now lunging at him. Makron raised his arm to try and block but Billy's jaws just sank down hard into his arm locking his jaws and stabbing all four of his paws into Makron's chest. He gave a hard tug and Billy could feel the high elves arm pop from its socket with one more tremendous pull Billy ripped Makron's arm clean off. Makron screamed in agony as Billy leapt off him and onto the floor holding Makron's arm in his jaws. Makron saw this as he stumbled to the edge of the battlement's and fell. Hilly pulled himself up hoping to see Makron's splattered corpse on the rocks below, but he had vanished. 'Damn his fathers saved him,' Hilly said.

'Don't worry about that come on we need to get the Princess to fix you,' Billy said dropping the arm.

'Where is she?' Hilly asked as the pair looked down to the courtyard. Their allies were fighting bravely, but the dark elves still had the greater numbers and were pushing them back. 'There she is.' Billy shouted as he saw the Princess running to the old well by their shack. She placed her hands on the well and focussed her energy on trying to draw the water from it, but she still hadn't recovered from having the collar on. Hilly grabbed Makron's arm and pulled the King's ring from its lifeless finger. 'Quick get this to her,' Hilly said.

'What about you?' Billy asked.

'It's just a scratch, go on!' Hilly said. Billy took the ring in his mouth and ran.

Lord Balmoth raised his lightening blade and fired a beam directly at Oshan, but his armour just absorbed the blast. Oshan reached out grabbing the blade of Balmoth's sword with his iron clad hand. He pulled Balmoth towards him and slammed his head into Balmoth's, shattering Lord Balmoth's nose. Oshan released the blade and gripped the ranger by the throat lifting him from the ground and throwing him back down. 'You can't defeat me watcher, the Dark Seer gave me more power than I need to end you,' Oshan roared as he towered over Lord Balmoth. Maybe he was right, he could feel his jaw was broken and blood was now building behind his eyes, worst of all his sword was now useless against him. He looked down to see his children side by side still fighting. 'Maybe I can't, but I'll make sure I give them the power to stop you, just as Wasiz did,' Balmoth said pulling himself up and putting both hands on the handle of his sword. With a warrior's cry the sword burst into light and sparks began to fly from the blade forcing Oshan to step back, as it transformed into a beam of light. Balmoth pulled his hands apart splitting the light into two, then he released them sending the two bolts of light shooting into the sky like arrows. James and Maggie saw this and looked to hear him cry, 'I'll be watching,' as Oshan's axe slammed down imbedding itself into him. Tears instantly filled Maggie's eyes, she tried to scream, but no sound came out. She turned to her brother, but before they could say a thing the two bolts of light shot back down from the sky and engulfed each of them. Maggie looked at her shield and saw it beginning to transform, the white light had turned to a great red glow. The same was happening to James's bow and with a flash the light vanished. James looked to his bow which was now solid silver but was as light as a feather. He placed his hands on the bow string and pulled it back slightly and a bright silver arrow magically appeared. He released the arrow into an approaching dark elf. The arrow shot through it and then through another two dark elves before it hit a wall and evaporated. 'It's father's sword,' James said as a dark elf charged Maggie. She raised her now solid silver round shield emblazoned with a white horse and the dark elf's sword slammed down onto the shield, but she didn't even feel the blow. Instead, it absorbed the force of the dark elf's attack quadrupling it and then fired it back at the dark elf, disintegrating every bone in its body. James grabbed Maggie's shoulder. 'He's given us the power to end this. Come on,' James said firing his bow clearing their way to the stairs. Oshan had been watching the young Balmoths and was now worried. He then saw the door to the tower beside him beginning to glow. He knew it was his master calling him back. He walked through the door and was gone long before the siblings made it to the top of the battlements. They stood over the body of their father both with red eyes and tears streaming down their faces.

Meanwhile, Billy had gotten to the Princess. She was covered in sweat from trying to use her powers to draw water from the old well. 'Princess take this,' Billy said, showing her he had her father's ring. She quickly put it on and felt a rush of power pulse through her veins. She held her hand back over the well, and the surrounding ground began to shake. Then a tower of muddy water flew from it. The Princess immediately began transforming the water into ice spears and firing them down onto the dark elves, giving the orcs much needed relief and forming shields of ice around the wounded. Mor looked to the orcs around him they were beginning to falter. 'With me my brothers,' Mor roared and stood beside Ore 'Stand with your War Chief, stand with me. The Queen to be shows us her might we must show her ours, fight now orcs of the Blood Works, claim your glory as warriors,' Mor rallied the orcs. With renewed strength and the aid of the Princess they ripped into the now broken dark elves. Then James began to fire silver arrows from the battlements as his sister joined

# The Unlikely Allies

Landon. 'There you are my lady with you by my side victory is for sure,' Landon said.

'Stop staring at me Landon, look to the enemy,' Maggie snapped as she blocked an axe blow, firing the power back at the wielder, but Landon could not look away her brown hair shone like gold in his eyes, and even though still in her graduation gown she fought as if she wore a full suit of armour, seeming to stand taller than any man there. Captain Roian and his rangers were now out of arrows and using whatever was to hand as they charged into battle fighting side by side with the orcs. Hilly watched from the battlements as his unlikely allies destroyed what was left of the dark elf army, but his eye was caught by the open door to Leonardo's workshop.

Ore Ash stood in the centre of the now calming courtyard he looked around at the corpses surrounding him then to the soldier's still standing. 'Everyone here. Everyone of you hear me. The day is ours my mighty brothers,' Ore cried out. Cheers of glory filled the courtyard but the cry's began to fade as Mor walked to his brother carrying the body of Lord Balmoth. 'What are you doing?' James said running over.

'This is the greatest honour us orcs can give,' Mor said looking into his friends eyes. James stepped aside. 'Brother this vessel belonged to Lord Richard Balmoth,' Mor spoke louder, so all would hear. 'This wood elf was one of the greatest enemies of our people. He has more glory than any orc,' Mor said, laying the Lord's body at the feet of his brother. 'Yes brother, for many years mothers have told their young of this man. An enemy, yes, once. But a glory follows him like none before and an honour few have known. I hear by name this one, I name him Richard Balmoth saviour of the damned,' with that Ore fell to his knees and put his head to the ground. It was silent in the courtyard as Orc after Orc fell to their knees to show respect to the fallen Lord, only clinking of armour could be heard. Ore then turned to the Princess and threw his sword to the floor, 'We are no longer puppets of the Dark Lord, do what you will with us,' Ore said remaining on his knees before her. She turned to Captain Landon. 'Captain the town of Eccos its still deserted right?' she asked.

'It is my lady,' he replied.

'Then you have it you'll need somewhere 'till we liberate the Blood Works,' the Princess said, looking back at the War Chief who had a look of shock over his face. He had expected a much harsher fate much like his brother had the first time he had met King Elidom. 'I don't want to rule over orcs or anyone. My... My father's dead and with him the old ways will die too. We must make something new. A new alliance, a republic even,' she said looking around at the variety of different faces in front of her. 'A republic what's that?' Ore asked.

'We shall talk later. Right now you need to move your injured into the infirmary,' she said as Hilly came stumbling out of Leonardo's workshop with Ernest flung over his shoulder. 'What happened to you?' the Princess said seeing the blood covering Hilly's chest as he placed Ernest down in front of her. 'Don't worry about me,' Hilly said. Ernest didn't look hurt, but his body was frozen, and his eyes were totally white. 'What did you do to my mage, he was fine when we brought him,' Ore said.

'I don't know what this is? It looks like some sort of spell?' Emma said.

'He had this in his hand,' Hilly said, handing a crumpled piece of paper to her. 'Prof taken,' she said, reading the note aloud. Captain Landon quickly turned to his guards. 'Find Professor Leonardo check everywhere, Go!' he ordered as his guard and a group of rangers began searching the castle for him while the Princess began to heal Hilly's wound. 'If Marlos has taken him.' Hilly mumbled.

'We don't know that he could be anywhere,' she said, but she knew what he was going to say. 'The things Leo can make we've both seen his designs, his machines. The things that science of his can do, we need to get him back. If Marlos has taken him its unthinkable what he might get Leo to create,' Hilly said. 'I can track him I know his scent pretty well,' Billy said.

'If we go now we may be able to cut them off before they reach the Lavender Lake unless, damn. Unless he uses the

# The Unlikely Allies

Headmistress hair clip, they could be anywhere now,' James said joining them. 'Come on then we need to move,' Hilly ordered waving to Jerrest. James whistled and Jenna came running from the stables where she had been hiding, after following the others from Lonas. 'Find a horse Mor,' James shouted.

'What's happening?' Mor asked, walking over.

'You can't do this you can't just run off after all that's happened,' the Princess protested. Hilly took Emma's hand and pulled her close. 'I'm coming back I will always come back to you, but we have to, you know we do,' he said. She threw her arms round his neck and kissed him sending a warm comforting feeling over the pair. 'I'll be here waiting, and I won't be idle. I'll do what others couldn't. Here today we all fought as one and I'll keep it that way. The next time the Dark Seer attacks we will be ready.' Most were watching the pair, she turned and spoke louder. 'And today a new bond is formed by all here, one of elves courage and orc's glory, wolves speed and human wit. Today the heart's of Alidor are one and all here are bound to keep it so,' she said as Hilly turned and pulled himself on top of Jerrest. 'You're going to make a great Queen, and I shall ride out now as your valiant knight,' Hilly said.

'No never my knight, my loveable rogue,' she said Hilly smiled back. 'I love you, you know that right?' Hilly said.

'I know and that's why I know you'll come back,' Emma said with a smile that could hardy fit on her face as Hilly began heading for the gate. 'What about us my lady what should we do?' Landon asked

'Make ready whoever's able and prepare horses, we ride for Duniesa. I find it hard to believe Marlos did all this alone, when we get there we lock up the rest of the Seers and get the city ready for the war thats to come.'

'What's going on?' Mor asked joining the party at the main gate.

'We're chasing Marlos,' Billy said as Bob flew down and landed on Hilly's shoulder, making sure he wasn't left behind again. 'Just the four of us,' Mor said.

'Five,' Jerrest barked.

'Do we count mounts now?' Mor said in jest.

'We certainly do,' James said patting Jenna as Maggie ran to them. 'Wait,' she shouted and went to Mor's side taking the silver whistle from her pocket and blowing it. 'I don't want you to go, any of you, but I know nothing I can say will stop you now,' she handed the whistle to Mor as Caspian charged along the road to the academy. He had hidden himself close to the academy as Lord Balmoth had ordered. 'That is Caspian my father's steed, his bravery and strength can only be matched by his own daughter, father will have wanted him to go with you,' Maggie said looking to Mor as Caspian stood beside them and looked to the body of his master. With a roaring neigh he bellowed out as Maggie put her hands around the steed's neck to comfort the animal. Then Mor spoke, 'I am a mighty warrior, but your Lord was even mightier than the great Mor. I will make a pact with you now steed, ride with me, aid me as you did him and I swear I will bring you the head of the one responsible for his death.' With another roaring neigh he agreed and allowed Mor to climb up into his saddle, to the surprise of all in the courtyard. Many orcs had never seen one of their own on horseback. The party then charged through the gates, as Ore and others ran after them as they did Ore cried, 'The Princess's pets ride for us,' he cried out as orc and elf began to sing songs of glory. 'Do you think they will be back?' Landon said standing beside Maggie. She took his hand in her own and looked at him. 'They will be back and we will be waiting.'

Hilly smiled and looked to his friends as they began to ride away from the Ranger's Academy. 'So where exactly are we going?' James asked. 'We ride around Alidor 'till Billy or Jerrest pick up Leo's scent,' Hilly said. 'Wait I thought you had more of a plan than that, that cannot be the whole plan,' Mor grunted.

'If what Marlos said about his army's moving over the world is true, I think we will find plenty to keep your hammer busy,' Hilly said. Smoke then caught their attention wafting into the air far away to the South. 'Speaking of busy hammers,' Mor said. 'Reckon there's someone crying for help wondering if some hero will save them. Oh well, best we keep going the other way,' Hilly joked smiling down to his brother. Billy smiled back but before he could speak Jenna shot off as if her hooves were wings. 'Come on, last one there finds dinner,' James said.

    'Let us fly Caspian, I'm not waiting on the woody,' Mor said as Caspian ran off matching his daughter's speed riding off after James. The brothers looked at each other, than with a grin and a laugh they sped off and the ones known as the Princess's pets and the unlikely allies of Tailor's Hope now went forth. Not knowing but knowing, unsure, but at the same time certain that the path they followed would lead to the peace they were now all fighting for.

Printed in Great Britain
by Amazon

69458030R00122